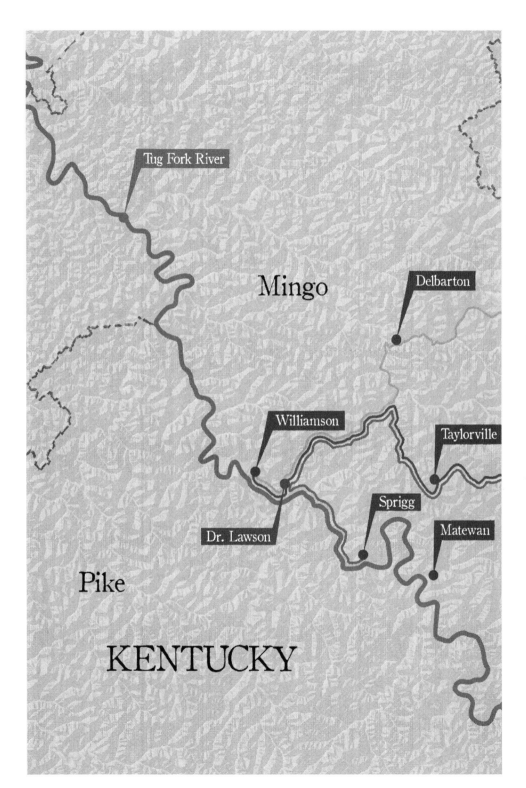

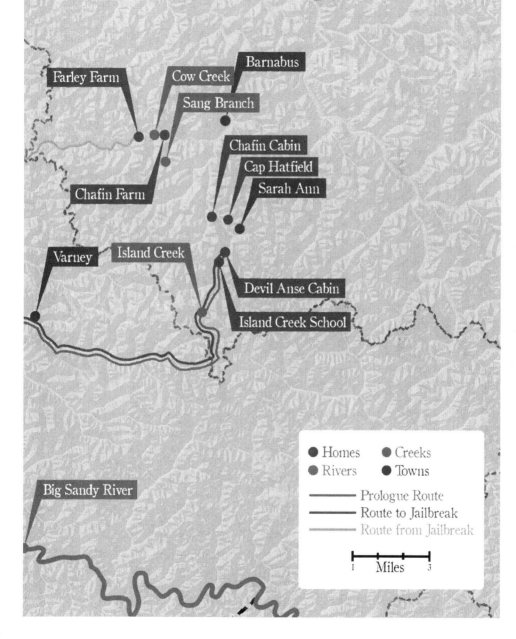

Also by Claude L. Chafin

Always Start with a Clean Kitchen

The Messenger

CLAUDE L. CHAFIN

iUniverse LLC
Bloomington

The Messenger

Copyright © 2013 by Claude L. Chafin.

All rights reserved. No part of this book may be used or reproduced by any means, graphic, electronic, or mechanical, including photocopying, recording, taping or by any information storage retrieval system without the written permission of the publisher except in the case of brief quotations embodied in critical articles and reviews.

iUniverse books may be ordered through booksellers or by contacting:

iUniverse LLC
1663 Liberty Drive
Bloomington, IN 47403
www.iuniverse.com
1-800-Authors (1-800-288-4677)

Because of the dynamic nature of the Internet, any web addresses or links contained in this book may have changed since publication and may no longer be valid. The views expressed in this work are solely those of the author and do not necessarily reflect the views of the publisher, and the publisher hereby disclaims any responsibility for them.

Any people depicted in stock imagery provided by Thinkstock are models, and such images are being used for illustrative purposes only.
Certain stock imagery © Thinkstock.

ISBN: 978-1-4917-1082-1 (sc)
ISBN: 978-1-4917-1084-5 (hc)
ISBN: 978-1-4917-1083-8 (e)

Library of Congress Control Number: 2013918768

Printed in the United States of America

iUniverse rev. date: 11/12/2013

To my sister, Betty Lee Chafin Avril, for her endless knowledge
of the Chafin, Browning, Dempsey, and Hatfield family histories

To my brother, Andy Chafin for suggesting this book, and persuading
my granddad to tell the stories,
and my sister, Betty Avril, for their travel and firsthand research into
Andrew Lee Chafin's life in Mingo County

To my son, Bradley Dean Chafin, for the map he researched
and provided, which is the true backbone of this book

And to my adorable wife, Tay, who not only suffered with me
through this writing ordeal and encouraged me,
but also had the idea to record my grandfather in the first place.
Without her this book would not exist.

To Sarah Sutfin, Andrew Chafin's great-granddaughter, for the picture
of the forest on the front cover, filmed on Island Creek, WV. And
to Cole Chafin, Andrew's great-great-grandson, for standing in for
Andrew in the scene. Also, to Rich Guglielmo, for the front cover
composition and lighting.

To son Allan Chafin, Andrew's great grandson, for restoring most of
the pictures found in this book.

My deepest thanks

In West Virginia, you don't steal a man's horse, his land, his wife, or his pigs. Now that's just all there was to it.

Andrew Lee Chafin

Andrew Lee Chafin, The Messenger,
with the author, Claude L. Chafin, age 4
Circa 1942

Contents

Preface xiii
Introduction xxiii
Prologue xxvii

1 Holbert and Lucinda, the Wedding 1
2 William Anderson "Devil Anse" Hatfield 11
3 Island Creek School, a New Life
     (The School in the Bottoms) 16
4 Officer Stanley Portous 27
5 The Raccoon Kill 38
6 The Lantern Ploy 44
7 The Eyewitness 55
8 Cap Hatfield 67
9 The Assault 74
10 Fuel, a Mountain Staple 87
11 The Jailbreak 95
12 Bounty Hunter 115
13 Andrew, the Teacher 126
14 Pinkerton Detective Agency 136
15 Humphrey "Doc" Ellis 144
16 Troy Hatfield 153
17 The N&W Railroad 158
18 Boomer, West Virginia 170
19 Sarah Richards 178

Epilogue 189
Sources 193

PREFACE

This is the story of a young boy growing up in one of the most remote areas of the country, the mountains of West Virginia, during the latter years of the nineteenth century. It is the story of my grandfather, Andrew Lee Chafin. Most readers will likely find it difficult to comprehend the motives of the people in this story from their perspective in the twenty-first century. In some cases, it will be impossible. So as you read, try to project yourself back to the nineteenth century in an attempt to accept as real the actions of the participants.

The time period of this book is precise, beginning with the marriage of Andrew's parents in 1881 and ending with Andrew's marriage in 1905. Before and after those dates, numerous events occurred for which no records can be found to verify them. Therefore, they are not included. The stories included are those that are verified by on-site visits and interviews with my grandfather or relatives of those who lived in the area at the time.

I write these stories in my own voice rather than in my grandfather's voice, even though they are based on his memories. I do so because my grandfather would not consider the stories important enough or unusual enough to put down on paper. He told them to me, both in recorded form and in light conversations, as a grandfather reliving his life. As a grandson, I was fascinated by them and felt the need to record them.

I do not consider this book a perfectly true history, because I do not have all the details and facts to do so. There were numerous gaps in my grandfather's telling, including things he could no longer remember or, frankly, chose to forget. So in some cases I also used information he did not have or could not have known—that is, information from other books and from historical archives. I did this to enhance the storytelling rather than simply to give a record of historical facts. I had hundreds of articles and books written about that time period, which substantiated all his stories. And in some cases my grandfather's stories give answers to questions the history books are not able to answer.

As an example, my grandfather remembered going to live with his "uncle and aunt" to start school. But he could not remember at what age. Today, that age would be five or six years old. But in the mountains of West Virginia at the time, he could have been seven or eight before he started school. Also, the school year in the mountains was not regulated. It started in the fall immediately after the crops were harvested, whenever that work was completed. The school year ended when it was time to plant, whenever that work began. In Mingo County, West Virginia, where most of the stories in this book occurred, there were only a handful of schools before the turn of the twentieth century, and most of those schools likely went only through the sixth grade. By the time young men and women finished the sixth grade, they were teenagers and expected to pull their own weight on the family farm or in other jobs.

Without visiting the area, it will be difficult for the reader to fully understand the dynamics of the West Virginia mountains. I was born and raised in Williamson, West Virginia, and can attest that the mountains in Mingo County are beautiful, but they are also rugged and, at least in the nineteenth century, unforgiving. Being lost in those mountains or purposely hiding in them rendered a person nonexistent. It is impossible to accurately describe the conditions that my grandfather, his family, and the characters in these stories lived through. Words cannot do that. But the imagination can bring these stories to life.

The main character in this book is Andrew Lee Chafin, my grandfather. There was nothing special about Andrew at birth, and there was nothing special about his parents, Holbert and Lucinda, that made them stand out from other people living in Mingo County at the time. Every family spent their days trying to feed themselves in rocky, hilly soil through bitterly cold winters without public support. There were few stores, even fewer doctors, no hospitals, few schools, and no roads.

What made Andrew special was the period and place where he lived as a youth. Of course he had no say in where he lived or when, and by today's standards, his treatment would be considered child endangerment and abuse. He became involved in brutal and murderous activities, sometimes with his parents' knowledge and sometimes without, but at least with their understanding that those activities were necessary.

The second most important character in this book is William Anderson "Devil Anse" Hatfield, the "uncle" my grandfather went to live with to start school. Anse Hatfield is known by historians as the patriarch of the Hatfield family, which was involved in a bloody feud with the McCoy family of Pike County, Kentucky. Before and after the feud, Anse was known as a community leader; the largest landowner in the county, owning four to five miles of land on both sides of Island Creek; and an officer in the Confederate army. He was involved in numerous battle victories during the Civil War and yet is recorded in some history books as a deserter.

By his own admission, Anse left military service on his own. But for the times, that was not unusual. While the able-bodied men were off to war, their families were at risk at home. And so it was that Anse left his company in Virginia during the latter part of the war and went back to Mingo County to protect his family and his own property. He started an unauthorized band of ex-Confederate soldiers called the Logan Wildcats, whose sole purpose was to look out for the best interests of the community during and after the war.

Anse was also credited with building at least three public schools for the children of his communities, one on Beech Creek, another on Island Creek, and a third (the one my grandfather attended) known simply as the School in the Bottoms. Anse was also actively involved in local politics, serving as a commissioner for a loosely organized school board. He was a successful lumberman and businessman and was well respected by all who knew him.

But he could also be brutal if crossed.

History books vaguely record the start of the Hatfield-McCoy feud as the killing of Asa Harmon McCoy, by the Logan Wildcats. Asa was a Union sympathizer and had fought with the Union during the war, an unwelcome allegiance to the Union for those in Mingo County, West Virginia. But the real instigation of the feud was the killing of Anse's brother, Ellison, by three sons of Randolph McCoy, patriarch of the McCoy family. Ellison was stabbed to death by the McCoy brothers over an alleged unpaid debt: a meager sum for a used fiddle.

When Anse heard the news of the stabbing, he rounded up the three brothers and held them for three days, waiting to see if Ellison would die from the wounds. When Ellison died, Anse and a group of his supporters took the three brothers back across the Tug River (the Kentucky-West Virginia state line) to Kentucky, tied them to paw-paw bushes, and brutally murdered them. Historians differ as to whether or not Anse himself actually shot any of the three. Some say he did; others say he did not. But they were killed on his word. Should Anse have decided that they should live, they would have lived.

It is important for readers to know that this area of the country was lawless at the time. There were no police officers, no state troopers, no criminal courts, and, frankly, no laws. If you were harmed, it was your obligation to right the wrong yourself. If you did not, you would be harmed again. Weakness was not an attribute in the mountains of West Virginia at the turn of the twentieth century.

The lawlessness of the area brings us to two other important characters of the book: Anse's sons, Cap and Johnse. By all accounts, Cap Hatfield, in his midtwenties at the time of the feud, was the most brutal of the Hatfield clan. Some even suggest he was psychotic. Most of the killings in the feud involved Cap in some form. He himself was shot several times, and the autopsy at the time of his death revealed bullet fragments pressing on his brain. It was Cap's demeanor to show no weakness, and he did not.

Johnse, Cap's older brother by almost three years, was not as interested in fighting as Cap but was equally brutal if crossed. Some would suggest that he was brutal whether he was crossed or not. Johnse's reputation was his lust for women. His attraction to women was notorious and, surprisingly, was returned by many of the Mingo County women of the time, as they found him exciting, good looking, and, as a bonus, a Hatfield, the most respected name in the valley. He even stole a McCoy girl, Rosanna, during the heat of the feud and took her to Anse's home with his stated intention of marrying her, but Anse refused to allow it. Anse did allow Rosanna to live there with

Johnse, unmarried, which resulted in the McCoy family disowning her. Later Johnse abandoned her himself and married her sister.

The inhumane brutality of Johnse was apparent in what must be considered the most offensive act of the feud. Johnse and a group of his supporters traveled to Pike County, Kentucky, on a bitterly cold New Year's Eve night to attack the Randolph McCoy home. They burned the McCoy home to the ground and violently murdered young Alifar, one of Randolph's daughters, an unspeakable and unforgivable act.

The death of Alifar and the burning of the McCoy home was a final straw for Kentucky officials. They had seen enough. Up to that point, the feud had reaped a dozen dead or wounded on the Hatfield side and twenty dead or wounded on the McCoy side, and state officials in Louisville wanted it to end. The Commonwealth of Kentucky demanded that the State of West Virginia arrest and extradite Johnse, Cap, Anse, and numerous others for the murder of McCoy family members. The state returned the favor and demanded that the commonwealth extradite McCoy family members for the murder of Hatfield family members. Both West Virginia and Kentucky refused.

Kentucky then sent Commonwealth representatives into West Virginia, who rounded up, arrested, and transported back across the state line a dozen or more Hatfield supporters to stand trial for murder. West Virginia sued Kentucky for what the state considered an illegal act, and the disagreement went to the Supreme Court for consideration. The Supreme Court ruled that Kentucky had no right to cross state lines to arrest the Hatfield supporters, but it also ruled that Kentucky was under no obligation to release them or send them back, a clear victory for Kentucky.

The Supreme Court decision emboldened the Commonwealth of Kentucky, and encouraged bounty hunters to travel back across state lines to capture (or show proof of killing) Hatfields or Hatfield supporters. As word spread of the rewards, unauthorized agents joined the hunt, wearing what has been described as mail-order badges. Mingo County became infested with bounty hunters, some of whom were known criminals. Cap and Johnse took to the hills and for a while left the county, doing all they could to avoid capture. Anse's

Claude L. Chafin

supporters meanwhile made it almost impossible for those bounty hunters to get near his home.

The two remaining principals in this story were Anse's two younger sons, Elias and Troy, who were too young to be involved in the feud itself but became important in the years following. From Andrew's stories, it would seem that bounty hunters tracked them as well, simply because they were Hatfields. And in the end they play a major role in these stories.

In 1888, the last official battle of the feud took place within a mile of Anse's home on Grapevine Creek. When it ended, both the Hatfields and the McCoys called an unofficial truce. Both families were worn out. Anse sold his property on Grapevine Creek and moved north a few miles to Island Creek, in Logan County, to get away from the feud area.

But some folk in Kentucky did not give up. They continued to fund numerous bounties on the heads of the Hatfields, and the bounty hunters continued to come to Mingo and Logan Counties. The Supreme Court's ruling that Kentucky had no right to send individuals into West Virginia was law; but without punishment, it did not matter.

It was at that time, sometime around 1892 or 1893, that Andrew Lee Chafin went to live with Anderson "Devil Anse" Hatfield. The stories of his life there were incredible then and remain so today. Anse took advantage of the fact that Andrew would probably be overlooked because of his youth and not suspected of assisting the Hatfield family. At the same time Holbert, Andrew's father, consciously allowed some of Andrew's exploits for reasons that remain a mystery; but he apparently felt that those exploits were necessary. Levicy, Anse's wife, and Lucinda, Andrew's mother, seemed disengaged from Andrew's endangerment, because they would not stand firm against Anse and his all-powerful image.

From Andrew's perspective it was just a part of growing up. He saw no danger in the errands he ran for his uncle and would not for a second think that he had done anything wrong. And according to the values of that time and place, he probably didn't.

The stories recalled in this book were relayed to me reluctantly by my grandfather from 1962 to 1970, culminating in a recorded interview in 1972 when Andrew Chafin was eighty-six years old. My grandfather did not like talking about those days and indeed changed the subject as often as it came up. But while I lived in Tampa, Florida, as a Sunday ritual I would travel to Seminole, Florida, where he lived, to mow his lawn. As a reward, my grandmother would bake a carrot cake for me, and I would sit with my grandfather and talk to him about those years he spent with Anse, while he smoked his pipe and I ate my cake.

My granddad chuckled often during those conversations, sometimes for things he remembered well and sometimes for things that, try as he might, he could not remember at all. All the stories were fascinating to me, mostly because they occurred while my granddad was so young. I could not imagine those events happening to my sons or grandsons when they were nine or ten years old. However, they happened to my grandfather, and those stories should be told.

Often during our conversations, he would choke up slightly and look away. I would wait for the conversation to continue without pressing him. Sometimes the conversation would continue, and sometimes it wouldn't. When they did not continue, in our next session he would pick up again, with a comment such as "I was telling you about . . ." and he would continue a story. (Some of his quotes have been placed at the beginnings of chapters.)

I felt as though he was anxious to get things off his chest, and although he often disliked talking about those times, he seemed to feel a need to do so. My grandfather was a kind and gentle man for all of his adult life, and I think his experiences in the Tug Fork Valley as a boy made him realize how important life is and how lucky he was just to be alive. He had an absolute devotion to the Hatfield family and felt it was his responsibility to protect them. To some measure he did just that.

Historians and state officials, from both Kentucky and West Virginia, have speculated for years about how Anse's sons, Cap and Johnse, could hide in the rugged mountains of West Virginia for months and years on end without access to food or communication from home. There is an answer to that speculation, and it begins with a young boy named Andrew Lee Chafin.

The life-size statue of Anderson "Devil Anse" Hatfield, made of Italian marble and paid for by family and friends, stands atop his gravesite.

The Hatfield Family
Circa 1897

Front row: Tennis, Louvisa, Willis
Second row: Mary Hatfield Simpkins, Anse, Levicy,
Nancy Glenn Hatfield, Louisa, Cap
Standing: Rosy, Troy, Betty, Elias, Tom Chafin, Joe, Ock
Damron, Shepard, Coleman, Emma

This picture was taken when Andrew Chafin was eleven years old and lived a mile north of the Hatfield family on Island Creek. Mary Hatfield Simpkins was married and did not live with the family at the time. Louvisa, her daughter, lived with her. Betty was married and did not live at home. Nancy Glenn Hatfield and the son she is holding, Robert, as well as Cap, Coleman, Shepard, and Levicy Emma lived across the bottoms from Andrew Chafin, north of the Hatfield family. The oldest son, Johnse, is not pictured. Shortly after this picture was taken, Shepard Hatfield died from what was reported to be malnutrition. The picture was not taken at the Hatfield home but was staged several miles away at a state park. Ock Damron (or Dameron) was a handyman who worked in Anse Hatfield's lumber business and around his home.

All of the family members who lived at the Hatfield home at the time this picture was taken are principals in Andrew Chafin's stories and played an important role in his life.

This is a picture taken around 1900 when Andrew would have been fourteen years of age. A group of visitors wanted their picture taken with Devil Anse Hatfield and his family. They probably brought their own photographer. All of the ladies in the picture are visitors. The only Hatfield family members are Devil Anse Hatfield, sitting in a chair holding a small child in his right arm and a rifle in his left. To his left is his son Tennis. Standing slightly behind Tennis and to his left is Anse's son Willis. Standing in front of Willis and to his left is Andrew Chafin. Standing next to Andrew and slightly behind him is Ock Damron, a hired hand. The lady standing beside Ock is one of the visitors. Directly behind Andrew, on the porch and holding on to the porch support post is Holbert, Andrew's father. We have been unable to determine if the lady sitting next to Anse is Levicy, but it is doubtful. We have no information on the small children or the other men on the porch.

INTRODUCTION

Historians record the start of the Civil War as April 12, 1861, at Fort Sumter in Charleston, South Carolina. They record the end of the war as April 9, 1865, at Appomattox, Virginia. However, historians are not quite as precise in recording the aftermath of the war. In fact, with a few exceptions, there is very little written, precisely or otherwise, about the war's aftermath, although it was longer lasting and often as brutal as the war itself. Without any knowledge of the aftermath, the general public would assume that the war ended peaceably on April 9, 1865, and everyone went back to their daily lives on April 10, as if the war never happened. That is hardly the case.

The Tug Fork Valley, an isolated area between massive mountain ranges along the Kentucky-West Virginia state line, is a place where a great deal has been written of the aftermath—specifically, the account of the most famous of all feuds, the Hatfield-McCoy feud. The valley is divided by the Tug Fork and Big Sandy Rivers, which are also the natural boundary between the two states. Written accounts give a less-than-precise beginning or end to the feud. They mark the probable beginning as the killing of Asa Harmon McCoy in 1865 and the probable end as the Battle of Grapevine Creek in 1888. The reality is that the feud, or at least remnants of the feud, extended well past the turn of the century.

History books also argue over the actual cause of the feud. Some suggest that it was a direct result of Civil War loyalties among the locals, with some residents supporting the Union and others supporting the Confederacy. Other historians lay blame on the theft of a pig, and still others on the illicit love affair between Rosanna McCoy and Johnse Hatfield. The reality is probably a combination of all three, one incident building on the others.

The killing of Harmon McCoy, however, is easily a good starting point of the feud. As stated in the preface, Harmon was a Union soldier who returned to his home on the Kentucky side of the Tug Fork Valley after the war to some disfavor among local residents who were loyal to the Confederacy. Even Harmon's own family was not pleased with his Union loyalty, as his brother, Randolph McCoy, fought on the Confederate side, alongside Anse Hatfield. Not only did Harmon continue to verbalize his Union support, he continued to wear his Union uniform through the streets of Pikeville, Kentucky, flaunting his attachment to the Union. Harmon was eventually killed by the Logan Wildcats, the marauding band of West Virginia Confederate sympathizers led by Anse. No one was ever brought to trial for the killing, and not one of the Logan Wildcats was ever accused.

The Tug Fork Valley, as in other areas of both Kentucky and West Virginia at the time, was inhabited by aggressive, lawless, free-living mountain people who were largely uneducated and mostly non-Christian. Killings after alcohol-induced arguments were not at all uncommon. And nothing brought on arguments or killings in the valley quicker than Civil War loyalties and politics. Every family living in the valley was actively involved in both.

The feud itself involved multiple families, not just the Hatfields and McCoys, including the families of Vance, Smith, Cline, Evans, Staton, Trent, Varney, Mounts, and my own family, Chafin. Anse was married to Levicy Chafin, commonly called Vicy. Several Chafins worked on his timber crews, including John and Moses Chafin. And Tom Chafin was one of Anse's longtime business partners.

This story, however, is about my grandfather, Andrew Lee Chafin, great-nephew of Vicy Chafin Anderson, Anse's wife. This suggestion that Vicy was my grandfather's great-aunt is, in itself, fuzzy. In tracing the family tree of the Chafin family and discussing the bloodline with other family members, it appears that, in reality, Vicy was a first cousin to Holbert Chafin, Andrew Lee's father, making Vicy my grandfather's third cousin.

Mountain folk traditionally consider older family members as aunts and uncles whether they actually are or not. And so it was with my grandfather, who probably went to his grave thinking that Vicy was Holbert's aunt and his great-aunt. And since it has no bearing on

The Messenger

the realities of the stories in this book, I will allow my grandfather that discretion.

In 1893, at the age of six or seven, Andrew went to live with his uncle Anse and great-aunt Vicy to start school. There were no schools near Andrew's home on Cow Creek outside of Barnabus, West Virginia, leaving his parents, Holbert Chafin and Lucinda Browning Chafin, few options for educating their son. Anse had been instrumental in the construction of the Island Creek School (or School in the Bottoms) in his neighborhood south of Sarah Ann, West Virginia, and that school seemed like a possible solution. Holbert discussed the possibility with Vicy and Anse, and they agreed to take Andrew. The feud hostilities had been over for almost four years, and Anse had moved from the Tug River area and onto Island Creek, an area closer to Logan, West Virginia.

Anse's move to Island Creek (some call it Main Island Creek) was motivated by two events. First, Anse lost a long court battle over his Grapevine Creek land, which he had acquired through the courts, and had to sell it to settle his debts. After settling his debts, he traded some of the Grapevine Creek land for the large swath of land on Island Creek. Second, he wanted to get his family farther away from the Tug Fork Valley and all of the feud remnants. Anse and Holbert felt that there would be little danger to young Andrew if he came to Island Creek to go to school. As Andrew's recollections will prove, they did not give enough consideration to the armies of state and federal agents, or bounty hunters, who descended on the valley in search of the Hatfield brothers and "Devil Anse" himself.

For the next twelve years, Andrew became deeply involved in some of the most brutal remnants of the feud. He became a confidant of Anse and a loyal friend of Anse's sons Joe, Willis, Tennis, Troy, and Elias, and of Anse's daughter Rosanna. Most importantly, he became a messenger between Anse and his sons Cap and Johnse, who were hiding in the rugged mountains from state officials and bounty hunters. Cap and Johnse both had bounties on their heads—some say as much as $2,000—for the murders of McCoy family members. Anse's bounty reached $5,000, although he was never officially charged with a capital offense. He was charged as an accessory to murder on numerous occasions as patriarch of the Hatfield family.

Claude L. Chafin

Young Andrew would have been oblivious to the past deeds of Anse Hatfield and his sons Cap and Johnse, to a nine- or ten-year-old boy, they were simply family. And when called on to offer assistance to family members, he would do so. It would not have occurred to him to consider right from wrong. In his mind, if he was asked to do something by someone he loved, he would do it without consideration or second thought. If it was family, it was always right.

Prologue

Sitting out of reach on a fragile poplar tree branch, Andrew stared down at the black bear. The bear, standing on his hind legs and grasping the tree trunk, was threatening to climb. Andrew wasn't frightened of the bear; he was used to black bears, having fed and cared for his uncle Anse's bears for months now. He knew the bear was interested only in the slab of ham Aunt Vicy had packed in the sack he carried over his shoulder. And he knew the poplar tree was too small to hold the bear if it did try to reach him.

Still, the sun had been down for hours, and the bear was getting harder to see in the pitch-black forest. Even the light of a full moon could not penetrate the thickness of the underbrush. Andrew saw eyes and teeth, nothing more. Andrew was concerned about spending the night in the tree, as it was flimsy, and he chanced falling while he slept. He needed to find a better spot.

The standoff with the bear had lasted for better than an hour, and Andrew's legs were getting numb from holding them in an awkward position. He was afraid of shifting his weight, and he was afraid of dropping the sack. Andrew knew that Cap Hatfield would not be happy if he arrived without the food. He had seen Cap's temper when he was not happy. Andrew would sit a little longer.

Andrew nodded off to sleep, jerked wide awake again, and looked down to see if the bear was still there. He was. Now Andrew was getting scared. The bear could outwait him, and he knew it. He was faced with a decision: climb out of the tree and face the bear or settle in and take the chance of falling. He could not stay in that position any longer. He regretted climbing the first tree he saw when the bear came after him. He should have used better judgment and found a stronger, taller tree. It is interesting how little attention is given to details when you are running from a bear.

Andrew took the gunnysack off his shoulder and tied it to a branch above his head. He braced himself against the trunk of the poplar tree and pulled a small rope out of the sack. The branch he was standing on was not the biggest branch he could see, but it would have to do. He wrapped the rope around the trunk of the poplar and around his chest. He sat on the branch, leaned against the tree trunk, and tied a knot in the rope as high on his chest and under his arms as he could. He tied himself to the tree, hoping he would not fall off in his sleep. At the moment he was glad that he was no bigger than he was, or the branch would not hold him.

Andrew did not sleep much during the night; he awoke often to make sure the rope was secure and that he was still in the tree. On each occasion he looked down to check on the bear, but it was so dark he could not see. He looked up, trying to find the moon or stars. He saw nothing. At one point he worried that he had awakened blind. He held his hand up in the air, trying to see it. He could not. He thought he was going to cry, but he would not allow himself to do that. After all, he was nearly a grown man.

Andrew was nine years old.

At daybreak Andrew opened his eyes and looked down. The bear was gone. He quickly untied the rope around his chest and recovered the gunnysack from the branch overhead. He knew the bear would be back, so he had to get out of that tree as fast as he could. He scurried down the tree and took off running as fast as his aching legs would allow. He went back forty or fifty yards and into a thicket where he had constructed a corral of branches and brush to protect his horse. The horse was safe. He pulled away the loose branches and cleared a path. He untied the rope he had wrapped around the horse's front legs and untied the bridle straps he had tied to the corral. He led the horse through the opening and walked him to a tree stump. He would be glad when he grew tall enough to get on a horse without using a tree stump.

An hour into his ride, he stopped in a clearing by the Big Sandy River to water his horse. He sat under a shade tree and thought again about his errand. This was not the first errand he had run for his uncle. There had been two or three others. But this was the first one that

The Messenger

required him to sleep out in the forest overnight. His uncle Anse had not prepared him for the anxiety he felt at the moment. He thought again about his uncle's instructions.

"Andrew."

"Yessir."

"Do you think you can find Sprigg Township from here?"

"Yessir, I think so."

"I need you to take some things to Cap and Johnse for me."

"Yessir, I can do that. When do you want me to go?"

"You leave after school tomorrow. You'll head south on Island Creek and then go west in the valley till you get to Taylorville. You'll find a pass just out of Taylorville that will take you straight to the Tug River. Keep the Tug in sight, and go east. Just before you get into Sprigg, you go down to the riverbank and listen for the bark of a squirrel. Cap knows you are coming, and he will find you from there."

The squirrel bark was very familiar to Andrew. His uncle used it often in hunts and in signals to his family members. He even taught Andrew how to bark like a squirrel and how to tell the difference between the signaled bark and a real squirrel bark.

"Yessir," Andrew said confidently.

"Vicy will fix you enough food for four days. And she'll have a sack of stuff for Cap. If anybody asks you where you are goin', tell 'em you're on your way home."

"Yessir, I understand."

"You take the big bay; he's the calmest horse we got, and he won't run off at night."

Andrew wasn't afraid of his uncle, and he trusted him completely. He had no reservations about his journey, and he had no reservations about living with his aunt and uncle. But he missed his family. And he missed his mother's cooking and stories by the fire at night. He sometimes wished he hadn't agreed to live with his aunt and uncle to go to school. He wished there were a school closer to his home. He even wished he didn't like school so much, because then he just wouldn't go. None of his friends back home went to school, but his parents insisted that he would. He hadn't asked his aunt or uncle why Cap and Johnse were hiding or who they were hiding from when he was told of his errand. It never entered his mind.

Andrew's thoughts were interrupted by a man approaching on horseback.

"Mornin'," said the rider.

Andrew looked up but stayed seated under the tree. "Mornin'," he said.

"You're out mighty early this mornin'," said the stranger as he dismounted.

"Yessir, I am."

"Where you goin'?"

Andrew panicked when he realized that his visitor was huge. He had to be over six feet tall, and he wore a gun belt and a badge. The officer stood there holding his horse with one hand while the other hand rested on a silver-handled pistol. He was watching every move Andrew made. Andrew assumed he was looking for any reason to be suspicious. The officer asked again, "I said, where you goin'?"

"I'm on my way home to Cow Creek."

"Cow Creek?" replied the officer. "That's quite a ways for someone your age, ain't it? Are you by yourself?"

"Yessir."

"Where have you been?"

"Williamson," Andrew said, trying to be as calm as he could.

"Okay, what were ya doin' in Williamson?"

"I was delivering some stuff to Dr. Lawson for my pa."

"What's your name, young man?"

"Andrew Chafin."

"Are you Vicy's kin?"

"Yessir, she's my aunt. I live with them during school."

"Well, that's nice," replied the officer. "What ya got in the sack?"

"Some food Mrs. Lawson fixed for my ma."

"Well, ain't that nice. Can I look at it?"

"Yessir."

Andrew watched as the officer took the sack off the horse and opened it. He was so glad he told the truth about having the food. He waited for a reaction. The officer closed the sack and circled the horse. He ran his fingers around its rump and walked around to the other side as if contemplating his next move. Andrew, acting as casual as he could, started throwing pebbles into the river, ignoring the officer.

"Do you know Cap Hatfield, Andrew?"

"Yessir, I know him. Most everybody knows Cap."

"You seen him lately?"

"No, sir, I ain't."

"Do you know where he is?"

"No, sir, I don't."

"And if you knew, you would tell me, wouldn't you?"

"Yessir, I would."

Andrew sat and waited. He watched as the officer put the gunnysack back on the horse and then walked down to the water's edge. Andrew thought, *Is he trying to catch me in a lie? Does he believe me?*

Andrew just sat. He said nothing, and he did not look at the officer. Finally, the officer walked back to him. "What is your pa's name?"

"Holbert Chafin."

Andrew was doing all he could to keep from looking nervous. He stopped throwing pebbles, stood up, and looked straight at the officer. "Can I go now?"

The officer looked back at the tree line and then back to Andrew. "Sure, go ahead. You got a long ride ahead of you. You be careful now, and say hello to your pa for me."

"Yessir, I will. What's your name?"

"Tolbert. Just tell 'im Tolbert."

"I'll tell my pa."

"You do that, young man."

Andrew led the big bay to a tree stump and swung his leg up over the horse's back. He turned the horse's head away from the river and walked away. Officer Tolbert watched closely. Andrew started due north. He knew that Officer Tolbert would be watching, so he had to go in the direction of Cow Creek for a while, and then he would backtrack.

Once inside the tree line, Andrew turned to see if Officer Tolbert was still there. He wasn't. Andrew continued north until he lost sight of the river. Then he stopped the big bay and waited. He listened for rustling leaves or cracking branches. No sounds.

After several minutes, Andrew continued north. At the first opportunity, he turned back to the east and looked through the trees to see if he could find the river. Finally, a mile from his encounter with Officer Tolbert, he came to a clearing and looked to the south. There was the Tug River, a few hundred yards away and much lower in elevation than where he was. He looked up to find the sun; it was almost directly above him.

Andrew figured he had lost more than an hour trying to avoid Officer Tolbert. He thought it was near noon, and he had a long way to go. He slapped the bay across the shoulder with the reins and started down the incline toward the Tug. He pushed the bay to a near gallop; he did not want to spend another night in the mountains alone. The black bear had taken a toll on his nerves, and he did not want to sleep in a tree again anytime soon.

It was nearing dusk when Andrew saw the first signs of civilization ahead. He was on the outskirts of Sprigg Township. Uncle Anse had told him to go down to the Big Sandy and wait. He found a clearing and walked down to the water's edge. He held the big bay's reins while the horse drank from the river. Andrew looked around; no one was in sight. *This is as good a place to wait as any,* he thought. He tied the horse to a tree branch and sat down under the tree to wait.

He didn't have to wait long. Within minutes he heard the faint bark of a squirrel. He jumped up and listened. First there was silence and then another high-pitched, barely distinguishable squirrel bark coming from the trees behind him.

Andrew untied the horse and walked toward the barking sound. There were no more distinguishable sounds. He heard the rippling of the water but nothing from the squirrel. As he neared the tree line, he stopped and looked around. And he waited. Finally he heard another high-pitched bark coming from inside the trees over his shoulder. He walked toward the sound. About ten yards inside the tree line, as he passed a chinquapin bush, a hand grabbed his arm, pulling him to the ground. He looked up to find Cap with his finger across his lips, indicating silence. Andrew froze. Cap did not move. The horse just stood there, his tail swishing against the chinquapin bush. Cap got up, moved the horse around the bush, and tied him to a branch out of sight. They sat for what seemed to Andrew to be a long time, though it was less than ten minutes. Finally Cap said, "Let's go!"

Cap Hatfield, Anse's twenty-eight-year-old son, had been hiding in the mountains for nearly a year, avoiding bounty hunters and

Kentucky officials, who wanted his arrest for his part in the feud with the McCoy family, including numerous killings. Cap had a permanent snarl on his face that spoke clearly of evil. His left eye moved constantly left to right, right to left, but his right eye did not move at all. Andrew did not fear Cap. Cap was family and had always treated him with kindness. He needed Andrew, and it showed in his actions.

Cap grabbed the horse's reins and led it off through the thick underbrush. Andrew followed. A half mile into the forest, Andrew saw Johnse sitting on a log. Andrew did not know Johnse as well as he knew Cap, and he was nervous around him. Johnse was Anse's oldest son, and while he did not have Cap's reputation for brutality, he was equally brutal. But he needed Andrew as well. Neither of the Hatfield brothers were particularly friendly, but they were not threatening either, especially to Andrew. They knew that Andrew was their life blood to Anse, and they would protect him at all costs.

"Where you been, boy?" Johnse asked.

"I got stopped by an officer."

"What did you tell him?"

"I told him what Uncle Anse told me to tell him, that I was on my way home."

"Did he believe you?"

"Yessir, I think so. He went back toward Matewan."

Cap took the horse's reins again and said, "Let's go."

Johnse got up and followed Cap. Both men had two guns strapped to their sides, and both carried long-barreled rifles. Cap had two ammo belts crisscrossing his shoulders. They were dressed in dark clothing and tall boots, with wide-brimmed hats pulled down over their eyes.

Andrew fell in behind the two as they went deeper into the woods. A hundred yards or more from where they met Johnse, they came upon a lean-to built out of tree branches and shrubs. It was barely visible. Cap tied the horse to a tree branch, and they sat under the lean-to. By now the sun was gone, and it was getting dark. Cap opened the sack of food, and the two men ate like they had not eaten in a week. Andrew chewed on his dried beef. Cap passed a mason jar full of water around, and all three took a long drink.

"Did Ma pack us any fuel?" asked Johnse.

"Nope," Cap said.

"Damn."

Andrew looked at both men. He thought, *What does he mean by fuel?* But he didn't ask. Nancy Hatfield, the biggest bootlegger in Mingo County, had given moonshine the name "fuel" to disguise her wares. It sounded innocent when discussing a price with customers.

Cap said, "You spend the night here, Andrew, and then head out in the morning,"

"Yessir." Andrew was glad to have the company in the deep forest. He did not like sleeping in the woods alone, but he would not let the Hatfields know it. Cap took the saddle off the bay and dropped the blanket down on top of it. Andrew laid his head on the blanket and closed his eyes. He was asleep in seconds.

At daybreak, Andrew felt a nudge and opened his eyes. Cap was standing over him, gun in hand. "Take off, Andrew," he said. "We're breaking camp."

Andrew jumped up immediately; he was very uneasy and ready to go home.

Cap and Johnse turned and walked farther into the forest. Andrew took the reins of the big bay and turned south toward the river. There was a heavy mist in the air, and a chill that made Andrew pull his light jacket tighter around his shoulders. He walked the bay to the south until he saw the river. With the river in sight, he turned west and then to the north, on his way back to Taylorsville. He had a two-day ride in front of him, and he was not looking forward to it. *What if I run into Officer Tolbert again? How will I explain why I'm here?*

Andrew thought about his errand a lot on the way home. He did not fully understand what Cap and Johnse had done or why the officer seemed to be looking for them. He did not understand why Anse had sent him with the food when there were others who were older and could have done it. He wondered again if it was wise to be living with Aunt Vicy and Uncle Anse. And he wondered why they called his uncle "Devil"; he didn't seem like a devil. And as far as Andrew was concerned, he never would.

1

HOLBERT AND LUCINDA, THE WEDDING

And Dad was a gentle man too. He had a great sense of humor and he loved making fun of himself. And I tell you what, he loved us kids, loved us. There wasn't anything he wouldn't do for Mom or us kids.

It was a simple wedding, as weddings were in those days, with a justice of the peace presiding. The ceremony, conducted in a small office inside the Logan County Courthouse in Logan Courthouse, West Virginia, was very short and very sweet. Holbert Chafin wore a three-piece, dark brown suit, a white, high-collar shirt, and a silver-tipped, string tie. His high-top, laced, brown boots were neatly polished. Lucinda Browning wore an ankle-length, dark blue, high-necked dress with white buttons, puffy shoulders, long sleeves that buttoned tightly around her wrists, and high-top, black shoes with black buttons. Her hair was in a tight bun at the back of her head. The wedding was witnessed by the bride's older brother, L. H., and her younger sister, Perlina Browning.

"Holbert Chafin, do you take this woman, Lucinda Browning, to be your lawfully wedded wife?"

"Yessir," said a very agreeable Holbert.

"You should say 'I do,' Holbert."

"I do," repeated Holbert.

"Lucinda Browning, do you take this man, Holbert Chafin, to be your lawfully wedded husband?"

"I do."

Lucinda was a quick study.

"Then by the power vested in me by the great state of West Virginia, I now pronounce you man and wife. You may kiss the bride."

Odds are that Holbert had never kissed Lucinda before that kiss, but considering the time, that would not be unusual. The engagement had been short, one week. Holbert had asked her father, Edmund Browning, for permission to marry his daughter on Sunday morning after church, and he asked Lucinda while walking her home from church on the same day, probably while positioned on one knee. They were married the following Saturday, June 9, 1881. Holbert was eighteen and Lucinda was nineteen.

Holbert was the only child of Joshua Chafin and Emeranda "Amanda" Dempsey. His father, Joshua, was born in 1841 and married Amanda in 1860, when she was fifteen. He enlisted in the Confederate army in 1862, at twenty-one, in Abb's Valley, Virginia. Amanda was pregnant with Holbert when Joshua went off to war. Joshua had been gone only a few months when Amanda went into labor, delivered Holbert, and died in childbirth. Joshua was released from the military in early 1864 and came back to Logan to raise Holbert alone.

In the short period of time that Joshua was in the military, he fought twenty-seven battles and became known as a hardened, disciplined soldier who worked hard and paid attention to detail. He instilled those same qualities in Holbert.

Holbert did not have the advantage of a nurturing mother and had to fend for himself for most of his young life. Joshua was an attentive father but at the same time demanding and strict. Holbert did not attend school formally, but he learned to read and write while young, and he quickly learned that hard work brought success. As a young man, he went to work for Edmund Browning, who was impressed with his determination and work ethic, his serious demeanor, and his intelligence. Each task that was given to Holbert was handled quickly and efficiently. It was understandable, therefore, that Edmund had no objection when Lucinda caught Holbert's eye.

At eighteen, Holbert already wore a signature bushy mustache that he would eventually take with him to his grave. He was not a big man, either in statue or girth, but he was lean and strong, a by-product of his father's military influence. Lucinda found him attractive.

Lucinda was raised with L. H. and Perlina on a farm in Logan County, West Virginia, by parents well along in their years. Edmund was forty-six years old when she was born, and her mother, Jane, was forty-three. They were hardworking and disciplined, and they expected the same from their offspring. Lucinda's young life was spent doing farm chores during the daylight hours, mending, sewing, and cooking during the evening hours, and going to church on Sunday mornings. Few of the Browning children had a formal education, but they had the advantage of loving parents, a stable environment, and an ethic of hard, honest work.

At nineteen, Lucinda was razor thin. Her long, dark hair was constantly in a tight bun—her way of keeping it out of the way for her numerous chores and kitchen duties. Her figure would best be described as tight, with no important curves anywhere. She had long and shapely legs that embarrassed her, so she kept them hidden under a full-length skirt most of the time. There seemed to be a self-conscious side to both Holbert and Lucinda, a trait that would attract them to each other.

Lucinda, or as Holbert called her, Lucindy, was the cutest thing he had ever seen, with dark blue eyes, dark brown hair, and olive skin that stretched over a thin but vibrant body. And she was no bigger than a heifer calf. Holbert figured she wouldn't eat much.

Holbert was leaving Logan Courthouse in a few days, and he wanted to take Lucinda with him. Her father was not too happy about it, but Lucinda had made up her mind to go. Her father was providing them with a place to stay and employment, but he felt that Lucinda should stay at home until Holbert was settled and working. Holbert was determined to purchase a few acres near Barnabus, West Virginia, as quickly as he could, but in the meantime he would work for Browning and save his money. He was young and ambitious, and having Lucinda with him just made everything better.

Bright and early on Monday morning (a concession to Browning not to travel on the Sabbath), Holbert and Lucinda set out in a wagon carrying all their worldly possessions. The wagon was pulled by two two-year-old mules, following two rutted dirt paths that resembled a very narrow road. Their worldly possessions probably included a pistol, a rifle, several rounds of ammunition, an ax, a plow, hand tools and kitchen utensils, a wash tub, lye soap, a few changes of clothes, blankets, maybe a few bales of hay, a sack of corn grain and wheat grain, bridles, a tent, food provisions for a couple of weeks, a copy of the Holy Bible, and as many US silver dollars as Holbert could have saved. These were bare essentials in the mountains.

They spent the first night in a small clearing, sleeping under the wagon, two blankets under them, one on top. For dinner Lucinda heated the ham hock her mother had packed, simmering it in a skillet over an open fire of twigs and branches. They drank cider from a small mason jar. After dinner they began their very first postwedding conversation. Holbert had their future firmly planted in his mind, but he never got around to talking about it. Lucinda was going on pure faith, but she had questions for which she needed answers.

"Holbert, you said we're going to buy a farm? What kind of farm? What will we raise?"

Holbert was anxious to respond to Lucinda—and he would tell the story often to his young children around an evening fire. "Cows, pigs, chickens, corn, depending on how much land I can buy. Lucindy, the land is beautiful! We will have huge trees, grass, and a creek of fresh water. It will be the perfect place for a home. We will raise lots of kids to help with the chores, and we will build our own home."

Lucinda was not as enthusiastic. It sounded like a lot of work to her, but she was impressed with his enthusiasm, and at some point she might even fall in love with him. But she was not there yet.

Lucinda had slept with Holbert on the night of their wedding, her first night alone with a man, but both had been too anxious to enjoy their time together, and both were unsure of what to expect next. They went immediately to sleep. This night they would do the same. She had more questions, but they would wait for another day.

Holbert was not sure of what he was promising, but he was short only in the details. He knew the land, he knew farming, and he knew what resources were available in nearby Barnabus. He was confident he could make it work.

"I'll take care of you, Lucindy; you'll see. We'll be fine."

At daybreak they repacked the wagon and continued south through the rugged West Virginia mountains on the expanded logging trail toward Barnabus. The distance, some twenty miles, would seem trivial later, but for two newlyweds, it was ominous. The farther they went, the more determined they became. They were going to make a new home and raise lots of kids. This trip was a minor inconvenience.

At four that afternoon, they pulled to a stop in front of a general store in Barnabus, West Virginia, exhausted but excited and full of energy. Holbert helped Lucinda from the wagon, and they walked into the store as nervous newlyweds and new residents. They were welcomed by a jovial storekeeper. "Good afternoon, folks. May I help you?"

"Yessir, we would like some milk and a small tin of butter, please, sir."

"Comin' right up. Are you folks new in town?"

"Yessir, we're going to work on the Browning farm a few miles south of here on Cow Creek. We hope to be here for a long time."

"Well, we are mighty glad to have you. I think you will like Barnabus and Cow Creek; mighty nice folk here."

"Thank you, we are glad to be here. Can you tell us of a place to pitch a tent for the night? It's raining a little outside, and we won't be goin' on till mornin'."

"Sure, there is room right behind the store. Pitch it there, and welcome to Barnabus."

"Thank you, sir. We appreciate it. We'll see you in the morning."

Neither Holbert nor Lucinda slept well that night; both were anxious to get on to Cow Creek and survey their new home. By the time the sun was peeking through the treetops, they were on their way. They followed the rippling Cow Creek stream through a wide valley surrounded by tall, tree-covered mountains on both sides. At midmorning Holbert stopped the mule team by the side of the logging trail and said, "Come with me, Lucindy."

Holbert walked around the mule team, reached up, and helped Lucinda off the wagon. She was still wearing an ankle-length dress to conceal those long legs that embarrassed her. They walked to the edge of a clearing, and there in the distance, fifty yards away, sat the most beautiful piece of land Lucinda had ever seen. The tall trees surrounded an open field of green grass, bordered on one side by a narrow expanse of water. "That is Cow Creek over there, and this pasture is going to be our farm." Lucinda was amazed, and she finally understood why Holbert was so excited. She turned and faced him, her hand over her open mouth and a tear in her eye.

"Holbert, it is beautiful!" she said.

"I knew you would like it. I want to build a house right over there under that tall oak tree. And over there I want rows and rows of corn. Back over here I'll build pens for chickens and hogs, and over there . . ."

Lucinda stopped him. She was having trouble keeping up, he was talking so fast. "Let's work on the house first," she said. Holbert knew he was dreaming big, but he was determined. Browning was to pay him twenty dollars a week, and he was sure he could save half of it toward his land purchase. He told himself that when he had saved $200, he would buy the land and have enough left to build a house. He worked on a half-dozen homes while in the employment of Browning, and he was confident that he could build one for himself.

Holbert was a good employee, and Browning was pleased with his work and that he was taking such good care of his daughter. By Christmas, Holbert was nearing his $200 goal, and he began looking for land. He wanted to stay near Cow Creek and Barnabus, and he wanted land he could farm, not the mountainous terrain that surrounded Barnabus. He was anxious to get on with building his house, because he knew he had to hurry. Lucinda was beginning to show.

Lucinda spent her days planting and caring for a small garden of essentials. They had a dozen rows of vegetables that would serve them well in the spring and summer. She drew water from the creek and boiled it until their well could be drilled. The days were full and hard, but they were at home and happy. The one-room cabin that Browning provided them was comfortable and would be a pleasant place for the birth of their first child.

Jane Chafin was born on May 16, 1882. She was a beautiful little baby girl, and Holbert was pleased. She had the look of a Browning, with a full, round face, long fingers, and long legs.

There was a slight twinge of disappointment in Holbert that his firstborn was not a boy, but he hid it well and pampered Lucinda and Jane with all the love he could muster. He knew that there would be other children, and he could only hope that a few of them would be boys. West Virginia farms need boys, lots of boys.

By summer, Holbert finally settled on a piece of land. It was twenty-eight acres, three miles outside of Barnabus, and it included a dozen acres he could farm. He paid $2.50 an acre for the tillable land and thirty cents an acre for the mountainous terrain. He told Mr. Browning that he was going to start on his new home immediately, and as soon as it was built he would leave Browning's employment and work his own farm. It was August 1882.

At the same time that Holbert and Lucinda were settling in on Cow Creek, and during the same week that Holbert closed on his twenty-eight acres of land, his uncle Anse's brother Ellison died after being stabbed during an encounter with the McCoy family of Pike County, Kentucky. While Holbert and Lucinda were isolated in the Cow Creek Valley, working at their farm, the Anse Hatfield family continued their decade-long war with the McCoy family, south of them on the Big Sandy and Tug River. On more than one occasion, Holbert was tempted to travel south to assist his uncle, but Lucinda would hear none of that. Her strong will and determination prevented Holbert from becoming involved in the Hatfields' fight with the McCoy family that was spilling blood all along the Tug River from Williamson to Matewan.

By spring of 1883, Holbert, Lucinda, and baby Jane were moving into a brand-new, one-room log cabin a hundred yards off Cow Creek. They had their big trees, their green grass, and room for a garden. The clearing in front of their house allowed for plenty of early-morning sunlight and late afternoon shadows. The clearing through the mountains, carved by the creek traversing their property, allowed them an extra thirty minutes of sunlight a day.

The house was a split-log, single-story house with a small, covered porch on the front. There was a large, open-faced fireplace along one wall on the west side and a long loft for sleeping along the east wall. There was an open kitchen in the back with a door leading out to a newly dug well up the hill from Cow Creek.

The Cow Creek farm grew over the next few years to include a barn, a chicken coop, a hog pen, a stable and corral, acres of corn, a vegetable garden, and an orchard of apple trees. The farm began producing more goods than Holbert and his family needed, so they began selling to neighbors. Holbert's hog population had grown considerably over the years, and he began selling a few hogs to the residents of Barnabus. He even traded two hogs for a heifer calf.

Holbert concentrated on his hog population, because hogs meant survival in the mountains of West Virginia. They could graze anywhere. Most of the land in West Virginia was drastically sloped and not tillable, but hogs could eat on it. So hogs became a staple in the lives and on the tables of West Virginians. If one had enough land for a few rows of corn and a few hogs, living was cheap. And so it was on Cow Creek.

The Holbert Chafin family had almost all they needed on their Cow Creek farm, except they had few neighbors, no stores closer than Barnabus, no church, and most importantly, no school. Holbert and Lucinda began to worry about the issue of school as they watched Jane grow, and they knew that other children would follow. It was a consideration they would have to face. Holbert felt, as most of his neighbors felt, that school was not as important for little girls as it was for the boys. And since families needed lots of boys for farm duties, there was little incentive to have a school that would take away the time needed for chores.

Holbert and Lucinda realized that while they could basically read and write, they missed out by not having a formal education. And they had decided that their children would go to school. Holbert knew that he had to figure something out before they had a son. It was a problem they would have to face soon, as their first male child was on the way. Andrew Lee Chafin was born on March 30, 1886, four years after Jane. Andrew was clearly a Chafin boy. He had none of the Browning features. His hands were small, his feet were small, and he had short, almost birdlike legs. His head was tiny, with oversized eyes, and thin hair. He was clearly a Chafin.

Holbert had successfully hidden his disappointment with the birth of his daughter; he had so wanted a boy. Farming is a difficult business without lots of help, and every farming family needs lots of sons. Jane would be a great help with Lucinda in the home and garden, but he needed help in the fields.

But his disappointment continued. Holbert had the son he wanted, but Andrew was born prematurely and was no bigger than Jane at her birth. He worried that all their children would be small. Holbert held Andrew often and examined his feet and hands; they were tiny. Over the next few months, he became even more concerned. Andrew had little appetite, and feeding him was a challenge. He would fall asleep while breast-feeding, and Lucinda had to wake him constantly. Andrew was a quiet baby who hardly ever made a sound, and he seemed happy. He was just not growing.

By the time Andrew started walking at fourteen months, Jane was being taught reading and writing by a circuit teacher who came to the house once a week. Andrew would sit quietly by his sister and watch, never making a sound. He seemed more interested in the lessons than Jane did. He was mesmerized by the sound of the teacher's voice and by all the marks she made on paper.

A year later Andrew began to involve himself in the lessons. He asked questions of Jane and the teacher. He got his own piece of paper and tried to duplicate the marks that Jane was making. He listened intently as Jane read, and when she put a book down, he picked it up and flipped the pages. It was becoming clear that Andrew was far more interested in books than he would ever be in farming.

Andrew was three years old and Jane was seven when Lucinda gave birth to her next child. Oliver was born on January 13, 1889. He was full term and much larger than either Andrew or Jane at birth. He was more Browning than Chafin, with long fingers, big feet, and long legs. Holbert was encouraged, knowing he had his first real farmhand.

By then the one-room home had been doubled in size, made necessary by their ever-expanding family. Holbert added a duplicate single room adjacent to the original structure, separated by a covered walkway, known locally as a dogtrot. The second room was used for sleeping quarters and the original room for living and eating. It was a typical West Virginia mountain home, in a not-so-typical West Virginia setting—on level ground.

Andrew was fascinated with Oliver. He loved holding him and playing with his fingers. They were so long and delicate. He fought with Jane constantly over who could hold him next or play with him while he was in his crib. They both lost interest at diaper time. Andrew could not wait until Oliver grew up. He just knew that he and Oliver would be best friends.

Holbert, now a twenty-eight-year-old farmer, blacksmith, and lumberjack, had big ideas to improve the family's well-being. He traveled back to Logan Courthouse in the spring of 1891 to see about the possibility of a loan for a grain mill he wanted to build over Cow Creek. He had the land and easy access to flowing water; he just needed the funds to build the turbine and housing. If he owned the mill, he would save the cost of having to haul his corn to Barnabus, pay a fee to mill his grain, and then haul the grain back to the farm. If he worked at it, he felt he could sell milling services to his neighbors for enough to pay the loan note. The bank listened, asked questions, checked his banking record, and agreed to front him the money. By summer, Holbert was beginning the third grain mill in Logan County, West Virginia.

The homestead that Holbert had dreamed of and sold so easily to Lucinda was becoming a reality. All his hard work was beginning to pay off, and all his plans for the future of his family were coming to fruition. In the mountains of West Virginia at the turn of the century, nothing took the place of hard work and honest dealings. Holbert had learned that lesson from his father, Joshua, and he would pass it on to his own offspring.

But Holbert's family would not live in isolation. In Mingo County, West Virginia, in the late 1800s, everyone's life involved William Anderson Hatfield in one way or another. As a relative of Anderson, Holbert would be even more involved.

2

WILLIAM ANDERSON "DEVIL ANSE" HATFIELD

I remember watching this big man ride up on a black horse, and I thought, Wow, this is somebody really important. *He just had an air about him that made me pay attention. Dad walked over to him, reached up, and shook his hand while the man was still sitting on his horse. I walked up and stood behind my dad, and Dad said, "Andy, this is your uncle Anse."*

Holbert was developing a countywide reputation as a general handyman. He could fix anything, and neighbors began bringing him their saddles, yokes, plows, harnesses, and other farming equipment for repair. And he was quite obliging. He spent his days farming or working on his mill, and at night he worked on his neighbors' broken implements. It was at one of these neighbor visits that six-year-old Andrew first met his uncle Anse.

Anse rode up to Holbert's barn, dismounted, greeted Holbert, and walked over to Andrew. He stuck out his hand and said, "Nice to meet you, young man." Andrew extended his hand, which was not much bigger than Anse's index finger. Andrew didn't actually shake Anse's hand; he simply extended it, and Anse did the rest. Anse could have done serious damage to young Andrew's hand with that handshake, but it was as soft and gentle as if he were holding a bird.

Anse was big, over six feet tall, but his face had a frail look to it. He had dark bags under his eyes and deeply sunken cheeks, hidden as much as possible by a full beard. It was the longest and blackest beard Andrew had ever seen. And his eyebrows matched the beard. They were long, bushy, and seemed to go off in numerous directions. There were tuffs of coal-black hair sticking out in all directions from under a wide-brimmed, black hat. Andrew noticed, with interest, a single bullet stuck in the hat brim just above Anse's right ear. It seemed both out of place and necessary at the same time.

Anse had on dark slacks that were neatly tucked into boots that came up nearly to his knees. He wore a wide leather belt and a holster that had his initials, WAH, burned into the side. The belt was filled with ammunition. And the holster, which was held to his right leg by two leather straps, held a silver-handled gun. The holster dropped slightly to his right, putting the gun within inches of his long fingers when he stood. He wore a dark gray shirt, buttoned all the way to his neck, disappearing underneath the long, shaggy beard. In contrast to his clothes, he had a warm smile and bright, penetrating, blue eyes. There was strength evident in Anderson Hatfield's look, and it was funneled through those eyes.

Andrew watched and listened intently as Uncle Anse made comments about what a fine-looking young man he was and how he would grow up to be a big help to his dad around the farm. Andrew loved the attention. Anse walked back to his horse and got a bridle out of his saddle bag and walked off with Holbert to the barn. Andrew followed. The two men discussed the problem with the bridle and came to a conclusion that Andrew didn't understand, but Anse seemed satisfied. He shook Holbert's hand again and walked back to his horse.

Holbert kept the bridle and went back to the plow he had been repairing when Anse rode up. Andrew followed Anse back to his horse and stood quietly while he remounted. Andrew stared at the long-barreled rifle that was strapped in a leather case that extended from the saddle bag to the big, black horse's neck.

"Young man, it was nice to meet you," said Anse. "I am sure I will see you again. Have your pa bring you over to meet my kids one day soon. You be a good help to your ma and pa, and you will grow to be a fine man one day."

"Yessir, I will," Andrew said.

And with that comment, Anse Hatfield turned his horse and rode away. Andrew watched until he was out of sight and then joined his dad in the barn. "Pa, where does Uncle Anse live?"

"Oh, he's got a place a few miles from here on Island Creek."

"Can we go see him sometime? He said he wants me to meet his kids."

"Sure we can. You can go with me when I take his bridle back to him."

Andrew looked forward to the trip. He didn't know where Island Creek was, and he didn't know how far "a few miles" was, but it sounded like an adventure to him, and he was anxious for the adventure.

Later that night, after Andrew, Jane, and Oliver were in bed, Holbert told Lucinda about Anse's visit earlier that day. He told her that Andrew wanted to go with him when he took Anse's bridle back and that he planned to take him.

Holbert decided this would be a good time to talk to Lucinda about the school issue. He told her about the school Anse had built for the neighborhood kids and suggested that they talk to Anse and his wife, Vicy, about the possibility of Andrew living with them and going to school there. Vicy was Holbert's aunt and Andrew's great-aunt, even though Andrew would never quite understand what all that meant, so he would simply call them Aunt Vicy and Uncle Anse.

Lucinda was not enthusiastic about the idea of Andrew leaving home. And she was uncomfortable with him living with the Hatfields. She knew of the Hatfield family's fights with the McCoy family, and she knew of all the bounty hunters and detectives who roamed through the mountains looking for Cap and Johnse. She was greatly concerned for Andrew's safety if they made such a move, and she expressed as much to Holbert.

Holbert did not push the issue with Lucinda, but he knew they would have to talk about it again soon. Both Holbert and Lucinda knew that if their children were going to attend school, Island Creek School might be the only option. It might take years to get a school closer to their home. There was no incentive among the neighbors to invest in a school that would take the young boys out of the fields and put them in a classroom.

The late-night conversation ended with an agreement that they would discuss it further before Holbert took the bridle back to Anse. But it was obviously important. Andrew continued to show an interest in books and reading. He pestered Jane constantly, asking her to read to him or share her books. Jane did not have Andrew's interest in reading or in books generally. She was reluctant to spend time with him when she much preferred playing with her dolls or being outside with her mother. At the same time, Andrew showed little interest in farm chores; they seemed boring and hard. He much preferred sitting in front of a fire, reading Jane's books.

Holbert and Lucinda decided not to mention the school to Andrew or even to bring the subject up again until after Andrew's visit to Anse's house. They knew that if Andrew did not like Anse's home, Aunt Vicy, or their children, it would not work anyway. If the Island Creek School was indeed an option, Andrew's visit to the Hatfield home had taken on a much bigger meaning.

A week after Anse's visit, Holbert found Andrew flipping pages in one of Jane's books and approached him with the news. "Andy, I am taking Uncle Anse's bridle back tomorrow if you still want to go with me."

"Yessir, I do. When are we going?"

"We'll head out after breakfast. I want to get an early start so we can be back before dark. You get in bed early tonight so I can get you up early in the morning."

Holbert had made a mistake mentioning the trip to Andrew before bedtime. Andrew did not sleep a wink all night. Not long after he finally dropped off to sleep, his dad was shaking him to get him up. But the lack of sleep did not matter to Andrew. He was so anxious to make the trip that he was on the floor and running for the kitchen before Holbert could get out of the way.

As the sun cleared the treetops to the east, Holbert and Andrew finished their hot biscuits-and-gravy breakfast, and Holbert saddled the mare. Andrew was doing all he could to assist; for the first time in his life he was helping with a farm task without being asked. Lucinda watched from the small porch as Holbert mounted the mare and pulled Andrew up behind him. They headed northeast toward Barnabus.

Uncle Anse's visit to the Chafin farm more than two weeks ago left Andrew with numerous questions. *Why was this man so important? What was his family like? How many kids did he have?* His trip to Island Creek would help answer many of those questions and introduce many more.

3

ISLAND CREEK SCHOOL, A NEW LIFE
(THE SCHOOL IN THE BOTTOMS)

When I first saw Uncle Anse's house, I was surprised at how old it looked. I was used to our house, which was pretty new, and Anse's place looked like it had been there for centuries. And then I saw the bear! Uncle Anse had a black bear chained to a tree in his front yard. The bear was just pacing, two or three steps to the left then two or three to the right, and all the time dragging a chain behind his left rear leg. He never took his eyes off us.

The trip to Island Creek was, in itself, an adventure for young Andrew. They passed through Barnabus just as the sun formed shadows across the front of the general store, where Holbert and Lucinda had spent the night eight years earlier. The town had grown by a dozen cabins, several stores, and two stables. Each of the stables had a corral visible in the back. Horses stood at the corral fences, watching Holbert and Andrew ride by. People walked the dusty street, all going in different directions and all seeming to be in a hurry. Smoke drifted upward from several cabins, and the smell of bacon made Andrew hungry.

As they left Barnabus heading south, the buildings and people disappeared. There were trees, bushes, and undergrowth—nothing more. They were on a wide path that allowed horses and wagons to pass each other if they were going in opposite directions, but even that would be difficult in rainy weather. And it was quiet. Andrew could count the number of birds flying around by the different sounds they made. There was no movement except for those birds and an occasional rabbit or deer that appeared at the tree line.

Andrew was getting tired holding on to Holbert's waist, and his head fell into Holbert's back when he dozed off. Holbert turned his head, looked down at him, and said, "Let's take a break, Andy." He stopped the mare, held on to Andrew's arm, and helped him slide down the side of the mare and stand for the first time in two hours. His legs were unsteady.

Holbert dismounted and led the mare to the rolling creek that lined the trail. The horse drank while Holbert recovered a canteen from his saddle bag, unscrewed the top, and handed it to Andrew. Andrew took a long swig from the canteen as he sat by the stream, watching the mare enjoying the clear, fresh water. Holbert took several strips of dried beef from the saddle bag and handed one to Andrew. Andrew fell back into the tall grass and looked up at the trees as he bit into the beef strip.

All of a sudden he was dreading getting back on the horse.

"Not much further, Andy," his father said. "We should be there in an hour. Are you doing all right?"

"Yessir, I'm doing fine."

"We'll rest here a little while and then move on."

Fifteen minutes later, Holbert was hoisting Andrew up behind him on the mare, and they were on their way once again toward the Hatfield home.

An hour later Holbert looked back at Andrew and said, "I see the house, Andy, and we'll be there in just a few minutes." They couldn't be there soon enough for Andrew's aching back.

Holbert and Andrew rode up to the front gate of Anse's home and dismounted. The gate was a primitive array of stripped tree branches strapped together vertically and held together by one horizontal branch at the top and another at the bottom. The gate was attached to a split-rail fence post by three pieces of leather. There wasn't a nail in the whole assembly, just branches and leather. The rest of the yard was enclosed with a two-tiered split-rail fence that disappeared into the tree line in both directions. The front yard was not really a yard; it was a sloped clearing where numerous trees had been cut down to the ground with parts of stumps clearly visible through the weeds and undergrowth. Anse was obviously not a gardener.

Holbert reached for the leather loop that attached the gate to the fence post and lifted it over the top. As he was about to push the gate open, a deafening growl engulfed them. Andrew jumped back and hid behind his father's leg. Holbert grinned and said, "It's all right, Andy. That is one of your uncle's pet bears; he keeps one or two around to scare off other animals or unwanted guests. He keeps them chained to that oak tree. Just don't go near 'im."

Anse was sitting on a front porch that stretched from one corner of the cabin to the other, watching Holbert and Andrew make their way up the slope to the house. The house was a primitive, unpainted clapboard structure with a single door in the center and a small window on either side. The porch was high enough off the ground to require two steps, but there was no railing around it, and there was sufficient trash under it to suggest that there may be animals under there as well. As Holbert and Andrew walked the horse to the front steps, Anse got up from a rocking chair and greeted them. A short, chubby woman came out of the front door, wiping her hands on a full-body apron. She was followed by a young girl and two boys.

"Welcome, Holbert," said Anse, "good to see you. And I'm glad you brought your son with you. Andrew, this here is your aunt Vicy, and this here's Rosanna. The shorter one there is Willis and that young feller is Joe. Y'all come on in and sit a spell. Joe, take Holbert's horse over to the barn and fetch 'im some water."

Vicy was dressed in an ankle-length, floral-print dress with a wide-laced collar tight around her neck. She wiped her hands on her apron constantly. Her hair was tied in a bun behind her head, pulled back tightly to expose a dominant forehead. She frowned. Even in greeting Andrew for the first time, Vicy could not muster a smile. Her years of living with Anse Hatfield, raising sons who were nearly impossible to control, and all the emotions and trauma that those years carried, made a smile a difficult task. She was indeed warm and welcoming, but the expression on her face would never show it.

Rosanna was cute, and Andrew took a liking to her immediately. She looked to Andrew to be about his age—seven or eight years old. Andrew would eventually shorten her name to Rosy, which was easier for him to say—and besides, she looked like a Rosy to him. She also had on a long dress with a high collar. But, in contrast to Aunt Vicy, she had a quick smile and was outgoing. At least for West Virginia women of the time she was outgoing, meaning that she didn't run in the house when a stranger appeared. She stood on the porch and stared at Andrew.

Willis seemed to be near Andrew's age as well. And, as would be expected, he was dressed more for playing in the barn than receiving company. He wore dirty, gray slacks, suspenders, and a floppy cap that fell to one side, stopped only by an oversized ear. His hair, sticking out from under the side of his cap, was as coal black as his father's.

Joe looked older than Andrew and wanted to show it. He gave Andrew a half smile, half smirk. He wore dark felt pants and a work jacket, buttoned all the way up. He had on a thin-brimmed hat that he pushed down over his eyes in a defiant manner. Andrew was not sure he was going to like Joe.

Holbert was quick to speak. "We can't stay long, Uncle Anse. I want to get home before dark. I just wanted to drop the bridle off and have you try it out to see if it is all right."

"I'll do that, Holbert. Come sit a bit. Joe, y'all take Andrew with you and show him around. I want to visit with his dad for a little while."

Andrew was not anxious to leave his father, but on the other hand, Rosy was kinda cute, so he didn't resist when she took his hand and led him away. They followed Joe around the corner of the house and disappeared. He could not have known about the conversation that was about to occur, some of which would alter his life completely. Anse would spend part of that conversation trying to persuade Holbert to work for him in his lumber business, and Holbert would spend the rest of the time asking if Andrew could live with his uncle and go to school. Andrew would not be pleased.

Holbert listened as politely as he could for Anse to finish talking about the lumber business so he could talk about the school. Anse, impressed with Holbert's work, his ambition, and his ability to make decisions and solve problems, was interested in luring Holbert into the lumber business. Anse did need help; his lumber business had suffered immensely since his move from Grapevine Creek to Island

Creek. He had lost most of his lumber acreage in a lawsuit, and he was having difficulty competing with the new lumber companies moving into the valley that were larger and better equipped.

After Anse finished his proposal, Holbert politely asked him if he could delay his answer until his mill was completed and their fourth child was a little older. Andrew's second sister, Louisa, was but one year old. The reality was that Holbert had no interest in working for Anse, but he did not want to jeopardize his chances of getting Anse and Vicy to keep Andrew either.

After Anse finished his offer of employment, Holbert raised the subject of school, explaining how important he felt the school was for Andrew. He explained how Andrew showed more interest in books than the farm and that he was still too small to be much help. Anse listened intently and excitedly agreed to keep Andrew. But Holbert needed Vicy's approval too. He knew that Vicy would be the one with the additional work, and he wanted her in the conversation. Anse was very reluctant; he never included Vicy in decisions. He rarely included her in conversations. That was just not done in the Hatfield household. But finally he agreed. They walked into the cabin, found Vicy at the sink, and asked her to join them.

Vicy walked into the room hesitantly, sat in a chair on the opposite side of the room, and folded her hands in her lap, which was still covered by the apron. There were specks of fresh blood on the side of the apron, which Holbert attributed to the stack of chicken parts he saw on the counter. Holbert explained the school situation and raised the possibility of Andrew living with them to go to school. Vicy was clearly reluctant to voice an opinion. Any opinion from Vicy would have been unusual. Holbert had known his aunt Vicy for years, but he had never known her to speak more than a few mumbled sounds at the end of a question or a few hallelujahs at a church service. She was easily intimidated by Anse and only spoke when he seemed to give her permission. She looked frightened.

Holbert began his explanation, telling her about the lack of schools in the Cow Creek area, Andrew's interest in school, and the possibility of his living with them and going to Island Creek School with the Hatfield kids. He even offered to pay for Andrew's keep. Vicy was very quiet and clearly hesitant. When Holbert asked her directly for her opinion, she brought up the issue of bounty hunters and state officials who came looking for Anse and their sons, and she said she was worried for Andrew's safety.

Anse became defensive and dismissed her fears as nonsense. This was 1893, he pointed out, and the feud had been over for years. He let Vicy and Holbert know that he had the support of the community, which would make it impossible for bounty hunters to get near him. Vicy said no more. She did not even change her expression. She knew that Anse was mad, and she was not about to make it worse.

Yet Anse became more aggressive. He told Holbert that he thought Andrew would be good for his kids, especially Rosanna, Joe, and Willis, because they had no close friends and they were always fighting with each other. He insisted that he would love to have Andrew stay with them and said he would talk to the school immediately to make sure there was room.

The conversation ended abruptly when Joe, Rosy, and Andrew walked in the front door. They were laughing and teasing each other in a manner that would suggest they had known each other for a much longer time. Holbert decided it would be a good time to make their departure. He got up and walked across the room to hug his aunt. "Thanks for your thoughts, Aunt Vicy. We'll talk again." He walked over and shook Anse's hand and then walked toward the front door. "Andy, it's time to go home. Say good-bye to your cousins and let's head out. Anse, I appreciate your offer. We'll think carefully on everything you said."

Anse followed them to the door. "Can't y'all stay for a bite? Vicy can fix up some chicken and her famous biscuits in no time."

"Thanks, Anse, but Lucindy fixed some things for us, and we'll eat on the way home. I want to be home before dark."

"Holbert, remember what I said. Everything will be fine."

"I will, Anse. I appreciate it. We will see you soon."

"Holbert, tell Lucindy I'll drop by for a visit the first chance I get."

"I'll do it, Anse." Holbert mounted the mare, leaned down and picked Andrew up by the arm and dropped him on the horse behind him. He turned the mare's head and walked toward the gate.

Their horse walked slowly by the black bear and the poplar tree where it was chained. The bear continued his back-and-forth pacing, dragging the chain as he went. He made no move toward Holbert's horse, but the horse made a wide arc, staying out of reach of the bear. Andrew was fascinated.

Holbert waited until they were out of sight of the house before he brought up the short visit to the Hatfields.

"Andy, how did you like your cousins?"

"Fine."

"Were they nice?"

"Yessir."

"Did you like the barn?"

"Yessir."

Andrew was a boy of few words. It was clear that Holbert was not going to get anything out of him one way or the other. He and Lucinda would have to make the decision without any input from their son and deal with a reaction when they got one. The subject was not mentioned again on the long ride home.

Anse did not wait long for his visit to Holbert and Lucinda. He was so anxious to talk to Lucinda about Andrew and the Island Creek School, the School in the Bottoms. He arrived in Cow Creek two days later. While the Chafin kids were outside playing, Anse brought up the subject. He told Lucinda that the disagreements with the McCoy family had been over for years and that there were no hard feelings with that family anymore. He explained how he felt that Andrew would be good for his own kids and the other kids in the neighborhood, including Cap's four. Anse told Lucinda that he was going by the school the next day to make sure there was room for Andrew. After thirty minutes of conversation the decision was made; Andrew would move into the Hatfield home and go to the school.

Holbert and Lucinda put Oliver down for the night and then sat at the kitchen table with Jane and Andrew. Holbert knew that Lucinda was reluctant to send Andrew off to school, but they both agreed it was the right thing to do. Holbert felt the tension in the room before a word was spoken, and he could tell that Jane felt it too, but not Andrew. Jane sat quietly and watched her parents, her eyes glancing back and forth between the two. Holbert had agreed with Lucinda that he would be the one to let Andrew know what had been decided.

Lucinda wanted no part of that task. Holbert wasn't excited about it either, but he knew it had to be done.

Finally, Holbert built enough nerve to speak. "Andrew, it is time for school to start next week, and we have decided that you need to be in school."

Andrew looked up from Jane's book but said nothing. Jane looked at her dad and then Andrew. Andrew looked at his dad and asked the question they all knew was coming, "Where is school?"

"It is down the road from Uncle Anse's house," Holbert said. "You are going to stay with them during the school week, and we will pick you up on weekends and bring you home."

"I'm not going," said Andrew sharply.

"You'll be fine, Andy. We have talked to Uncle Anse about it, and they are glad to have you."

"I'm not going."

Jane had heard enough. She jumped up from her chair and ran out the door.

Lucinda had heard enough too. "Andy, you are a bright boy, and it would be a sin for you to miss school and maybe ruin your life forever. We don't want you gone so much either, but it is best for you, and you're going to do it."

It was now two against one, and Andrew was not winning. He slammed the book shut and ran out the door. Holbert and Lucinda decided to let him be. They knew this would be his reaction, and they were determined not to make a fight out of it. They had said all they were going to say at the moment. They would simply make the necessary arrangements and bring it up again in a few days. They hoped that eventually he would be fine with it.

Lucinda didn't go with Holbert to take Andrew to the Hatfields. She decided that if she were going to cry, she was going to do it alone. Jane wanted to go, but both parents said no to that; it would have been much harder on Andrew. Jane and her mother simply waved good-bye from the front door. When Holbert and Andy were out of sight, Lucinda and Jane walked back inside. Lucinda cried while standing at the sink, and Jane cried on her bed.

Vicy and Anse were waiting at the gate when the wagon arrived. Andrew was doing his best to be brave. He showed no fear as they pulled into the yard. Rosy and Joe ran to the wagon to greet them. It was clear that they had been instructed to make Andrew's arrival as painless as possible. Holbert offered his greetings and began unloading Andrew's things, including several of Jane's books and as many of Andrew's things as he wanted. Holbert was going to spend the night with Vicy and Anse to ease Andrew's anxiety. Unfortunately for Holbert, there was nothing to ease his anxiety.

Rosy and Joe did a good job of keeping Andrew busy for the afternoon and most of the evening. They ran, they played, they crawled around in the barn, and they pestered the black bear—anything to keep Andrew busy. For dinner, Vicy had cooked Andrew's favorite meal, chicken and dumplings, with apple pie for dessert. After dinner Rosy and Joe took Andrew to the loft, where they would sleep, and began telling stories of their neighborhood friends and the school. Anse and Holbert went out to the front porch to smoke their pipes. Vicy went to the kitchen with the dishes.

At bedtime, the Hatfield kids and Andrew climbed to the loft, laughing and giggling. Andrew had settled in and was no longer anxious, which made everyone more at ease. Vicy joined Holbert and Anse on the porch, where all three smoked their pipes. Vicy was as much a pipe smoker as either of the other two and probably enjoyed it even more than they did. Holbert and Anse talked about the neighborhood, about Nancy Hatfield, Cap's wife, and her struggle to raise four children by herself, and about the weather. They avoided any talk about the school. It was clear that Holbert was struggling with his decision to allow Andrew to live with the Hatfields, and it was not discussed anymore for the evening.

Early the next morning Holbert and Andrew had breakfast with Anse, Vicy, and their children. Then Holbert got up from the table and said good-bye to Andrew as casually as he could. He did not want to show any emotion. Andrew followed him out the front door and waved good-bye from the porch. Holbert could sense that Andrew wanted a hug, so he waited; he did not want to make the first move. Andrew finally ran from the porch to the wagon, climbed up, and gave Holbert a big hug. He then jumped down and ran to the barn. He did not turn around. Holbert waved good-bye to Anse and Vicy, slapped the mules with the long reins, and headed out the gate. And then he cried.

Soon after Holbert left, Anse picked up his Winchester, which he carried with him every time he left the house, and joined Rosy, Joe, and Andrew on the quarter-mile walk to the school. It was late September 1893, and Andrew would start the first grade. Rosy was starting the second grade, and Joe was starting fifth. For the first time, Andrew wished that his sister Jane was with them. He needed her support. But his parents knew Jane was not interested in books and would probably have fought them if they had attempted to send her to school full time.

The one-room school sat at the base of a steep mountain slope on the west side of Island Creek, with a wide expanse of flat yard in the front. There was plenty of space for young children to romp between the schoolhouse and the creek, and they used every inch of it. The school housed grades one through six and had a single teacher. She directed an assignment to the first grade and then moved to the second grade and then on through the room until all were working. She would circle the desks to make sure everyone was busy and then start the process all over again. Andrew had three classmates in his first-grade class, Rosy had three in her class, and Joe had two in his. There were no more than a dozen students in the entire schoolhouse. With the economics of the time, it would be unusual for any of the classmates to finish the sixth grade.

As Andrew walked into the building with the Hatfields, all eyes were on them at the front door. There was a new kid in class, and all the students were very curious. Andrew was embarrassed. Rosy went to her assigned seat, as did Joe. Andrew stood at the front door with Anse. The young teacher walked over to them, leaned down, put her hand on Andrew's shoulder, and welcomed him to the school. Andrew shook the teacher's hand as she extended it. The teacher put her arm around Andrew's shoulder and took him to an empty chair in the first row. As Andrew and the teacher walked away, Anse made his exit.

Andrew was relieved to be sitting down as he now seemed more out of sight. The teacher began her instructions. Whether he was willing to admit it or not, Andrew knew he was going to love school, and he could not wait to get his first book.

The school's single room had a large pot-bellied stove near the back. The teacher had a small desk at the front, elevated on a platform so that all could see her. The exterior clapboard walls were insulated with crushed paper and lined on the inside with flat, unpainted planks, installed horizontally. There were two windows at the front door, which was the back of the classroom, as well as a window on both sides of the room. There were no windows on the wall behind the teacher, which backed up tightly to the steep mountain slope. That wall was heavily decorated with row after row of student art.

Andrew's first school day finished at noon, and Rosy, Joe, and Andrew began the short walk back home. Andrew felt as grown-up as Joe. He had completed his very first day of school, and he was very proud. He even had his first book, a reader with large pictures and large print. He considered his new arrangement quietly on his way home that day: living with Aunt Vicy and Uncle Anse was not what he wanted, but going to school would be a good thing. His classmates were friendly enough. They thought he was a big deal because he was in Uncle Anse's family. But they also troubled him. On two or three occasions during the day, he heard someone refer to Uncle Anse as "Devil Anse," and he did not understand.

On the way home, he brought up the subject, "Rosy, why does everybody call your dad Devil Anse?"

"Some people call him that but we don't. He doesn't care though, 'cause he says his mother gave him that name."

"Why?" asked Andrew.

"She said that Pa was not afraid of the devil hisself," Rosy said.

"Then why don't y'all call him that?"

"It sounds funny," replied Rosy. "And besides, he's not a devil!"

Andrew did not like the name. He was not going to use that name and he was not going to listen if anyone else did. Uncle Anse was a nice man. The Island Creek home would be his home for a while, and he wanted to be happy there. The name "Devil" did not make him happy.

4

OFFICER STANLEY PORTOUS

I don't remember being scared. But I had a sense that something wasn't right. I was just going to do what I was told.

Andrew finished his first year of school at the School in the Bottoms as peacefully and quietly as a school year should be for a first-grader. He spent the summer on Cow Creek at the Chafin farm, doing light chores and playing in the creek with his siblings. Life was good on Cow Creek. In September 1894, he was to begin his second year at the school and was looking forward to seeing his friends and the Hatfield children.

Holbert delivered him to the Hatfield home on the evening before the first day of school and watched as Andrew scampered off into the woods with the Hatfield kids—happy children seeing each other for the first time in months. Unlike Andrew's first year, there was no anxiety, no tears, and no dread. He was happy, and Holbert made a quick departure back to Cow Creek.

The next morning Andrew, Rosy, and Joe left the Hatfield home for the quarter-mile walk along the creek to the one-room schoolhouse. Anse and Vicy waved good-bye from the front steps. Twenty minutes later, as Anse was sitting on the front porch in his rocker, Andrew came walking back toward the cabin by himself. Anse got up and met him at the front gate. "Andrew, is something wrong? Why aren't you in school?"

"We have a new teacher, Uncle Anse, and she said she did not have room for me this year."

"She did?"

"Yessir. She didn't even know my name."

"Come with me, Andrew. I want to meet this teacher."

Anse walked back to the porch, picked up his Winchester rifle, and walked out the front gate with Andrew on his heels. They walked south toward the school. With every step Anse's pace quickened. By the time they reached the schoolhouse door, Andrew was practically running.

Anse opened the door and stood in the middle of the doorway as every eye in the room turned to look at him. Joe grinned. Rosy dropped her head in anticipation. The new, young teacher got up and stood behind her desk. Anse quietly motioned for her with his index finger and then backed up and stood just outside the door. The young teacher walked outside and closed the door behind her.

Anse did not waste time with small talk. "Ma'am, do you know who I am?"

"Yessir, Mr. Hatfield."

"I understand you do not have room for my nephew. Is that correct?"

"Mr. Hatfield, his name was not on my list. I—"

"Ma'am, let me explain. Young Andrew here will be taught in this school, this year. You may not be the one teaching him, but someone will, and it makes no difference to me who that is. Am I clear?"

"Mr. Hatfield, I did not know he was your nephew, and I am sorry for the confusion. Of course we would love to have Andrew in our school. Andrew, come in and find a seat."

Anse rubbed the top of Andrew's head as he walked by, and said, "She didn't mean nothin', Andrew; it was just a mistake. You go on in and learn sumpthin', you hear?"

Andrew walked through the door to the smiles of all his classmates, who slapped at him and pushed at him with open affection. He walked to an empty chair, appropriately in the second row.

The young teacher attempted to continue her apologies to Anse, but it was too late. He had turned his back and was walking briskly back to his front porch. She turned and walked back inside, trembling slightly. Andrew began his second year at the School in the Bottoms.

The Messenger

As much as Andrew liked school, he looked forward to the quarter-mile trek home from school each day almost as much as he did the classroom work. It was a happy walk. The cool, rolling creek made a soothing noise; rabbits, squirrels and an occasional deer slipped in and out of the tree line as they walked by; and the sky was filled with noisy, chirping birds. And best of all, he knew that Aunt Vicy would have a treat for them when they got home. On this day, their arrival at home would be different.

There was a chill in the air that fall day as Andrew followed Rosy and Joe home. They were taking their time, throwing rocks in the creek, chasing squirrels, pushing each other, and laughing constantly. When the three laughing kids reached the front gate of the Hatfield home, Joe reached up and removed the leather strap that held the gate to the post and pushed the gate open. They walked into the familiar opening that served as the front yard of the Hatfield home, staying as far away from the black bear as they could.

As usual at this time of day, Anse was sitting in his rocking chair on the front porch, holding his Winchester across his lap. As Joe walked toward the front porch with the others close behind, Anse stood up and walked to the top of the steps. Vicy, sitting in a rocker next to him, continued to sit, shucking ears of corn. Tennis and Willis were playing in the yard. Anse dropped the butt of the rifle onto the porch, stood the rifle straight up in front of him, and rested his arm across the top of the barrel. He looked down at Joe, Rosy, and Andrew. "Joe, come over here. Rosy, you and Andrew come too."

No one argued. They all went straight to the steps. All three were familiar with Uncle Anse's instructions. No one questioned those instructions; you did as you were told.

"Joe, sit on the top step right here. Rosy, you and Andrew sit beside him. Vicy, take Willis and Tennis inside and shut the door." Anse said nothing more. Joe, Rosy, and Andrew took their assigned seats without comment or complaint. They faced the yard, their backs to Anse. Anse returned to his rocker, sat, and placed the Winchester back across his lap. He started puffing on a long-stemmed corncob pipe. Vicy walked slowly to the front door, cradling numerous ears of corn in her apron. She walked inside, with Willis and Tennis following, and slowly closed the door behind her. Andrew heard the door latch.

Anse continued, "Joe, y'all sit still. Don't move and don't make a sound. And whatever happens, don't say a word. You understand?"

In unison, all three said, "Yessir."

Andrew wondered, *Are we being punished? What did we do?* He was the only one who seemed concerned. Rosy leaned over and watched an ant crawl across her shoe. Joe took off the ever-present hat and started running his fingers through his hair. A dog started barking. Anse yelled, "Dog! Quiet!" The dog stopped barking.

Andrew looked around for a clue. *What are we waiting on?* He wanted to turn around and look at Anse. He thought better of it. He leaned over and watched the ant that Rosy was watching. Anse sat motionless. Even the squeaking of the rocking chair had stopped. The only sound that Andrew heard was the rattling of the chain the black bear pulled around the poplar tree, and flies, lots of flies.

The black bear continued to pace: two steps to the left, two steps to the right; back and forth around the poplar tree, the bark of which had been stripped bare months ago. Andrew, Rosy, and Joe continued to wait. But they had no idea for what. Anse took the Winchester off his lap and stood it straight up, supporting it on his leg, with his finger resting on the trigger.

Finally, in the distance, from the south on the familiar path from school, they watched a single rider approach the Hatfield home. He sat comfortably in the saddle as if he were accustomed to long rides and dusty trails. He did not seem to be in a hurry. Within minutes he was at the front of the Hatfield gate, looking up at the group on the front steps. Andrew, Rosy, and Joe watched him intently.

The rider stopped, dismounted, and opened the gate. He was clearly attempting to be nonthreatening. Anse and the three kids sat and watched. There was no movement on the steps other than the widening of their eyes and the grinding of their teeth. Anse sat completely motionless, as though he had seen this before. He showed no emotion.

The rider glanced over at the bear, which was pulling at his chain, trying to get nearer, and walked slowly toward the porch holding the bridle of his horse with his left hand, his right hand swinging slowly back and forth across a holster holding a black-handled gun. He had an impressive-looking badge on his chest, partially hidden by a brown leather vest. He wore a wide-brimmed hat that was weatherworn and dirty. When he was within ten yards of the porch, Anse broke the silence. "That's far enough."

The visitor stopped.

Anse was first to speak, "What can I do for you?"

"Mr. Hatfield?"

"Yes."

"Mr. William Anderson Hatfield?"

"That's right."

"My name is Officer—"

Anse interrupted. "I don't care what your name is. What do you want?"

"Mr. Hatfield, I have a warrant issued by the Commonwealth of Kentucky which I would like to read: 'The Commonwealth of Kentucky, having examined the submitted evidence, and following listed protocol and procedures as they relate to the following crimes against the Commonwealth of Kentucky and Commonwealth citizens, does hereby—'"

Anse interrupted again. "What did you say your name was?"

"I didn't say, sir, but my name is Kentucky Officer Stanley Portous."

Anse continued, "Officer Portous, you got off the 7:15 a.m. train from Catlettsburg yesterday morning in Williamson, rented a horse from the Williamson Livery, and have spent the last day and a half making your way here."

The officer looked confused but said, "That is correct, sir."

"Officer Portous, if you look up, you will see that the sun is almost exactly over your head, which tells me that it is just a little after noon. In this part of the country this time of year, the sun drops out of sight around three o'clock, and it is nearly pitch black by five or six. Now, I know that you are on a paid mission from the Commonwealth of Kentucky and that you mean me no harm. And I don't mean you no harm either, but if you ain't well on your way out of these hills by the time darkness sets in, you may never see the sunlight again. Do I make myself clear?"

Officer Portous stood motionless for several minutes. Anse watched, his finger on the trigger of the Winchester. The kids watched. The horse flipped his tail back and forth. The bear paced back and forth. The only sounds were the sounds of flies buzzing around the officer's horse. Officer Portous glanced down at the three kids sitting on the steps and then back to Anse Hatfield. He looked over his shoulder at the tree line, just outside the split-rail fence, and then back to Anse. He tipped his hat ever so slightly in a polite gesture and said, "Good day, Mr. Hatfield." There was a slight look of relief in his eyes.

Anse said, "Good day, sir."

Officer Portous turned and walked his horse through the gate and closed it. He remounted the horse, glanced over his shoulder at the group sitting on the porch, and turned to the south. Officer Portous was on his way back to Louisville, Kentucky, never to return.

Anse did not suggest to Andrew that he should not mention the episode with Officer Portous to his parents. He did not want to imply that anything had been improper. Andrew, on the other hand, could not wait to tell his parents. He had been captivated by the entire experience, not realizing the danger he could have been in.

Holbert and Lucinda were not quite so captivated. They listened politely to Andrew's version of the encounter and changed the subject quickly, lest Andrew think they were upset. But Holbert decided to have a conversation with Anse about it when he took Andrew back to the Hatfield's on Sunday afternoon.

When they arrived at the Hatfield home on Sunday, Andrew took off immediately for the barn when he heard Rosy and Joe playing. Holbert walked onto the porch to greet Anse and Vicy. He sensed that Anse expected a discussion about Officer Portous, which would make things easier. Holbert sat and a casual conversation began, turning almost instantly to the visitor from Kentucky. Holbert explained to Anse that Andrew told him about the visitor and he wondered why Anse would allow the children to be present when things could clearly have gotten out of hand.

Anse was prepared for the question and explained that things could not have gotten out of hand because his sons, Cap and Johnse, had rifles trained on the visitor the entire time. If the officer had made a move for his gun, they were to shoot. The livery hand had let Johnse know about the officer's arrival, and Johnse had come immediately to Anse. They were ready for him.

Anse explained that the kids were there to keep things from getting hostile. He told Holbert he knew that the officer would be hesitant about pulling his gun with children sitting in front of him and that he was convinced that without the kids sitting there, either he or the officer would be dead right now. When Holbert asked why Anse sent Vicy into the house, he was ready for that question as well. He explained that Vicy had a tendency to get aggravated when she felt that someone was out of place, and he did not want her to get involved in the argument and do something that might make things worse.

More than a year had passed since Andrew had come to live with the Hatfields, and it had been a peaceful year. Holbert and Lucinda had begun to believe that their fears about the McCoy family feud and the remnants of that feud were unwarranted. They had almost completely forgotten about the bounty hunters chasing Cap and Johnse, and the officers from Kentucky trying to arrest Anse for the murder of the McCoy brothers. But now those fears were back, and they were rightfully concerned.

After the incident with Officer Portous, Anse could only agree with Holbert's concerns. And he had a solution. Anse owned a cabin just over a mile north on Island Creek that had not been used in years. He invited Holbert to move his family into that cabin, free of charge, and live there for as long as Andrew and his brothers and sisters were in school. A move to the cabin would get Andrew away from possible dangers in the Hatfield household, and he could still go to school.

Holbert was immediately excited. Moving into Anse's cabin would allow the family to be together again and allow his children to be near a school. He thanked Anse for the opportunity and said he would talk to Lucinda about it and get back to him as quickly as possible.

Holbert was anxious to talk to Lucinda about Anse's offer. It seemed to be the solution to their school problem. But he realized that such a move would introduce a new problem: what to do with the farm. That farm would not run by itself, and he still had the mill to think about. He expected to be through with construction on the mill by spring, and operating it might be a full-time job. He and Lucinda had lots of things to think about.

Back on Cow Creek, Lucinda's reaction to the cabin option was more reserved than Holbert had hoped. She was reluctant to relocate the family, especially with a newborn. Louisa was just turning two. And while she was excited about having the family together again, the timing was terrible. A move right then would be hard. She suggested that Andrew finish out the year with Anse and move after school was out in the summer. Then, she argued, Oliver will be ready to start school at the same time. She suggested that they look at the place first and see if Andrew could finish the school year with the Hatfields. Lucinda had lots of questions, but deep down she knew that this was the best move they could make for the family.

Holbert agreed with Lucinda's points. A move right now would be difficult. He told Lucinda that he would drop by and see the cabin for himself, and he would ask Anse if Andrew could finish out the year with them. Holbert asked Lucinda if she wanted to join him, but she declined. She felt the buggy ride would be too hard at the moment, as they would have to bring all the children with them. Holbert agreed.

Early on Friday morning, Holbert was on his way back to Island Creek. His survey was to include the travel time to Island Creek from the Cow Creek farm. Could he make that trip daily? Would the new place on Island Creek be suitable for a family of six? And how difficult would it be for the kids to walk back and forth to school? There were lots of things to consider.

Anse had instructed Holbert that if they were interested in the cabin, he should stop by Cap's house and see his wife, Nancy, and she would show him the cabin. Holbert resolved not tell Lucinda that Cap and his wife lived a few hundred yards across the bottoms from the cabin. (West Virginia locals call the land surrounding a creek bed "the bottoms," meaning the lowest land in the valley.) With Cap's problems, that might be a deal breaker for her. It would be best for that information to wait a while. Holbert had high hopes that all would work out. He wanted to keep the farm and allow the kids to go to school on Island Creek.

Holbert's trip to Island Creek took just under three hours, across what would amount to expanded logging trails along Sang Branch. According to mountain lore, Sang Branch was named for the extensive amount of ginseng root that bordered the creek as it wandered through the mountains. The name had been shortened colloquially to Sang Branch a generation before. Holbert's trip had answered one of his questions; trips back and forth to the farm from the cabin would have to be on a weekly basis, not daily.

Holbert arrived at Nancy's cabin before noon on Friday, and she greeted him with a friendly hug. She wore a solid-black, ankle-length dress with the high collar that West Virginia women wore at the time in an attempt to show as little skin as possible. She wore her hair in bangs. The rest of her hair flowed freely across her shoulders, framing her face. Nancy was an attractive woman but was showing signs of stress from looking after four kids without much help from Cap. Three of those children stood beside her as she greeted Holbert on the porch. Her fourth, young Shepard, was a year younger than Andrew and would be a perfect playmate, except for health problems that kept him indoors most of the time.

Nancy gave Holbert directions to the cabin, and he set off while she watched from her front door, three kids clinging to her apron. Holbert felt sorry for Cap's kids and the meager conditions forced on them. He hoped that his kids would be better fed, clothed, and cared for. At the moment, he was sickened by what Cap's family was going through and wished there was more he could do about it.

The cabin Holbert's family would move into was almost a duplication of the Hatfield family's current home. They must have had the same architect. It was a rustic, unpainted, clapboard structure with a front door in the center and a small window on either side. There was a small porch across the front. Inside was a loft for sleeping, a small kitchen in the back, and a single window on the side. There were no windows in the back of the house.

Anse had lived in this cabin before he acquired the house on Grapevine Creek in a lawsuit. After the feud and losing the land on Grapevine Creek, he built a new home a mile away, leaving this cabin unoccupied. It was in surprisingly good condition except for the tall weeds that surrounded it. Holbert was not excited about the cabin, but he could see that with some changes he could make, it would serve their purpose. He decided to withhold judgment until he completed his survey.

The trip from the cabin to the school was encouraging. The kids could easily walk to school in thirty minutes or less without danger. That was the biggest positive to sell to Lucinda. All things considered, Holbert concluded, if they could get accustomed to living in a smaller place, they could make it work. Holbert would have to travel back and forth to the farm, but if he spent three or four days on the farm and three or four days with Lucinda, they would be able to keep their children in school.

Holbert continued his survey, backtracking to Anse's house to the north. And on the way he decided he would make the decision by himself. He felt sure Lucinda would prefer that. He would take Anse's offer and move into the cabin.

Holbert found Anse in his familiar position overlooking his front yard and the creek below. But this time he had no rifle across his lap; it was leaning against the wall behind him. Anse was whittling a small piece of wood into the shape of a pipe.

Vicy came out the front door as Holbert rode up and sat beside Anse, drying her hands on the ever-present apron. Holbert stopped at the front gate, dismounted, and walked his horse to the porch. Anse waved; Vicy just sat. Holbert began the conversation with the normal pleasantries about the weather and the crops. He asked about the kids and whether or not Andrew was behaving himself—all questions one would expect a parent to ask. Anse responded when appropriate and smiled casually when the conversation dragged. Vicy just sat and rocked. Holbert was worried she would wear her hands out on that apron.

Holbert got to the real point of the conversation when he sensed that Anse and Vicy were growing impatient with small talk. He let them know that he had been by the cabin and that it would work nicely. He said that he felt Anse's offer was very generous and that he would take him up on it. Anse smiled. Vicy smiled, meekly.

Then Holbert brought up the issue that troubled Lucinda: would it be possible for Andrew to stay with the Hatfields until the end of the school year, several months away, while he prepared the cabin and Lucinda got the family ready for the move? For the first time, Vicy showed real emotion. She got up from her rocker, walked over to Holbert, and threw her arms around him in a massive bear hug. She then turned and walked back in the house without a word. Anse got up, shook Holbert's hand, and told him that Vicy had given him his answer. They were thrilled to have Andrew stay.

Holbert sat with Anse on the porch, continuing the small talk, waiting for the children to come home from school. Andrew would be expecting his father to be on the porch, talking to Anse, as he was most every Friday. Andrew, like most school kids, liked Fridays best.

On the way back to Cow Creek, Holbert decided to tell Andrew about the cabin. He wasn't sure what Andrew's reaction would be to the move, but he felt sure it would be positive. "Andy?"

"Yessir."

"I have some news for you that I think you are going to like."

"Yessir."

"Uncle Anse is giving us a place here on Island Creek where we can live while y'all go to school. You won't have to be away from home all week, and you can still see the Hatfields every day."

"We are leaving the farm?"

"No, we'll keep the farm. I will work the farm during the week while you and Oliver go to school. Your mother will stay with you. Then I will come home for the weekends as you did when you were living with Uncle Anse. What do you think?"

Andrew sat quietly behind his father on the mare. He said not a word. The mare continued her steady pace along the mud-filled ruts of the logging trail. There was dead silence. Holbert waited for a reaction but got nothing; Andrew was his typical quiet self.

Holbert began to worry. He was almost afraid to turn around and look at Andrew's face. *What does this silence mean? Is Andy unhappy about the news? Is he mad? Did I say something wrong? Would Andy prefer living with Anse, Vicy, and his cousins?*

Holbert could stand it no more. He pulled on the reins of the mare, and they came to a stop in the middle of a bright, sunny clearing. Holbert shifted his weight and looked over his left shoulder at Andrew's face. Andrew looked back. He had a tear on his cheek and a smile across his face that formed deep dimples. He leaned forward, threw both arms around his dad's waist, and laid his head against Holbert's back. He still said nothing. Holbert turned back around without a word and slapped the reins against the mare's neck. They continued their trip home, silent but happy.

5

THE RACCOON KILL

Now I tell you what, I could shoot; don't think I couldn't. Uncle Anse taught me how to shoot, and I could out shoot just about anybody but Uncle Anse. I would (chuckle), I would outshoot Joe, and I was just a little thing then. Joe was much bigger than I was.

The mountains of West Virginia are full of wildlife, and hunting was not a hobby; it was a way of life. In the rugged hills and mountains surrounding the Tug Fork Valley, the wildlife was even more abundant than in other parts of the state because of the remoteness of the area and the sparse population. So it was natural for every male to grow up shooting a gun. At the turn of the century, it was not unusual for boys as young as thirteen or fourteen to carry a side arm or a long-barreled rifle openly. Hunting was encouraged by the parents, and young boys were teased if they didn't know how to shoot or didn't hunt. It was no different in the Hatfield family.

The Hatfield men were known as expert marksmen, probably because Anse had them shooting early in life and hunting before they were twelve. The Hatfield boys preferred hunting raccoons, because they were slow-moving and easy to hit. Raccoons do not make good meals but would suffice in a stew if cooked long enough. The skin was the prize. The young Hatfield boys didn't particularly like to skin raccoons, but Anse insisted that they skinned their own kills. To the Hatfields, guns and hunting were facts of life.

Joe, Rosy, and Andrew came home from school on a bright, sunny day to find Anse behind the barn with a dozen bottles set up on the back fence. He called Joe over and handed him the long-barreled Winchester rifle. "See how many you can hit, Joe."

Joe placed the rifle against his shoulder and took aim. He fired and missed. He tried again. He missed again. Anse walked over and took the rifle from him. "Joe, look at this. Look through this slot right here, and put that tip at the end of the barrel between the slot and the target. And don't squeeze the trigger so hard; you're moving the barrel around. Try it again."

Joe replaced the rifle against his shoulder, took aim, and fired. A hit! Joe shot four more times and missed only once. Anse was pleased. "Good job, Joe, you're learnin'." He knew it was important for Joe to begin hunting and shooting. Joe had just turned ten, and he would need to be proficient in the art of hunting by the time he was twelve.

Andrew was watching, intently. "Uncle Anse, can I try it?"

"Sure, Andrew, come over here."

Andrew took the rifle, which was nearly as tall as he was, and tried to put it against his shoulder. He couldn't hold it up. Andrew was not quite eight years old, and he was very small for his age. Anse walked over and handed Andrew a single-shot pistol. "Here, Andrew, try it with this one."

Andrew took the pistol and started to aim. "Uncle Anse, show me how to aim like you were showing Joe."

Anse took the pistol and went through the same instructions that he had given to Joe. Andrew held it with both hands, extended his arms as long as they would reach, and fired. The recoil almost knocked Andrew off his feet, but a bottle exploded. Andrew reloaded and fire again. Another bottle exploded.

Anse set up more bottles, and Joe and Andrew took turns shooting. Andrew had found a new love. He asked Anse if he could try the rifle again. Anse handed Andrew the rifle and offered new instructions: "Andrew, don't put the butt of the rifle on your shoulder. It's too long. Put it under your arm. That will get you closer to the end, and you can hold it better."

Andrew tried the new technique, took aim, and fired. Another bottle exploded. Andrew was beside himself. He couldn't wait to shoot more. But Anse called a halt. "That's all for today, boys. We'll shoot some more tomorrow."

Andrew was growing up fast in the Hatfield household. The more he experienced, the more he wanted to experience. There was little doubt in Anse's mind that Andrew would be a proficient hunter by the time he was twelve. He seemed to be a natural.

A few days later, Anse, Troy, and Elias gathered their guns and walked toward the front gate. Joe and Andrew were in the barn when Joe saw his dad and brothers leaving. He yelled, "Andy, come on!"

Joe ran up to his dad. "Pa, where y'all goin'?"

"On a coon hunt," replied Anse.

"Can we go with you?"

"You and Andrew?"

"Yessir."

"Boys, I don't have enough guns for you, but you're welcome to come along. Andrew, go get that single-shot; you can bring that. Joe, you and Andrew can share the pistol."

Andrew was off to the house in a flash. He was back in seconds, and the group headed out the gate. Andrew and Joe were practically skipping with excitement. It was their first coon hunt. They didn't know what to expect, but they knew it had to be fun. They also didn't know that coon hunts are night hunts.

After an hour of hiking, the boys were getting tired. And it was getting dark. But there would be no complaining from those two. At dusk they came upon a clearing next to a small stream. Troy and Elias went immediately to two trees on the bank of the stream and climbed up to two low branches. Anse went to Joe and Andrew and said, "Joe, take Andrew to that tree over there near the creek, and get up off the ground. Sit quiet. Don't make a sound, and don't move around."

By the time the boys got settled in the tree, it was getting harder to see. They settled in and stared at the ground, waiting. An hour passed. The boys were really getting tired, and they had seen nothing. Joe looked at Andrew and shrugged a what-are-we-doing-here look.

Just as their patience was nearly gone, Andrew looked down to see two glowing eyes coming straight for him. A large male raccoon shuffled toward the stream just below him. He slowly raised his single-shot to take aim. Then two more eyes! Behind the male shuffled a smaller female. A shot rang out from Andrew's left. The male coon lifted a foot off the ground and then dropped to the ground with a thud. The female spun to the right and headed for the tree line. A second shot rang out, and she dropped like a stone. Two shots, two dead raccoons.

All of a sudden the boys were no longer tired. When they saw Troy leap to the ground from a tree across the clearing, both boys scampered to the ground and ran to the raccoons. Troy beat them there. He stood over the male and poked his side with his boot to see if there was any movement. There was none. The raccoon was dead. They walked over to the female and poked her side as well. No movement.

Anse and Elias joined the group and looked down at the game. Anse said, "That's it for the day, boys. Let's get these two back to the house and skin 'em."

Joe and Andrew forgot all about their tiredness, the long hike home, and the boring tree-sitting. They were now coon hunters. As they thought about Elias and Troy skinning and cleaning the raccoons, they were suddenly glad that they weren't the ones who shot them. They were not quite sure about the skinning part yet. But they sure looked forward to watching Elias and Troy skin them when they got home.

It was after midnight when the group got back to the Hatfield cabin. Anse opened the door and walked in, and the other four followed. Sitting across the room were three men, each one with a rifle standing up in front of them. They said nothing to Anse, and he said nothing to them. He just looked at them with a frown on his face. Andrew recognized two of the men as Anse's sons, Cap and Johnse. He did not recognize the third man.

Andrew had seen Cap only a few times in the two years that he had lived there, once or twice with his wife, Nancy, and once or twice at Uncle Anse's house. He had thinning, dark hair, a thick mustache, and one eye that wouldn't move. He had an ammunition belt across his shoulder, a holster around his waist holding a silver-handled gun, and a rifle standing in front of him. His tall boots had mud caked on them and had left a trail of mud on the floor with every step he took. Vicy would have quite a mess to clean up when the three were gone.

Johnse sat next to Cap. He was tall and thin, with a full mustache. He had Anse's sunken cheekbones, which made him appear even thinner than he was. He did not wear a full beard to hide the cheekbones as Anse did. Andrew thought, *Maybe he should.* His eyes were piercing and hostile. He also had a rifle standing in front of him and a side arm. Andrew knew that Johnse had been married a few times and lived near the Tug just off Grapevine Creek, but he knew little else about him. Like Cap, Johnse stayed hidden in the mountains most of the time to avoid bounty hunters and lawmen.

The third man, sitting off to the side, was surveying the room with eyes that screamed of violence. He stared intently at Anse and ignored the four boys. He was much larger than either Cap or Johnse and dressed in clothes that looked newer. He had a clean-shaven face with dark, thick eyebrows and thick, bushy hair. He wore a wide-brimmed hat. His name was never mentioned, and Andrew had no idea who he was. When he looked at Andrew with an expression that seemed to say, "What are you looking at?" Andrew decided he did not want to know who he was.

There was a nervous silence in the room. Rosy, Willis, and Tennis were in bed, and Vicy was standing at the sink, watching the room and staying out of the way. After a minute or more of looking all three men directly in their eyes, Anse said, "Joe, you and Andrew go to bed. Troy, you and Elias take the coons to the barn and skin 'em." Then Anse turned and walked out the front door, taking the Winchester with him. Cap, Johnse, and the stranger followed. Not a word was spoken.

Joe and Andrew climbed the ladder to the loft. The other Hatfield kids were fast asleep. Joe put his finger across his lips. They silently crawled to the edge of the loft, looked down, and watched Anse, Cap, Johnse, and the stranger walk out the front door. They stayed quiet, watched, and waited.

Ten minutes later, Anse walked back inside. The others followed. Anse walked over to Vicy and said something to her. Neither Joe nor Andrew could make out what they were talking about. She walked immediately out the back door. Cap, Johnse, and the stranger sat back down, holding the rifles in front of them, waiting. Minutes later, Troy and Elias walked back in carrying a blood-soaked sack full of coon meat. They were covered in raccoon blood. Anse stopped them at the front door and said, "Troy, you and Elias change clothes and go with Cap and Johnse and bring their horses back. And get two shovels out of the barn and take them with you."

Joe and Andrew looked at each other in silence.

Vicy walked back in the back door, carrying a gunnysack that was filled to the top. She handed it to Cap. He took the sack and walked toward the front door. Johnse and the stranger stood up and walked behind him. Anse followed. Troy and Elias reappeared minutes later and followed the others out the door. Joe motioned to Andrew to get in bed. He didn't have to ask twice. Andrew was exhausted.

6

THE LANTERN PLOY

The following morning, Andrew awoke and dressed for school. All the kids ate breakfast together without a word about the events of the past evening. As they were finishing their breakfast of country ham, honey, and biscuits, Anse walked up to the table and said, "Joe, you and Rosy go on to school. I need Andrew to run an errand for me. Tell his teacher he won't be in today."

Andrew looked at his uncle but said nothing. *What is this all about?*

After the Hatfield kids left for school, Anse approached Andrew with his mission. "Andrew, I need you to take the big bay over to Cap's house. Nancy's got some stuff for you to take to Cap. She'll tell you where he is. Take this lantern to Nancy, and she'll fill it up for Cap. He left it here last night. If anybody stops you, tell 'em you're takin' the lantern over to Cow Creek so your pa can fix it. Can you do that?"

"Yessir."

Andrew was confused. No one said a word about the previous evening or the man with Cap and Johnse. No one mentioned the shovels or what they were to do with them, and now he was being sent on an errand to take something to Cap and Johnse without any explanation as to what or why, or even where. And he was missing school to do it. But he wanted to go. He wanted to please his uncle and be a part of the Hatfield family. Even at eight years old, Andrew knew that a simple question like "Why?" might change his uncle's mind about sending him, so he decided not to ask.

The Messenger

His uncle answered without him having to ask. "Andrew, I would send Troy or Elias, but everyone knows they are my young'uns, and some folks would start askin' questions. They don't know you. You won't be in any trouble; my boys will see to that."

Andrew accepted his uncle's explanation, took the lantern, and walked outside to the horse that was already saddled and waiting. He wasn't happy about missing school, but he didn't want to disobey his uncle Anse either. He walked the horse to a tree stump, swung his leg up over the horse's back, and turned the horse's head toward the gate. As he passed Anse, Anse walked up and took hold of the bay's bridle. The horse stopped, and Anse looked up at Andrew. "Andrew, be careful. Don't talk to nobody unless you have to. Don't answer any questions about Cap or Johnse, and if anyone tries to follow you, turn back. Understand?"

"Yessir."

"You should be back before dark. If you ain't, I'm comin' to look for you." Anse reached up, took the lantern out of Andrew's hands, and dropped it into the gunnysack. He then tied the sack to the saddle horn. "Vicy put some lunch in the sack for you. It's under the lantern. Be careful now!"

Andrew rode slowly out the gate and turned the bay to the north. Cap's home was just a mile away and across the bottoms from where his family's cabin would be when he moved in the spring. He knew how to get to Cap's house, but he had no idea where he was going after that. As he approached Cap's house, he saw Nancy standing at the front door. She had a child standing on each side of her, and she was holding a third. The oldest child, Shepard, stood at the door but did not come out. Andrew knew that Cap and Nancy had a son his age, and he didn't understand why he never saw him outside. The bay came to a stop just beyond the porch and the two steps that led up to the front door. "Mornin', Andrew. Did you bring the lantern?" asked Nancy.

"Yes, ma'am." He twisted to the side and pulled the lantern out of a gunnysack. As he handed it to Nancy, he noticed that the handle was loose on one side and that the wick had a cap on it. It was a solid-brass lantern with a base on the bottom that held kerosene, a long handle on the top, and a large glass bowl that reflected light when the wick was lit. It was beaten up as if it had been well used.

"You wait right here, Andrew. I'll be right back." Nancy disappeared through the door, leaving the two small children staring at him. The younger one had three fingers in his mouth and what looked like oatmeal on his cheeks. The taller one, a cute little girl, had a runny nose, and the moisture nearly reached her lips. She didn't bother to wipe it. Their clothes were more rags than clothes, and they looked like they hadn't been washed in a while. They said nothing to Andrew, and he said nothing to them. They just stared at each other.

Nancy came back holding the lantern as if it was full and heavier. She also had a wool blanket over her shoulder. She walked around the horse, removed the gunnysack from the saddle horn, and gently placed the lantern upright in the gunnysack. Then she walked around behind Andrew and threw the blanket over the horse's rump. She tied it to the saddle with leather straps on either side of the horse. "Don't lose this blanket, Andrew. And make sure it don't fall off."

"Yes, ma'am. Where am I goin'?"

"Take Lizzies Creek back to the west a mile or so. When you come to a fence row, you take the path to the right and go up the mountain. When you get to the top, you'll see a loggin' shack back down the other side a little ways. Cap will be in that shack. Tell 'im this is all the fuel I got for the lantern and the only blanket I can spare."

"Yes, ma'am."

"Andrew, be careful. Don't take any chances, and if you see anybody you don't know just turn around and come back. You hear?"

"Yes, ma'am. I'll be careful."

Andrew turned the bay around and headed north to Lizzies Creek. He turned to the west on a trail no wider than the horse's width. Tree branches and weeds slapped against the bay with every step. Andrew wondered if he was on the right trail. A mile west of Cap's cabin, two riders came out of the trees right in front of him. One horseman leaned over and grabbed the bridle of Andrew's horse with his left hand. He held a rifle in his right hand. The horse stopped. The rider was chewing tobacco, and he leaned over close to Andrew and spit defiantly between the bay and his own horse. The thick, brown liquid nearly dropped on Andrew's boot. The second rider dismounted and walked behind the bay and around to the gunnysack. The rider holding the bridle said, "What's in the sack, boy?"

"A lantern," replied Andrew.

"Where you goin' with it?"

"I'm takin' it to Cow Creek. I gotta get it fixed."

"What you doin' with the blanket?"

"It's for my ride back home. It'll be after dark."

"You're kinda young to be goin' to Cow Creek alone, ain'tcha, boy?"

"No, sir, I live there. I go through here a lot."

"Do you know Cap Hatfield?"

"Yessir, most everybody knows him."

"You seen 'im lately?"

"No, sir, I ain't."

"What's your name, boy?"

"Andrew Chafin."

"What's your daddy's name?"

"Holbert Chafin."

Andrew thought, *I wonder what they would have said if it had been Joe.*

The second rider took the gunnysack off the horse, untied it, and opened it. The lantern was resting on the package of ham that Vicy had packed for his lunch. The rider rummaged through the sack, looking for other contents. There were none. He lifted the lantern out, took the package of ham, bread, and apples, and put the lantern back in the sack.

"We're keepin' the food, boy. You got a gun?"

"No, sir, I ain't."

"On your way, boy. Don't turn around and don't look back."

Andrew was shaking inside, but he tried not to show it. He nudged the bay along the trail, tempted to turn and look behind him. He needed to know if the two riders were following, but he was afraid to look. After an hour, Andrew decided to stop. He found a tree stump and slid off the horse. He tied the reins to a low branch and walked into the trees. When he was far enough into the trees that he could barely see the horse, he looked back down the trail in the direction of Cap's cabin. It was quiet. He sat down and watched; nothing. He waited ten minutes, still nothing. He went back to the trail and looked back down the trail for any signs of riders but saw nothing.

Then he looked down at the trail. *Hoofprints!* His horse was leaving hoof prints that were clear and easy to follow. The riders wouldn't have to follow him; they could pick up his trail any time they wanted. Andrew untied the horse and walked it into the trees. He retied the horse and walked back to the trail. He broke a branch off a small shrub and started walking backward down the trail, sweeping the branch back and forth across the trail. The hoofprints were gone. He continued back down the trail thirty yards and then turned and went into the trees.

He knew about where he had left the horse, but he did not take a direct path. He walked left, circled a tree, went right, and circled another tree, just like he and Joe did playing hide-and-seek. He walked straight ahead for twenty yards and then circled another tree. By then he was moving in the general direction of the horse, but he continued his zigzag path until he was back to the horse. He took the reins and walked farther into the trees.

Andrew stayed in the trees, parallel to the trail, for a half mile more before he finally saw the fence line. He kept the fence line in his sight but stayed in the trees. He walked the horse up the side of the steep mountain slope until he reached the top. He found a tree stump, mounted the bay, and continued down the other side of the mountain, looking through the trees for a logging shack.

A quarter mile down the trail he saw a small log structure on his left; it wasn't much bigger than the outhouse behind their home. It had a chimney on one side and a door on the other. There were no windows. He dismounted and walked the horse along the ridge above the shack, fifty yards below. He stopped and barked like a squirrel, which is not really a bark but more of a high-pitched squeal. He waited; nothing. He barked again; still nothing.

Now he was getting worried. *Did the riders find the shack? Did Cap leave?* Andrew was not sure what to do. He tried one more time; he did not want to go near the shack until he made contact with Cap. He barked and waited. Over his shoulder, behind him, he heard a squirrel's bark. He did not turn around. He barked again and waited. Another bark came from over his shoulder. He turned the horse and walked in the direction of the sound. Thirty yards away, sitting on the ground with a rifle pointed at Andrew's head, sat Cap.

The Messenger

Cap put his finger across his lips, indicating silence, and motioned for Andrew to join him. Andrew pulled the horse's reins and walked up beside Cap. Cap stared straight ahead in the direction from which Andrew had come. Andrew walked the horse a few more feet, tied it to a tree branch, and walked back to Cap. Cap continued to stare straight ahead. Andrew sat beside him, saying nothing, and stared in the same direction.

They sat together in silence for ten minutes. Finally, Cap barked again, three short, shrill squirrel barks. Johnse walked out of the woods behind Andrew. The stranger walked beside him. Cap did not get up. Andrew did not either. Johnse leaned down and put his hand on Andrew's shoulder. "Where's the lantern?" he whispered.

Andrew turned and pointed to the gunnysack. He said not a word. Johnse walked back to the bay and took the sack off the horse's back. The stranger sat down next to Andrew, which made Andrew very nervous. Johnse came back and sat next to the stranger. He opened the sack and pulled out the lantern.

And then he did a strange thing. He unscrewed the fuel bowl at the bottom of the lantern, tilted it up, and took a gulping swig that obviously burned his mouth. Andrew's mouth gapped open. He stared at Johnse as Johnse passed the fuel bowl to the stranger, who took a swig. The stranger then passed the bowl across Andrew and handed it to Cap. Cap put his rifle down and took an even bigger swig. The expression on his face made Andrew think that it must have been painful. "It ain't fuel, boy; it's whiskey," said Cap.

"Moonshine?" said Andrew.

"Yep, I told Nancy to send us some. We ain't had a drink in days."

"I've been carrying moonshine?"

"Hell, boy, ain't much different than kerosene. If anybody asks ya about it, just light the damn thing. It'll burn better'n kerosene anyway!" Cap laughed.

The fuel bowl passed across Andrew several more times, each time making him more anxious. Finally, after the bowl was passed to Cap for the fourth time, Andrew realized that it was time for him to move on. The voices were louder, the reactions slower, and the temperaments more hostile. Andrew dropped his hands to his sides and pushed himself up the steep slope of the bank several feet behind the three men. He moved away from the trio about ten feet and waited. He realized that things could get out of hand, and he wanted no part of it.

The stranger was the first to complain. "Goddammit, Cap, save some for us!"

"You've had your share, Rutherford. Quit bitchin'!"

That was the first time Andrew had heard the name of the stranger. He would, unfortunately, hear it again. Johnse waited at the other end. "Quit bitchin' and pass it over, John."

Rutherford was the most out of control. "There ain't no more, goddammit!" He lunged at Cap and took the bowl out of his hands, turned it upside down over his extended tongue, and waited for the last drop to descend. He savored it as if it were the last drop of water on earth.

Cap raised the rifle that had been resting across his lap and pointed it directly at Rutherford's face, not six inches away, and in a whisper said, "Say one more word, Rutherford, and it'll be your last."

Andrew had seen enough. He slid back down the slope to Cap. "I gotta go. It'll be dark before I get home."

Cap returned the rifle to his lap and turned to Andrew. "Take the lantern back to Nancy. Tell her I'll be home late Saturday night and that we'll need more fuel. And take the shovels back to Pa. If anybody finds those shovels up here, they'll wonder what we were diggin', so just take 'em back."

What were they using the shovels for? thought Andrew, but he didn't ask. *I guess it ain't none of my business.* "How can I take two shovels on my horse? I can't carry 'em."

"If you can't git all the way home with 'em, just drop 'em on the trail, I'll pick 'em up later. I need to get 'em away from the cabin."

Andrew walked to a fallen tree and mounted the horse. Cap followed. "Did Vicy fix you any food, boy?"

"Yessir, but two men took it."

"What?" said a very startled Cap.

"On the trail comin' up here, I got stopped by two men. They looked in the sack, found the food, and took it. I was afraid they were going to take the lantern too."

"Did they say anything?"

"Yessir, they asked me if I knew you, and I said yes, everybody knows you."

"Any chance they followed you?"

"I went back and cleared the trail and then stayed in the trees. I don't think they could have followed me. I made sure my tracks were gone."

"What'd they look like?"

"I didn't get a good look at one of 'em, 'cause one was holding my horse and I was watching the one going through the gunnysack. But that one was tall and skinny and had a bushy, yellow mustache. And he had a big silver buckle on his belt."

"Andrew, when you get home, you tell Pa about that, you hear me?"

"Yessir."

"And don't forget, tell Nancy I'll come in late Saturday night and I'll need some more fuel."

"Yessir, I'll tell her."

Cap slapped the bay on his hindquarter and set Andrew off through the brush.

The sun was gone, and it would be dark in two hours. Andrew knew he would not be home before dark. More importantly, he was afraid he would come across the two men who had stopped him on the trail coming up. He didn't have the blanket, and the lantern was still broken. He would have to rethink his story if he saw them.

Andrew followed the same trail down the mountain that he took going up. It was much darker now, and he couldn't see at all. The bay could see, so all Andrew could do was sit back and ride.

After a couple of hours, Andrew could see the lights of Nancy's cabin in the distance. He took the bay to the front of the cabin and stopped at the front door. Dogs were barking. Andrew sat on the bay wondering what to do next. The door cracked slightly open, and Nancy appeared. She looked at Andrew and walked out of the door alone. "Did you find Cap?"

"Yes, ma'am. He said to tell you that he would come in late Saturday night." Andrew pulled out the lantern and reached toward the door, extending the lantern as far as he could without falling off the horse. Nancy came off the porch, reached up, and took the lantern from his hand.

"Cap said to tell you he would need more fuel when he gets home," Andrew said.

Nancy took the lantern and looked Andrew in the eye with a look that said, "That bastard!"

Nancy turned and walked back into the cabin without another word. Andrew worried that she was mad at him for telling her what Cap had said. He shrugged and slapped the bay on the shoulder and started south toward Anse's house. He had another twenty minutes before he would be home. He looked forward to a soft bed.

Andrew had carried the shovels across his lap for more than two hours, and they were getting heavier. He had wanted to leave them with Nancy, but that was not the instruction Cap had given him. Andrew was afraid of Cap's reaction if he didn't do what he was told. He would keep them for the next twenty minutes.

By then it was pitch black, and if the bay did not know the way home, they were in trouble. Andrew could not see a thing.

Fifteen minutes later, Andrew could see a dim light in the distance. He could not make out the source, but the bay was walking directly for it. The closer they got to the source, the brighter the light became until, finally, Andrew could make out the outline of a building—Anse's cabin. He switched the shovels to the other arm, as he had done a hundred times in the last hour, and forced himself to stay focused. He could make it another few minutes, and then he would be home. He could crawl into his bed and sleep until morning. He would not think about the two men on the trail, the sad looks on the faces of Nancy's kids, the argument between Cap, Johnse, and Rutherford, or the two shovels he cradled in his arms. He would think about his pillow and breakfast.

Andrew dropped the shovels and slid off the horse in front of the barn. He led the bay into the barn and started taking off the saddle. Anse walked up behind him. "I'll do that, Andrew. You go get yourself to bed."

"Uncle Anse, Cap said to tell you—"

"It can wait till morning, Andrew. Go get in bed. You have a school day tomorrow. I was just about to come looking for you. You're later than I thought you would be."

Andrew didn't argue. He left his uncle with the horse and saddle. He didn't mention the two men or the lost lunch. He decided it would be better to wait until morning. He went to bed hungry.

Joe woke Andrew on schedule the next morning for breakfast and school. Andrew could easily have slept in and missed school, but breakfast was a strong incentive. He got up and got dressed. Joe and Andrew left the loft and joined Rosy and Willis at the breakfast table. Aunt Vicy was just putting another bowl of hot biscuits on the table when they sat down. Andrew was anxious to tell his uncle about the two men who stopped him, as Cap told him to, before he forgot all about it. But his uncle was not there.

Anse walked in the front door as the kids were finishing breakfast. Andrew went straight to him, but before he could say anything, Anse brought it up. "Andrew, you said last night that Cap had a message for me. What was it?"

"Cap said I was to tell you about the two men who stopped me on the trail yesterday."

"Two men?"

"Yessir. They asked about Cap, if I knew him, and they went through my gunnysack."

"Did they take anything?"

"Yessir, they took my lunch."

"They took your lunch?"

"Yessir."

"Did you know 'em? What did they look like?"

"I didn't know either of them. I didn't pay much attention to one of them, but I watched the one going through my sack real careful. I was afraid he was going to take the lantern."

"What'd he look like?"

"He was tall and skinny and he had a big silver belt buckle on his belt."

"Did he have a mustache, a heavy, thick, blond mustache?"

"Yessir, he did."

"What did they ask about Cap?"

"They asked me if I knew him, and I said yes. I said most everybody knows Cap. That's all they said. They told me to be on my way and not to look back. I didn't until I was farther up the mountain. Then I stopped and covered the marks the horse was making on the trail. I walked the rest of the way up the mountain in the trees. I was afraid they would follow me, but they didn't."

Anse said not another word. Andrew could tell he was riled, and he thought, *Uncle Anse must know the fellow with the silver belt buckle. I bet he has a talk with him.*

Anse said, "You go on to school, Andrew. We'll talk later today when you get home."

"Yessir. Cap also said to make sure I got the shovels back to you. I put 'em back in the barn last night."

"I saw 'em. Now get yourself on to school."

"Yessir."

Andrew thought long and hard on his walk to school to make sure he had told his uncle everything that Cap had told him to say. He worried that he had not said anything about the fight he saw between Cap, Johnse, and the man named Rutherford. He knew that Cap didn't tell him to tell Anse about it, but he wondered if he should anyway, especially since Cap put a gun in Rutherford's face.

During the day, while Andrew should have been listening to his lessons, he was trying to get the fight settled in his mind. On the one hand, if he told Uncle Anse about the fight and Cap did not want him to, he would have to face Cap. On the other hand, if he didn't, and Uncle Anse found out from someone else, then he may be in trouble with Uncle Anse.

Andrew decided easily once he had considered all the options. He would not mention it to his uncle. He would rather have Anse's fury than Cap's. Joe had told Andrew stories of Cap's temper and reputation. He said that Cap once beat a man nearly to death with a rifle butt in an argument over money, and during the feud with the McCoy family he had killed three or four more. Cap had always been calm and protective around Andrew, but Andrew had done nothing to rile him either. And he was not going to. The only people who could tell about the fight were Cap, Johnse, Rutherford, or Andrew. Andrew decided that it would be far better for the information to come from any of the other three than from him. He would say not a word.

He could study then.

7

THE EYEWITNESS

And they trusted me. Even Cap and Johnse trusted me. (Chuckle.) They thought I had a sixth sense about me, that I could see danger coming before it happened. I didn't have any sixth sense; they all lived with these strange and dangerous things all the time, so they didn't pay any attention to some things. It was all new to me, so I questioned things that didn't seem right.

Two weeks had gone by since Andrew delivered the "fuel" to Cap and Johnse. And in that two weeks, Andrew completed two other errands for Anse. He and Joe took a wagonload of corn to a still that operated on a hill behind Nancy's house, and he delivered the lantern of fuel to Johnse, who was hiding near Sang Creek. Andrew's fear was slowly going away. He looked forward to getting home from school each day, hoping that Anse had another errand for him. He loved the adventure, and it was more fun than playing in the barn. At the same time, Anse, Cap, and Johnse were depending on him more and more. And as they gave him more to do, he lost more and more of his fear. But his fear would come back.

The one-room school that the neighborhood kids attended had several advantages, not the least of which was that it was there. Otherwise, all the kids would have faced the same thing that Andrew faced on Cow Creek, not going to school at all. But it also had one big disadvantage: only one teacher. When that teacher was sick, school was out. And so it was on a warm fall morning when Andrew and the Hatfield kids arrived, on schedule, only to find that there was no teacher. They were sent home with instructions to come back the next day.

Andrew, Joe, and Rosy walked back home in a great mood, not unlike most students around the world with an extra day off. A missed school day was necessary sometimes, just to lift the spirits. They walked through the front gate at Anse's house, and Andrew went straight to the barn, while Joe and Rosy ran in to tell Vicy the good news.

As he turned the corner of the house, he saw Lucian, the handyman, peering around the corner of the barn, staring at the house. When Lucian saw Andrew coming, he ducked behind the barn. Andrew thought that was very unusual, so he went around the barn to find him. Lucian was gone. Andrew went looking for him. When he found him, Lucian was pitching hay into the horse's stall. Andrew went straight to him and said, "Were you looking for somebody, Lucian?"

"What do you mean?"

Andrew persisted. "When you were looking around the barn just a minute ago, were you looking for somebody?"

"I wasn't looking around the barn."

"I saw you watching the house."

"No, you didn't. Mind your own business."

Andrew realized that he was getting nowhere in this conversation, so he turned and walked out of the barn. But the whole thing troubled him. He didn't understand why Lucian denied even being there. He could have easily passed it off as looking for Vicy or Anse or somebody, but to say he wasn't even looking made Andrew very suspicious.

Joe came out of the house with Anse, and they walked directly toward Andrew. Andrew decided to leave the Lucian encounter alone for the moment. Anse walked up to Andrew and said, "Andrew, I'm going coon huntin'. Joe has some chores to do and can't go. Do you want to go?"

"Yessir."

"All right, we'll leave out right after lunch. Stay close to the house."

Andrew was thrilled; he was going on his first real coon hunt alone with his uncle Anse, and he couldn't wait. His schoolmates would be so jealous. Lunchtime could not come soon enough for Andrew, and when it did, he was more than ready. He went straight to the front step to wait for his uncle as soon as he left the lunch table.

Anse walked around the house from the barn, carrying two rifles. He handed one to Andrew and said, "You have to carry your own gun, Andrew. If you're old enough to hunt, you're old enough to carry your own gun."

"Yessir."

Andrew took the rifle and cradled it across his stomach as if it were a baby in a blanket. Anse corrected him. "Andrew, put the rifle across your shoulder like this and it won't weigh as much. We have a long walk."

Andrew shifted the rifle and plopped it down on his shoulder. The rifle was longer than he was, and he realized that balancing it was going to be a problem. He moved it several times until it felt more stable and then fell in line behind his uncle, walking toward the front gate. The rifle bounced, tilted, and then fell off his shoulder. Anse did not notice Andrew's trouble and kept walking. Andrew picked the rifle up off the ground and, while continuing to walk, tried to place it once again on his shoulder. Anse finally turned to see if Andrew was behind him and realized the trouble he was having. He walked back and took the rifle from Andrew.

"Here, Andrew, try this."

Anse placed the rifle behind Andrew's neck and showed him how to hold it with a hand on each shoulder. That position was easier for Andrew, and he proudly fell in line behind his uncle, balancing the rifle and feeling like a real grown-up. When they reached the clearing near the creek where Andrew had witnessed his first hunt, Anse began his instructions. "Andrew, you take that first tree over there on the creek bank. Keep the rifle quiet, and don't move it around. Keep it pointed to the ground. I'll be on the other side of the clearing. If you see a coon, take a shot. I'll wait until you shoot first. Aim for the front shoulder and take your time. Don't rush your shot; you'll have plenty of time."

Andrew climbed the tree and settled in for what he realized would be a long wait. He would have hours to ponder the Lucian episode. He laid the rifle across his lap and stared down at the open field. He watched the tree line on the far side of the clearing and tried to stay focused. He nodded off once and then opened his eyes with a jerk. He knew it would be embarrassing if he went to sleep and fell out of the tree. He shook his head, trying to stay awake.

It was nearing four o'clock, and the sun had been gone for almost an hour. The shadows were gone and dusk was settling in. From the tree line, Andrew watched as a large male raccoon stuck his head out into the opening, looked in both directions, and then backed up into the trees. Andrew watched. Moments later the coon was back. He looked in both directions again and disappeared again.

This time Andrew did not wait. As the raccoon backed up out of sight, Andrew carefully pulled the rifle off his lap and placed the butt underneath his arm as Anse had shown him. He looked through the groove on the top of the barrel and sighted down to the tip at the end of the barrel. He put the tip squarely in front of the opening through which the raccoon had appeared twice before. He waited.

The raccoon reappeared, and this time he did not back up. He took three or four steps into the opening, completely clearing the tree line. Andrew squeezed the trigger as gently as his small fingers would allow. A shot rang out, and the raccoon dropped to his shoulder and rolled over on his side. There was no more movement. Andrew started climbing out of his tree, but he was much slower than Anse. By the time Andrew reached the ground, Anse was looking over the coon to make sure he was dead. There was no doubt.

Andrew ran up beside Anse and looked down at the raccoon, grinning from ear to ear. Anse reached down and slapped him on the shoulder. "Good shot, Andrew. Your first coon!"

"Yessir!"

"Let's get him home; it'll be dark soon. It's your coon, Andrew, so you gotta carry him home."

Now Andrew had a real problem. He had struggled with just the rifle. How would he carry both? Anse pulled a sack out of his hunting jacket, picked the coon up by its tail, and dropped it into the sack. He walked over to Andrew and tied the sack around Andrew's shoulder and slid it around to his back. Anse had solved Andrew's problem. Now he could carry the rifle with both hands as he had done before. His grin returned.

Anse and Andrew started home, and Andrew felt ten years older than his eight years. He felt emboldened, so he decided to bring up the Lucian incident. "Uncle Anse, where did Lucian come from?"

"I hired him a while back to work on the tree crews. When they ain't busy, I let him work around the house. Why?"

"I don't know. He acts funny sometimes."

"How's that, Andrew?"

"Well, this morning when we got home from school, I went to the barn and when I walked around the house, I saw him peeking around the back of the barn, watching the house. When he saw me, he backed up and went in the barn. I went to him and asked him who he was looking for, and he said he wasn't looking. I told him I saw him looking, and he said he wasn't. And then he told me to mind my own business. I just thought it was strange."

Anse did not respond to Andrew's observation. In fact, he said nothing the rest of the way home. They walked the two miles in complete silence until they reached the front gate. Then Anse turned to Andrew and said, "Andrew, after dinner you'll learn to skin a coon. Go wash up and get ready for dinner. I'll take the coon to the barn, and we'll fix it later."

"Yessir."

Andrew walked in the house to find Joe sitting at the table. Willis and Rosy were playing on the floor. Joe looked up at Andrew. "Did you get a coon?"

"I did. I got my first coon!"

"Dang it, I wish I could've gone."

"We're goin' again. You have to go next time."

Anse walked in, and Vicy ordered everyone to the table for dinner. All sat down in their usual spots, with Vicy at one end of the table, Anse at the other, and all the kids lined up on both sides. Vicy folded her hands in her lap, bowed her head, and said a silent prayer. Andrew bowed his head and waited. Joe, Rosy, Willis, and Tennis did not bow their heads, but they patiently waited on Vicy to finish her silent prayer. Anse started eating.

When Vicy finished her prayer and the rest started eating, Anse started the conversation. "Vicy, what did you fix Andrew for his lunch yesterday?"

"Several slices of ham, some bread, and two apples," she replied. "Why?"

"Just wondered. He didn't get to eat it."

Vicy looked at Andrew. "Why not?"

"Two men stopped him on the trail on his way to find Cap. They took his lunch."

"What? Who was it?"

"Don't matter. They won't bother him anymore."

Vicy said, "Andrew, did you eat anything yesterday?"

"Yes, ma'am, I had breakfast."

"And after that?"

"I had breakfast this morning."

Vicy looked at Anse but said nothing. She was fuming.

Anse just kept eating. He didn't look up.

Joe and Rosy looked at Andrew and then to Anse. They said nothing.

Willis said, "Can I have more peas, please?"

Andrew wondered about the fate of the tall, thin man with the silver buckle. *Did Anse hurt him?* He was not about to ask.

Andrew walked up on a conversation between his uncle and Lucian in Anse's front yard the following afternoon after school. Anse and Lucian were looking at rifles. They were deep in conversation when Andrew walked by. He did not stop, and he did not acknowledge their presence. After his encounter with Lucian, he decided it would be best to stay away from him for a while. Anse had other ideas.

Anse waited until Andrew had passed and then he called to him. "Andrew, me and Lucian are going coon huntin' this afternoon. You wanna come?" Clearly, Anse did not want Andrew involved in their conversation; he just wanted a short answer on the hunt, and that was all.

"Yessir," replied Andrew.

After Andrew answered, he wondered why he did. He really didn't want to go anywhere with Lucian, so why did he agree to? He was disappointed in himself for not just telling Anse that he didn't want to join them. But there was something in the way his uncle asked the question that made Andrew think that Anse wanted him to go. Whether that was really the case or not, he was committed. He was going hunting with Anse and Lucian.

Anse said, "Good, we'll head out right after lunch. We are going to a new place up above the cabin. You go eat your lunch and let Vicy know you're goin' with us. I'll get your rifle ready."

Lucian said, "Mr. Anderson, I ain't got no rifle neither."

"You can use Troy's gun today, Lucian. I'll get it ready too."

Andrew left the two and walked into the house. "Aunt Vicy, Uncle Anse said to let you know that I was goin' huntin' with Lucian and him after lunch."

Vicy turned her head sharply and looked at Andrew. She said nothing. She backed up from the sink and dried her hands on her apron. "Where is your uncle, Andrew?"

"He's out front talkin' to Lucian."

"I put your lunch on the table. I'll be back in a minute." Vicy walked toward the door, out the front door, and went straight to Anse. Anse saw her coming and told Lucian to go about his chores and he would let him know when it was time to go. Andrew got up from the table and walked to the door. He watched as Vicy and Uncle Anse conversed. He could not hear what they were saying but just the fact that they were talking was strange. Uncle Anse and Aunt Vicy hardly conversed at all, especially when there were other people around. Andrew became even more puzzled.

Vicy walked back in the house but said nothing to him. She walked back to the sink and continued washing vegetables. Andrew finished his lunch and took his plate to the sink. "Thank you for lunch, Aunt Vicy."

"You're welcome, Andrew." As Andrew walked away she added, "Andrew, I let your uncle know that I am not happy about you goin' huntin' with them today, but he insisted. You be very careful, you hear? Don't say nothin' to Lucian and don't get separated from your uncle."

"Yes, ma'am. I'll be careful."

It was nearly two o'clock before the three had their guns and were on their way. They did not go through the front gate this time; they circled around the barn and headed up a steep slope behind the cabin. The slope was steep enough that Andrew had trouble balancing his gun and walking up the hill at the same time. On occasion he was on all fours just to keep moving in a forward direction. He hoped they were not going far up this mountain; it was slow going. The three hunters were in a straight line going up the incline, with Uncle Anse leading the way, Lucian in the middle, and Andrew in the back. Anse had assigned the walking order, and all three stuck to that order.

Twenty minutes up the incline, they came to a clearing where the ground leveled out. Beyond the clearing they still went uphill, but the incline was not as steep. In another twenty minutes they came to a clearing that was almost level. Anse stopped, turned to Lucian and Andrew, and said, "This is it. We'll hunt here. I watched two or three coons go through this clearing last week, so they should be back before long. Find you a tree and settle in. Spread out in a circle. Andrew, you take that tree over there, and Lucian, you come back over here next to me."

Andrew walked to the designated tree and climbed up to a low branch where he could see the entire clearing. Vicy had told him not to get separated from Anse, but he could see Anse from where he was sitting, so he was comfortable that he was doing what Vicy told him. They all settled in for what could be a long wait.

It was after four o'clock before they saw their first coon. A male stuck his head out in the clearing and then backed up. Andrew had seen that before. A few minutes later, he was back. He stuck his head out of the underbrush, looked both ways, and ducked back into the brush.

Andrew got his gun ready. When the coon reappeared, Andrew was ready. The gun was aiming right at the coon's head, and Andrew was gently squeezing the trigger when a shot rang out from across the clearing. Andrew looked across the clearing and saw a faint puff of smoke coming from Anse's tree. In an instant, Anse was on the ground and approaching the coon. Andrew followed.

Anse walked up to the coon and pushed gently against it to see if there was any movement. There was none. Anse took a sack out of his hunting shirt and was loading the coon in the sack when Lucian walked up. Anse glanced up at him and threw the sack up over his shoulder. Anse's gun was lying on the ground.

Lucian lifted his rifle to his chin, pointed the barrel directly at Anse's head, and said, "Drop the coon, Anse Hatfield!"

Anse looked at him but said nothing. He made no move to drop the sack or to pick up his rifle.

Lucian cried out again, "I said drop the coon, Anse!" Looking at Andrew, Lucian said, "Boy, git over there by Anse."

Andrew moved a few steps to his right and stood next to Anse's right arm.

Lucian continued, "Devil Anse Hatfield, I've been waiting a long time for this, you are under arr—"

Lucian could not continue. In one swift motion, Anse had quickly placed the sack on the ground and come up with a pistol he had tucked in his belt. The pistol went off, and a small hole appeared above Lucian's left eyebrow. A small trickle of blood flowed into his eye. The second shot rang out before the echo of the first subsided, hitting Lucian to the left of his breast pocket. The two shots from Anse's pistol came so fast that it almost sounded like one shot.

Lucian dropped immediately to his knees and then tumbled over onto his face, half in the mud, half out. Lucian's gun rested against his cheek, both hands still on it. He had no chance to fire it. Lucian's eyes never closed; his expression never changed. He stared out into open space as if he were waiting for something to happen. All that was going to happen to Lucian had already happened, and there was no going back.

Andrew stared at the dead body lying in front of him. Then he looked at Anse. Anse said, "Goddamn bounty hunter, Andrew."

Andrew started shaking. He had never witnessed a killing, and his mind and body could not comprehend what he had just seen. He dropped his gun. He was shaking so hard he could no longer hold it. Anse walked over to Lucian's body, took off his hunting jacket, and covered the top part of Lucian's body with it. He said nothing. Andrew was shaking uncontrollably.

"You all right, Andrew?"

"Y-yessir-r-r."

"Andrew, I want you to know that you were not in any danger. I wouldnt've brought you up here if I thought you were. Lucian was using Troy's rifle. Troy's rifle ain't got no firing pin in it, and he don't own no other gun. That feller has been waitin' for his chance to get me for months now, and he ain't nothin' but a common crook."

Andrew nodded. But he wondered why his uncle had brought him along. *Why am I even here?* he thought.

"Can you find your way home from here, Andrew?" asked Anse.

Andrew nodded again.

"All right, go back to the house and tell Vicy I'm okay. If Troy and Elias are at home, tell 'em I need 'em. Pick up two shovels and bring 'em back up here. Can you do that?"

Andrew nodded a third time. He was afraid to try to speak. He was afraid the words wouldn't come out. But he realized why his uncle had included him in the hunt. Anse couldn't bring shovels with him; he needed Andrew to go back and get help and shovels.

"All right, get goin'," Anse said. "It'll be dark soon. Can you find your way back up here?"

Andrew finally had the nerve to speak, hoping he wouldn't stutter, "Yessir, I'll-I'll be-be-be back as soon as I c-c-c-a-n." He left his rifle lying on the ground, turned, and ran across the open pasture.

Andrew crossed the clearing and started down the mountain. He was still shaking. Fifty yards down the slope he lost his footing, slid on his bottom, and came to a stop at a rotting tree stump. He just sat. He couldn't get up. And to his own embarrassment, he began to cry. Andrew sat on the trail, buried his head on his arms, and cried.

When he could regain his composure enough, he began to talk to himself. "I can't let Uncle Anse see me cry, or Aunt Vicy or Joe or Rosy or anybody!" He had to get it out of his system and get over it. "Stop being a big baby!" he said. He kicked the rotting stump; he picked up loose dirt and threw it down the trail; he pulled at his hair. He took a deep breath, and then another . . . and another. And then he got up with a look of determination on his face. He looked back up the trail to see if Anse could see him. He could not. Andrew started down the hill. He was breathing hard, but he was not shaking.

The lights were on in the cabin when Andrew walked around to the front steps. Vicy was sitting at the table with Willis, Joe, and Rosy when Andrew walked in. They all looked up at him. Andrew wondered if his eyes were red. "Aunt Vicy, Uncle Anse said to tell you that he would be down later. I gotta go back up the mountain with some things. Do you know where I can find Troy or Elias?"

"Troy is in the barn. Elias ain't here," she replied.

Joe looked puzzled and watched Andrew carefully for any sign of stress. "I'm going with you, Andrew," he said.

"No, you ain't," Vicy said. "Troy can help your pa. You're stayin' here."

"We'll be back later tonight, Aunt Vicy. Uncle Anse will probably be hungry too."

"I'll fix y'all somethin' when you get back, Andrew. You go on now, and be careful."

Willis and Rosy paid no attention to the conversation, but Vicy knew quite well what was going on. She had seen this before.

Andrew left the house and ran to the barn. Troy was sitting on a bale of hay, working on a saddle. "Troy, your pa needs you. He just shot Lucian."

"What?!"

"Lucian was a bounty hunter. Uncle Anse shot him when Lucian pulled a gun on him."

"Where is he?"

"He sent me down to get you. And he said to bring shovels."

"Let's go," Troy said.

Troy picked up the two shovels and a lantern and headed out the door. He motioned for Andrew to lead the way. Andrew said, "Troy, Uncle Anse said to bring you and Elias both if you were home. Where is Elias?"

"He's over at Cap's with Nancy. It would take too long to go get him. Pa and I can take care of this. Just show me where Pa is."

Andrew started back up the slope with Troy close behind. Troy had both shovels. Andrew started to ask him if he could carry one of them but thought better of it. They could make much better time if Troy carried them both.

It took over forty minutes to get back to the clearing where Anse waited. He was sitting on a tree stump, smoking his pipe, when Troy and Andrew came into the clearing. Anse stood up and walked over to Troy. They looked at each other with a look of complete understanding as to what had to be done. Words were not necessary.

Andrew looked around. Lucian's body was nowhere to be seen. Anse's hunting shirt was lying across the tree stump where Anse had been sitting. It had two bloody spots in the back, the only evidence Andrew could see of what had happened a couple of hours before.

"Where is Elias?" asked Anse.

"He's at Cap's. We didn't want to wait to go get him," replied Troy.

Anse looked at Andrew. "You all right, Andrew?"

"Yessir, I'm all right."

"You head on home then. Tell Vicy we'll be home in a couple of hours, keep our dinner hot. You go on to bed, and we'll talk in the morning."

"I'd like to stay and help."

"Best you head on home, Andrew. We can handle it from here," Anse said. "Be careful now. And Andrew, I didn't tell you not to tell your ma and pa about the deputy that came to the house, but I think it best that you don't tell them about this if you don't have to. They would take you home for sure."

"No, sir, I won't tell 'em."

Andrew started back down the hill. It was pitch black now, and he didn't have a lantern. But he was not going to complain. He would get home in the dark, and he would not be a "big baby" any longer. It was time for him to grow up. He was almost nine years old.

It was October 1894.

8

CAP HATFIELD

All school kids looked forward to Fridays, weekends, and summer vacation, whether they attended the largest school in the state or the smallest school in the county. And so it was with young Andrew and his schoolmates at the end of the school year in May 1895. But this year it was even more special. Andrew's family was to move closer to his school so that he could live at home. His father had spent the last few weeks working on the cabin, converting it from a single room into a two-room complex, complete with a sleeping loft for Jane, Andrew, and Oliver. Their newest sibling, Louisa would sleep downstairs with her parents.

Their new home was a mile north of Uncle Anse's cabin and across the bottoms from Cap and Nancy. The rolling, crystal-clear creek ran directly in front of their new home, and wild deer roamed freely in their backyard. At night, sitting on their front porch, Andrew and his family would look out on a valley that stretched for a mile to the north and a mile to the south. They could see chimney smoke and lights from three or four homes in the valley, including the lights from Nancy's cabin directly across from their front door. Andrew felt he had the best of both worlds: living at home with his family and seeing the Hatfield kids as often as he wanted.

Andrew realized that while he would now live with his own family, he was as deeply involved in the Hatfield family as he was his own. Uncle Anse depended on him, and he was proud of that trust. He had become the family's messenger, errand boy, and lookout. Andrew felt a pride in having the Hatfield families involve him, and he wanted to encourage it.

Kentucky officials and both authorized and unauthorized bounty hunters with mail-order badges were flooding the mountains of West Virginia, determined to make arrests or bring in some proof of death in order to collect the numerous bounties on the Hatfield boys and Anse Hatfield himself. There was also the incentive of name recognition. Authorized state employees, both in Kentucky and West Virginia, as well as the unauthorized bounty hunters realized that whoever captured or killed Cap, Johnse, or Devil Anse would be remembered in history books forever. It was a war, at least in the valley, equal to the tension and brutality of the Civil War.

Andrew was but an unsuspecting participant, unable to fully understand his actions or the actions of members of the Hatfield family that put his life in danger. Andrew's life was identical to the lives of everyone else in the Island Creek Valley at the time, where no laws existed except the law of survival. The strongest bond among individuals in the valley was family. Families stuck together and looked out after each other as the safest mode of survival, and to Andrew, the Hatfields were family.

Andrew and the Hatfield kids walked home from school in the final week of the school year to find Cap sitting on the porch with Uncle Anse, a most unusual sight. Cap was never around his parents' house. Anse noticed the surprised expression on Andrew's face and offered an explanation. "We've been waiting on you, Andrew. Do you have plans this afternoon?"

"No, sir, Pa is at the farm all week. Can I help with something?"

"Cap needs to go to the hunting shack we have over on Mate Creek for a little while. He'll need someone to go with him and bring the packhorse back home. Can you do that?"

"Yessir, I can do that."

"If you leave right now, you can get there before dark. Then you can come back tomorrow morning. Run home and tell Lucindy what you're doing, and then bring your mare back here. Cap will wait on you."

Cap sat motionless beside Anse throughout the entire conversation and did not add anything. He was letting Anse do the talking for him.

Cap was always quiet around Andrew, and while he seemed to like the boy, he was guarded and kept his distance. Andrew had delivered messages and food to Cap for two years, but the number of words they had said to each other in that time would not fill a page. At the same time, there seemed to be a bond and a mutual respect between the two. Andrew knew what was expected in his dealings with Cap, and Cap had the confidence that whatever was expected of Andrew would get done.

Andrew ran back through the front gate and headed north. He found his mother on the porch, churning milk. "Ma, Anse wants me to go with Cap to Mate Creek to bring a horse back. I'll stay there tonight and be home in the morning."

"What about school, Andy? You got a few days left."

"I am way ahead of the class, Ma. I can make up whatever I miss when I get back. This late in the year, we aren't getting much new work."

Lucinda knew Andrew well enough to know that he was telling the truth. It would be worthless for him to be in class anyway if she made him go; he might as well be doing something he felt good about. "All right, Andy, but do be careful. And don't start back until daylight."

"Yes, ma'am, I'll be careful."

Andrew saddled the mare and headed south for the Hatfield home. Cap was waiting with two horses, one saddled and the other a packhorse fully loaded with gear. As Andrew walked the mare through the front gate, Anse and Cap met him. Anse was carrying a Winchester inside a leather case. He walked up beside the mare, slid the rifle and case underneath the right side stirrup, and attached it to the saddle. He looked up at Andrew and said, "Bring this back here before you go home, Andrew. I don't want you going off without it, but until your pa gives you permission, I'd just as soon he didn't know you were carrying it."

Andrew didn't say anything, but he smiled in approval.

Cap rode past Andrew, leading the packhorse, and walked the horses through the gate. Andrew followed. They turned south with Cap in the lead, and Andrew followed the packhorse on his mare. They passed the Island Creek School and crossed the mountain ridge to the south and headed into the valley. Five miles into the valley, they turned south and headed up a logging trail. By then the sun was low on the horizon, indicating two or three more hours of daylight. The cabin was two hours away.

It was dusk when the cabin came into view, hidden in the shadows of tall, black pine trees and dense underbrush. The cabin had not been used in years, and the surrounding brush concealed the lower half, exposing only half a door and a single window. Cap had some work to do. Cap and Andrew dismounted, forced the door open, and walked into the dark, musty cabin that smelled of fireplace ash and wild animals. Cap lit a lantern—this one had real kerosene—and set it on a table in the middle of the room. Andrew thought, *I wouldn't want to stay here a few weeks.*

They began unloading the packhorse, finishing as the last strands of evening light disappeared. Cap started a fire in the large stone fireplace and stuck a mason jar filled with beans into a large cast-iron pot that swiveled in over the fire. When the beans were hot, they poured them over the ham shank that Vicy had packed and sat down at the table for the meal that they had anticipated for the last two hours.

After their meal, Cap unloaded two blankets and placed them on the two cots that lined the walls. Both of them settled in for the night. It had been a long ride, and Andrew had the same ride tomorrow, which was not a pleasant thought at that moment. He fell fast asleep.

Andrew awoke several times during the night, disturbed by the sound of an animal scratching at the door or the crackle of the slow-burning fire in the open fireplace. Twice he got up to add a log to the fire. Cap slept through all of it. From his cot, Andrew glanced over at Cap occasionally, amazed at how soundly he slept. He had no pillow, no blanket over him, and his rifle was securely cradled across his chest. It was clear that Cap was accustomed to sleeping in different places, and he had developed a mental shield against discomfort. He would just sleep right through it.

The sky was bright red in the east when Andrew mounted the mare for the trip home. The packhorse had a long rope tied around his neck and attached to the saddle horn in front of Andrew on the mare. Andrew held the reins from the packhorse's bridle. Andrew waved good-bye as he rode north and Cap waved from the cabin door.

Andrew and Cap had just spent the last twenty hours together and not a single word had passed between them.

Halfway up the southern slope of the mountain ridge, a small black bear cub darted across the logging trail right in front of Andrew and disappeared into the underbrush. It startled the mare, and she jumped away from the trail. Andrew stopped the packhorse and quickly pulled the rifle out of the case. *Where there is a cub, there is a momma bear,* he thought.

It didn't take long for Andrew to know he was right. A full-grown black bear darted into the path, saw the horses, faced them with a snarl, and stood on her hind legs. Andrew leveled the gun. The mare was backing up as quickly as she could; the packhorse was pulling against the rope. Andrew fired a shot into the ground in front of the bear, and dust and gravel flew. Andrew did not want to shoot the bear and leave the cub in the mountains to starve. He fired again, but the bear continued to come toward them on her hind legs.

Andrew fired a third shot, this time directly at her back paw. The bullet penetrated the thick fur, went through the foot, and dug into the dirt. The bear dropped to her front paws and rolled over on her side and off the trail. She scampered to her feet and disappeared into the underbrush. Andrew kicked the mare in her underbelly and slapped the reins against her neck. She took off up the slope, and the packhorse followed, almost at a dead run.

When he reached the crest of the ridge, Andrew looked back down the trail to make sure they were not being followed. He was shaking. He replaced the rifle into its case and looked down the northern slope toward the valley. He slid off and walked in front of the mare and began rubbing her nose to calm her down. The mare's eyes were still enlarged from fear. He walked back to the packhorse, which was equally spooked. He rubbed the horse's nose and whispered softly to calm the animal. After a few minutes both horses seemed to be calm.

Andrew was ready to remount when movement in the valley below caught his eye. *What is that?* he wondered. In the distance he saw three riders in the valley coming from the east. Each held a rifle straight up, resting on his hip, and all three were looking at the ground. *What are they doing? What are they looking for?* Then he realized that those riders were following the fresh trail left when he and Cap had come through the valley last night. Andrew panicked. He would have to pass right by them on the way home. How would he explain the packhorse or where he had been?

Andrew backed the horses up and off the trail. He tied them to a tree branch and went back to the clearing to watch the progress of the three riders. When they reached the logging trail that Andrew and Cap used coming up the mountain, they stopped. The lead rider dismounted, looked to the ground, and got down on one knee to get a closer look at something.

Andrew watched as a conversation went on with the three riders. *What? What did he find?* He knew he was in trouble if those riders started up the mountain. He had few places to hide. The lead rider remounted, and more conversation took place. *Keep going!* Andrew pleaded to himself. *Just keep going!*

They did. The lead rider turned his horse to the west, and they continued westward, still watching the ground. Andrew watched until they were near the western horizon before he rushed back to the horses and remounted. He knew that he had to get to the valley and head east as quickly as possible, in case the three riders changed direction and came back. He was shaking again.

When Andrew reached the valley and turned to the east, he looked over his shoulder to the western horizon. No sign of the riders. He looked at the ground to see how clear the tracks were that the three seemed to be following. He discovered their confusion; there were several fresh hoof marks on the trail, going in opposite directions. Luckily, others had used the same trail after Andrew and Cap had passed through the night before. The three riders had been distracted by other trails and picked up the wrong one. Andrew slapped the reins against the mare and went in a quickened trot. He wanted to get home as fast as he could.

By noon he was walking the mare and the packhorse through Anse's front gate. Anse was nowhere in sight. Andrew dismounted and walked the packhorse around the house and into the barn. He found an empty stall and walked the horse inside, took the bridle off, and closed the stall gate. He filled the hay rack with fresh hay and walked out of the barn. Anse met him at the door. "Any trouble, Andrew?" he asked.

"No, sir. I left Cap in that old cabin and got back a few minutes ago. Didn't have any trouble." Andrew was going to keep the episode with the bear and the three riders to himself; he didn't see it necessary to bring it up.

"Good," replied Anse. "Let's get that Winchester off your saddle, and you can head on home. I know Lucindy will be worried about you."

Andrew remounted the mare and headed north for home. Lucinda was waiting on the porch when he got there. Louisa was sitting on her lap, or what there was left of her lap, as she was eight months pregnant with their fifth child, Joshua. As Andrew rode up, Lucinda put Louisa down, stood up, and met him at the steps. "You hungry, Andy?"

"Yes, ma'am, I am."

"Come on in. I'll fix you something. Did you have any trouble?"

"No, ma'am, none at all." He still did not mention the bear. Where the Hatfields were concerned, everything was always easy as pie. Andrew walked in behind his mother, holding on to Louisa's hand and looking forward to a large plate of biscuits and gravy.

9

THE ASSAULT

I can't explain why, but Cap and Johnse hung out a lot with the Rutherford boys. They were customers of Nancy's, but I don't know why they had anything to do with them. John, the oldest, was the meanest man I ever met.

Andrew was determined to make their new home work for everyone, even if it meant he would be doing field chores when he would much rather be inside reading a book. So he needed no incentive to be up bright and early on the first morning of summer vacation to help with chores. At breakfast he asked what his dad was doing and was told that he was working on the fence behind their house. Andrew quickly finished his breakfast, said thanks to his mother, and headed out the front door. He found his dad in the back of the house, ax in hand.

"Pa, I'm here to help. What can I do?"

"Well, Andy, until I get some of these logs split, there isn't much you can do. After I split a few logs, you can help me put the fence up. But Nancy came by a little while ago and said she had an errand for you sometime today if you had time. Why don't you run over there and help her, and then you can help me when you get back."

"I'll be back as soon as I can!" With that, Andrew was gone.

Andrew seldom talked to his parents about his escapades with the Hatfield family. When he did, he was as casual with the explanations as he could be. Some of his descriptions of errands were simplified to protect his own involvement, and others were a result of simply not fully understanding how difficult or dangerous the errand was.

Andrew took off for Nancy's house across the bottoms on a dead run. If he was going to go somewhere for Nancy, he wanted to leave before lunch so he would be home before dark. Andrew stepped up on Nancy's front porch as she walked out the front door. Her two small children followed.

"Good mornin', ma'am. Pa said you had something you wanted me to do."

"I do, Andrew. Johnse came by night before last, and I gave him some food. I didn't have much to give him, so I know he needs some more by now. Do you think you could get him something from your ma?"

"Yes, ma'am, I'll ask her."

"He said to tell you he and Rutherford are back in the logging shack if you can get something to him. He took the only fuel I had when he left, and I ain't got no more. Tell him I ran out of corn. I gotta wait until Anse brings me some more before I can get them anymore fuel. You understand?"

"Yes, ma'am. I'll see if Ma can get him some food, and I'll take it up to him."

"Andrew, you be careful. I don't trust that Rutherford fellow any further than I can throw him."

"Yes, ma'am, I'll be careful."

Andrew raced back across the bottoms and back up to his house. He went straight to his dad. "Pa, Nancy said that Johnse needs food, and she doesn't have any to give him. She said to ask if Ma could get something for him. I told her I would take it to him."

"Where is he?"

"He's up in that ol' loggin' shack off of Lizzies Creek. I've been up there before. If I leave soon I can be back well before dark."

"Okay, go get the mare. I'll get some food from your ma."

"Yessir."

Holbert was more than aware that Cap and Johnse were hiding from bounty hunters. Everyone in the valley knew. They also knew that most of the bounty hunters were unauthorized and were themselves known killers. While the feud had been over for nearly six years, some folk in Kentucky continued to fund bounties for their capture, in spite of the Supreme Court decision. And the Hatfields were family. In his younger years, Holbert had threatened to join the feud along Grapevine Creek, but Lucinda had put her foot down. But Holbert still felt a need to help when he could.

Within thirty minutes, Andrew's mare was saddled and loaded down with food from Lucinda. He walked the horse across the bottoms and stopped by Nancy's to let her know he was on his way. He went north to Lizzies Creek and then headed up the same mountain path he had traveled before, when he was stopped by the two men who took his lunch. It was a much quieter trip this time.

The sun was directly over his head when he got near the cabin, telling him that was just after noon. He dismounted and walked the mare along the ridge above the cabin. When the cabin was directly below him, he stopped and barked like a squirrel. Within moments he heard a squirrel bark behind him. He turned the mare and headed in that direction. Thirty yards up the hill, he saw Johnse and Rutherford sitting near the same spot where he found them before. Each was holding a rifle pointed directly at him.

Andrew tied the mare to a tree branch, came back down the slope, and sat down beside Johnse. Without a word, Rutherford got up and walked to the gunnysack strapped across the mare's back. He opened it and looked inside. He turned and looked at Andrew with an expression that told Andrew he was in trouble. Rutherford walked over to him, leaned down to within inches of his face and said, "Where is the goddamn lantern, boy?"

"I didn't bring it. Nancy—"

Andrew didn't get to finish. Rutherford ripped the back of his hand across Andrew's face with a blow that sent Andrew crashing to the ground. Andrew was stunned. He felt something on his face and reached up to touch his lip. It was split wide open. Blood was streaming down his chin from his lip and his nose.

Johnse screamed, "John, what the hell are you doin'? Are you crazy? Anse will kill you for that!"

"Not if he don't go home. Anse'll never know what happened to 'im!"

Andrew panicked. He jumped up and ran for the horse. Rutherford grabbed him by the waist and held him up like a sack of flour. Rutherford drew his hand back to hit Andrew again when Johnse screamed, "John, stop! That's enough! Put him down!"

Rutherford looked over his shoulder to see Johnse's rifle just inches from his face. Johnse said, "I said put him down, goddammit. Now! Or so help me, God, I will blow your goddamn head off."

Rutherford dropped Andrew to the ground and turned to face Johnse, his hand on his pistol. Andrew sat up and pushed himself away from the two as quickly as he could. He started shaking. He could not see out of his right eye.

Johnse held the rifle to Rutherford's head and said, "Andrew, get on your horse and get out of here while I make sure this bastard doesn't come after you."

Rutherford said, "You can't let him go, Johnse. I'll be a dead man!"

"You're already a dead man, John. It's just a matter of time. You can hide, but Anse'll find you, and it won't be pretty. Andrew, I'm giving you an hour head start and then I am going to turn this bastard loose in the woods or kill him. Rutherford, you had better run your ass off and get out of Mingo County. Nobody can protect you up here anymore, and I sure as hell won't. Andrew, go home!"

Andrew dropped the sack of food, remounted, and turned the mare down the mountain trail. Blood had soaked his shirt and was still running from his nose and mouth. He would not cry. He pushed the mare as much as he dared without falling off or causing the horse to slide.

He made the trip back down the mountain in half the time it took to go up. He rode past Nancy's house without stopping and crossed the bottoms at a near gallop. By the time he reached his house, the blood had stopped, but it was soaked into his shirt and caked on his face. *There is no hiding this from mother,* he thought.

When he walked in the front door, the look on his mother's face was one of absolute horror. Jane screamed. Holbert jumped up and ran to the door. Lucinda followed. Holbert picked Andrew up and carried him to the sink. Lucinda started unbuttoning his shirt. No one said a word. Andrew sat, trying his best not to cry. The cold water felt good on Andrew's face as Holbert dabbed a cloth gently around his face, trying to figure out where the blood was coming from. By then Andrew's lip was swollen to twice its normal size.

Lucinda took his shirt off and examined his body for cuts. Holbert dabbed his face clean and gave Andrew a wet cloth to hold over his eye. Andrew's lip had a deep split in it that separated the lower lip into two pieces. Andrew sat, watched, and shook. Jane cried. Oliver was as close to his parents as he could get, making sure he didn't miss a thing. The blood did not bother him.

Twenty minutes after Andrew walked in the door, his face was clean, he had on a fresh shirt, and he was holding a wet cloth on his lip. He was sitting at the table before conversation even started. Holbert said, "How did this happen?"

"A man named Rutherford hit me."

"John Rutherford? Why?"

"He and Johnse were waiting on food and Nancy's fuel. Nancy didn't have any fuel for me to take 'em, and Rutherford got mad."

"Does Anse know what Rutherford did?"

"No, sir. I came straight home. But Pa, Johnse made Rutherford stop. Johnse told him he would kill him if he hit me again. Johnse told him he was a dead man as soon as Uncle Anse finds out about this."

"He may be a dead man before Anse finds out about this," said Holbert. "Do you know where he is now?"

"Johnse told him he was giving me an hour head start, and then Rutherford should get out of the county, because no one could protect him now."

"We're going to see Anse, right now! Lucindy, we'll be back later."

Holbert and Andrew walked out the front door as Lucinda and Jane watched in tears. Fifteen minutes later, Holbert and Andrew were opening the gate to Anse's house. It was almost dark, and the lights were on in the house. The dogs started barking, and the bear started pacing. Anse walked out of the front door, carrying his rifle, followed by Troy and Elias. They met Holbert at the front steps.

Anse looked down at Andrew, who was holding the wet cloth over his lip. Andrew's lip was badly swollen; his right eye had turned black and was swollen shut; and the entire side of his face was bloodred.

Anse gasped, "Andrew, what happened?"

Andrew repeated the story about Rutherford, Johnse, and the slap.

As expected, Anse was livid. Andrew had seen Anse when he was mad, but never like this. "Let's get in the house. Andrew, does Rutherford know where Cap is? That crazy bastard may go after him now. He'll know that we will all be lookin' for him."

"No, sir, I was goin' to tell Johnse where he was, but Rutherford didn't give me a chance."

Anse took Andrew by the shoulder and walked him into the house. Joe, Rosy, and Willis were sitting on the floor in front of the fireplace, and Vicy was in a rocking chair, knitting. Joe was first to see Andrew, and his mouth dropped open, but he said nothing. Rosy put her hand over her mouth and started to cry. Vicy dropped the knitting needles to the floor and walked over to Andrew, saying, "Oh my God." She took Andrew by the shoulder and walked him across the room to the fireplace. She sat in a chair, with Andrew standing in front of her, took the damp cloth out of his hand, and removed it from his lip to survey the damage. "He needs to see a doctor. This is a bad split." She did not ask how it happened.

Holbert said, "I'll take him in the morning, Vicy. It's too late to go tonight."

Anse said, "Elias, you and Troy go to Nancy's and see if Johnse is there. If he ain't, go up to that ol' loggin' shack off Lizzies Creek where Andrew left 'em. If Rutherford is still with him, bring him down here to me . . . tonight. If he ain't, we'll head out to Mate Creek in the morning. No tellin' what Rutherford will do now. We gotta get word to Cap."

Vicy could stand it no longer. "Andrew, did Johnse have anything to do with this?"

"No, ma'am. Johnse made Rutherford stop. He was gonna hit me again, and Johnse said he would kill him if he did."

Troy and Elias walked out the front door and headed for the barn. Rosy ran to Andrew and gave him a big hug. Andrew thought, *Hmm, maybe it was worth gettin' hit.*

Vicy wouldn't ask for details, but Joe was dying to get every one. He put his arm around Andrew's shoulder, and they walked out the front door together.

Andrew and Joe spent thirty minutes on the front porch going through every detail of the confrontation with Rutherford. Joe was sorry that he had not been there to help. Andrew was worried that it would now be harder for him to continue helping the Hatfield family. He realized that his dad would be less agreeable to letting him be so involved in their struggles. And he knew that his mother would stop him at every opportunity. But this gave Andrew a new resolve;

he would just be quieter about his activities. The Hatfield kids had become as much his brothers and sisters as were Jane, Oliver, and Louisa. And Vicy was almost as much a mother to him as was Lucinda. Deserting them now would be like deserting his family. He could not do that.

Troy and Elias mounted their horses, walked them through the front gate, and turned north toward Nancy's. Holbert said good-bye to Vicy, and he and Anse and walked outside to find Andrew.

Anse said, "Holbert, I hope you know how bad we feel about Andrew. I think of Andrew as one of my own, and I don't want anything to ever happen to him."

"We know that, Anse. It wasn't your fault, or Johnse's. But I sure would like to get my hands on Rutherford."

"Holbert, he can't hide forever. I'll find him. And when I do, God help him."

Holbert called to Andrew, who was sitting on the porch, talking to Joe. "Andrew, let's go home. We have a busy day tomorrow."

Holbert mounted the mare, reached down, and pulled Andrew up behind him. Joe waved good-bye and walked in the house with Anse. Holbert walked the mare through the gate and turned north, following the same dirt path that Troy and Elias had taken just minutes before. A hundred yards outside the gate, Andrew said, "Pa, let me carry the lantern. I'll put it under my shirt. If Cap is out there anywhere, he'll know it's me. I left him on Mate Creek, but he may be back by now. We need to get word to him to be on the watch for Rutherford."

Holbert handed Andrew the lantern and watched as Andrew unbuttoned his hunting shirt, put the lantern inside it, and buttoned it back up. Holbert said, "You're gonna get burned!"

"I do it a lot, Pa. It's kind of a signal. If Cap is out here he'll let me know." Andrew had developed the habit of putting the lantern under his hunting shirt on cold winter nights just to keep warm. The Hatfield kids would kid him about it, but eventually they all recognized it was Andrew as he rode on horseback. So it became a signal. The bright glow of the lantern became a muted horsehide color, covering his entire shirt.

They had ridden in silence a hundred yards more when Andrew heard the sound of a night owl. "Pa, stop!" Holbert pulled on the reins, and the mare came to a stop. "Listen!" They heard the owl again. Andrew made the exact sound of the owl. Holbert was amazed.

"Where did you learn that?"

"Anse taught me."

They listened again. They heard the owl again. Holbert turned the horse, and they walked in the direction of the owl. Twenty yards into the trees, Cap walked out from behind a tree, rifle in hand. "Lots happenin' at Pa's house. What's goin' on? What happened to Andrew's face?" Cap had obviously been watching.

"It's a long story, Cap," said Holbert. "Come on with us, and I'll tell you about what's happened—unless you think it is safe enough for you to go home or to Anse's. We've got plenty of food too, if you're hungry."

"Thanks, Holbert, I'll chance it at Pa's. Is there anybody down there?"

"Nobody there but family, Cap. Good luck!"

Troy and Elias stopped a hundred yards from Cap's house and watched. There were lights on inside but no sounds. Not even a barking dog. They walked their horses closer. Then the dogs started barking. Nancy came out of the house, and two small children followed. Troy walked his horse to the steps, greeted Nancy, and asked about Johnse. Nancy said that he was inside eating. Troy and Elias dismounted and walked inside behind her. They were both relieved that they did not have to make the journey to the logging shack that late at night, especially with John Rutherford on the loose.

Johnse proceeded to tell his brothers the story that Andrew had told Anse earlier. Troy and Elias were amazed that Rutherford was crazy enough to hit any kid, not to mention a relative of Anse. Johnse reminded them of Rutherford's demeanor, especially when he was drinking. He explained that Rutherford had been skittish all day, waiting on that whiskey. He had been pacing and short-tempered. He could not wait for Andrew to get there, and when Andrew showed up without the whiskey, it was more than he could take.

Troy asked Johnse which way Rutherford was headed when he left. Johnse said that he assumed that Rutherford would head home to Matewan, since he went off west toward Red Jacket. He was on foot and carrying a side arm and a rifle. Troy and Elias waited for Johnse to finish his meal, which wasn't much, considering Nancy's low food and fuel supplies, and then mounted the horses.

Nancy walked to the door with the three and asked Elias to let Anse and Cap know that she was out of food, and she needed corn for a new batch of whiskey. Troy said that they would bring her some supplies the next day and bring as much corn as they could gather. With Johnse riding behind Troy, the three headed south to Anse's house.

Thirty minutes after Holbert and Andrew left Anse's, Cap walked into the front yard. Anse was standing at the front door with a pipe in his mouth and a rifle in his right hand. The dogs started barking and then stopped when they recognized Cap. Anse watched Cap walk up the steps, walked out to meet him, and proceeded to tell him the story of Rutherford hitting Andrew and threatening him with his life. Cap was amazed. And Anse was still fuming. He told Cap he wanted Rutherford dead, and he didn't care who did it or when.

Troy, Johnse, and Elias rode up as Anse and Cap argued about the best way to settle things with Rutherford. Anse wanted a search party out early the next morning, but he got no support from any of his boys. Cap's argument was that he and Johnse were already at risk, and they did not want to make it worse by wandering off through the woods without knowing exactly where John was. And they especially did not want to go near Matewan. Johnse argued that he hated to see Troy and Elias get involved at all; they had been insulated so far from any of the hostilities, and if they were involved in a hunt for Rutherford, they would be at risk as well.

Anse did not respond. He walked to the rocker, sat down, and relit his pipe. He started rocking slowly as he looked out over the front yard. It was pitch black, so he couldn't see much, but he stared straight ahead anyway. Cap knew that the conversation was over, so he walked into the house to see Vicy about something to eat.

Anse sat and pondered. He knew that Cap was right about going after Rutherford, and he knew he had his own fights to worry about. Rutherford had just added to the list. He also knew that Cap was right about Troy and Elias. They would become targets, even though they had nothing to do with the McCoys or the feud.

Both Troy and Elias had shown a more responsible side than either Cap or Johnse. They finished their schooling, and they were working with their dad in the lumber business. Everyone knew that the N&W Railroad was coming through the county very soon, and both Troy and Elias looked forward to signing on to one of those good-paying jobs the railroads always brought with them. It would be a shame if they did not get that opportunity just because their name was Hatfield.

Anse also had his battles in court. With the railroad coming, his land holdings were a target for every lawyer this side of Charleston. The rich resources in the Tug Fork Valley—coal and timber—would become much more valuable when there was an inexpensive way to get those resources to market. The railroad would provide that cheap transportation. All the land in the valley would become more valuable, and Anse's land holdings would be under more pressure than usual, because he had obtained most of it, though the courts and an appeal was always a threat from the party who lost.

The more he pondered over Cap and Johnse, Troy and Elias, the more depressed he became. And now the incident with Andrew and Rutherford had taken a toll on his spirit. All of a sudden, he felt very old.

Anse came in off the porch and gathered his sons for another session. His mood had tempered, and he had concluded that his sons' arguments were sound; it would be a better strategy to wait for the right time to face John Rutherford. But just to make a point, he complained openly that Johnse should have settled the issue when it happened. Johnse was defensive. He told his father that he thought John was a friend and that he was not himself at the time because of his need for whiskey. Johnse said that after Rutherford dropped Andrew, he sat in front of Rutherford for an hour, holding the gun to his head, and they talked. Rutherford had made no threatening moves and was remorseful and at the same time scared for his life. When the hour was over, Rutherford picked up his rifle and headed out through the forest. Johnse said he left immediately for Nancy's house, afraid that Rutherford would come after him.

Anse dropped the subject. He had made his point: John Rutherford must be dealt with, and Johnse knew it. He had just delayed it.

By the time Holbert and Andrew got home, Andrew was holding on to his father with his head pressed against Holbert's back to keep from falling off the mare; he was exhausted. Lucinda met them at the front door, went straight to Andrew, and cupped his chin in her hand. She looked at Holbert and said, "He has to see a doctor. This looks bad."

Holbert agreed. "Vicy looked at it and said the same thing. I'm taking him to Barnabus in the morning. Anse is really upset. They all are. There is no doubt that they love Andrew as much as we do."

Lucinda was not consoled. "Holbert, I don't want Andrew getting caught up in all that goes on with the Hatfields. We should go back to the farm and find another way for Andrew to go to school."

Andrew had heard enough. "Ma, I love the Hatfields. You can't keep me away from them. They are family. I love all of Uncle Anse's kids. I want them to have a home like I have, and I want to help them. Remember, I didn't want to go there to live when you told me to, but I went. And now I don't want to stop helping them when I can, and it is not fair for you to tell me that I can't."

"Andrew, I love the Hatfields too. But I love you more. We'll talk tomorrow. I put some food out for you, and then I want you in bed. Tomorrow will be a long day."

"Yes, ma'am."

Andrew went to bed upset. His face hurt, but more importantly his heart hurt. He felt that his mother was going to try to keep him away from the Hatfield family. He could not allow that to happen. Joe was his good friend, and so was Rosy. There were people out there that wanted to hurt them, and he wanted to help. He remembered back to the Cow Creek farm, when his mom and dad told him that he was going to live with another family and leave his own. He had cried, thinking his parents didn't love him anymore. He realized now that they loved him a lot, which is why they wanted him to go. But now he had to convince his parents that they had made the right decision.

Holbert and Lucinda went to bed upset as well. They had been very lenient during Andrew's time at the Hatfield home, but now they worried that they had made the wrong decision. The Hatfield family was a focal point in the community, and everything that happened to them was part of the lives of all in Mingo County. Living a segregated life away from the Hatfields was not an option in Mingo County. If it happened to the Hatfields, it happened to the community. Church services were held at the Hatfield home; what employment existed in the valley was employment that Anse provided; he had built the school and hired the teachers; he loaned money to struggling farmers and sent his timber crews to help with planting and harvesting; his political preferences were always elected—he needed only to let his choice be known. It was indeed Anse Hatfield's community.

Early the next morning, Holbert and Andrew were on their way to Barnabus. Andrew's face hurt a lot more than it did when he went to bed, but at least he could see out of his eye again. For the trip, Holbert was carrying a gun, which was very unusual; Holbert never carried a gun. Andrew asked his dad if he could carry a gun as well, but Holbert said no. He did not know about Andrew's shooting skills or the amount of practice he had. Although Andrew had shared the stories of the coon hunts with his dad, he just left out the details as to who was shooting the coons. He wasn't sure his dad would object, but he did not want to take a chance. He knew his mother would really be upset if she knew all that Andrew had been involved in since he had gone to live with the Hatfields.

The doctor looked at Andrew's lip and advised stitches. Otherwise, the damage was minimal. His nose was not broken, and his eye was black, but the swelling had gone down considerably. After the surgery, Holbert and Andrew started the ride back to Island Creek. Holbert decided to use the time for a heart-to-heart talk with Andrew. "Andrew, the Hatfield family has been really good to you, and we know they love you. But there are plenty of folk out there that don't like the Hatfields, and they want to do them harm. Your ma and I are concerned that in harming them, they may harm you as well. We want you to stay in school, but we would rather you stay at home more and not go to the Hatfield house so much."

"Pa, Rosy can't leave, and neither can Willis or Tennis. If the Hatfields are hurt, they get hurt too. I am not afraid. Those people are not after me or Rosy or Willis or Tennis. They want Cap and Johnse and Uncle Anse. Troy, Elias, and Joe are all really good at looking out for us. And so are Aunt Vicy and Uncle Anse. I just want to help when I can. I promise I am very careful."

They rode the rest of the way in silence. Holbert had said all he intended to say.

As Holbert and Andrew neared home, they passed Elias and Troy in a wagon full of corn. Elias pulled the mules to a stop as Holbert approached on the bay. Andrew followed closely behind on the mare. Elias looked at the patch on Andrew's lip. "How's the lip, Andrew? Does it hurt much?"

"It's kind of numb right now. It's all right."

Troy added, "I sure wouldn't want to be John Rutherford right now. Ain't never seen Pa so mad."

"Well, at least I suspect we won't see him much around Island Creek anymore," said Holbert.

"Ain't likely," replied Elias.

Holbert changed the subject. "Where ya goin' with all the corn?"

"We're takin' it up to the fuel farm above Nancy's," Troy said. "She's been out for a while, so we've been gatherin' for her all mornin'. This batch should last a couple of weeks anyway. Pa's got a couple of hands up there waitin' on it."

Holbert knew that Nancy didn't make all of her own brew, and Anse didn't sell any. But he furnished the materials and the men to cook most of it. Nancy provided the sales and made small batches in a shed behind her house. It was a profitable system that kept Nancy in income and the children fed, so it was hard to object. Until new laws made it illegal, moonshine had been a way of life in the valley. Folks resented the Charleston politicians for passing laws against it so they could tax whiskey legally when it sold. The locals in the valley considered Nancy's operation as open rebellion against an unfair system, and they supported her strongly for it. Of course they liked the fuel as well.

10

FUEL, A MOUNTAIN STAPLE

Oh yeah, I made deliveries for Nancy a good bit. Especially to old man Garrett over there off Sang Branch near Barnabus. Garrett was a real ruffian until he got religion. (Chuckle.) He wouldn't go near Nancy's house after that, so I'd go over there a lot.

The start of the school year in 1896 was even more exciting to Andrew than in previous years. He would be starting the fifth grade, and Oliver would be starting the first grade. Andrew was truly a big brother, and he was anxious to have Oliver in the same classroom. He could not wait to introduce Oliver to all his friends. To Lucinda's disappointment, who so wanted to go with Oliver on his first day, Oliver marched off proudly with his big brother, leaving her waving from the front porch. They stopped to meet the Hatfield kids and continued their walk to the one-room school, a quarter of a mile south.

Oliver was understandably nervous on his first day of school, a typical first-grader. Having Andrew to walk into the schoolhouse with him made things a lot easier for him, but he was still nervous. Oliver was much bigger than Andrew had been at his age, and it probably wouldn't be long until Oliver and Andrew were the same size. But Oliver did not possess Andrew's adventuresome nature and was hesitant to try new things or to voice an opinion. He would not risk anything that seemed to be dangerous. Andrew, while small for his age, was far more aggressive, far quicker to voice an opinion, and more accepting of danger. Life with the Hatfields had brought a complete change in his demeanor.

After an uneventful and short first day of school, Andrew and Rosy led the trio of younger kids back up the dusty trail toward home. They walked to the front porch of the Hatfield home and were greeted by Aunt Vicy. She invited Oliver and Andrew in for a piece of apple pie, which was enthusiastically accepted. The five sat around the table, laughing and telling Vicy stories about their first day of school.

Andrew asked about his uncle Anse; Vicy said he was in the barn. Andrew jumped up, told Oliver he would be right back, and ran out the door to go see his uncle. Oliver was unconcerned. He was as infatuated with Rosy as Andrew had been on his first day of school, and he loved sitting by her side, eating apple pie. Rosy even held his hand for a little while.

Andrew found Anse in the barn, saddling Fred, his favorite horse. "Mornin', Uncle Anse. Where you goin'?"

"Mornin', Andrew. I'm goin' over to see Nancy for a few minutes to see if she needs anything. We took her some corn a week or so ago, and I'm just gonna check to see if she needs any more. How's your lip doin'? Have you gottin' the stitches out yet?"

"Yessir, the stitches fell out a few days ago. And my eye is back to normal. Uncle Anse, I can drop by to see Nancy for you, and if she needs anything, I'll come back and let you know. I'm going home anyway, and it'll save you a trip." Andrew was afraid that, after the episode with Rutherford, his uncle would be reluctant to have him involved in Hatfield business anymore, and he was going to make sure that didn't happen.

"That's kind of you, Andrew, but I want to check to see how she's doin', and I want to take her some more corn if she needs it. You're welcome to come over while I'm there, in case she needs anything."

"Yessir, I'm gonna do that. I'll be there as soon as I get my brother home."

"I'll see you then. And I'm glad your lip is better."

Andrew ran back to Vicy's house and in the front door. "Come on, Oliver, we gotta get home. Thanks for the pie, Aunt Vicy. Bye, Rosy. We'll see y'all tomorrow."

Andrew practically ran home, dragging his reluctant little brother behind him. Oliver was not as anxious to get home as Andrew, and he did not like running. Lucinda met them on the front step and was excited to hear stories of Oliver's first day at school. Andrew was anxious to get to Nancy's. He answered all of his mother's questions as quickly and as shortly as he could, giving Lucinda the big hint that he wanted out of there. As soon as Andrew could involve Oliver in one of her questions, he made a hasty retreat out the front door. He ran down the hill, across the bottoms, and back up to Nancy's house.

Anse was inside talking to Nancy when Andrew walked in the front door. The conversation ended when Andrew walked in.

"Good mornin', Andrew," Nancy said.

"Mornin', ma'am. I came over to see if I could do anything. I don't have anything to do today, and Pa is at the farm this week."

"Well, there is something you can do, Andrew, if it is all right with your ma and Anse don't mind." Anse looked unprepared for Nancy's comment and looked at her with a what-is-this-all-about look.

"You won't mind, will you, Uncle Anse?" Andrew asked.

"Don't know. What is it you want him to do, Nancy?"

"I gotta get a jug up to ole man Garrett. I can put it in a gunnysack, and Andrew can take it up there. I don't think his mother would mind. It ain't that far, and it's not on your way home."

"Fine with me, Andrew, if you want to go, but you gotta ask your ma first. Stop by there on your way and make sure she don't mind. And if you go, tell ole man Garrett I said hello."

"Yessir!" Andrew was excited to be able to run another errand.

Nancy got up from the table, picked up a clay jug, and dropped it into a gunnysack, which Andrew threw over his shoulder. Nancy said, "Andrew, Mr. Garrett may give you some money. If he does, bring it back here when you can."

"Yes, ma'am."

The sack was heavier than Andrew had thought it would be, but it was lighter than carrying a coon and a rifle at the same time, so he didn't care. He went back to his house and found his mother sitting in a rocker, sewing buttons on one of his shirts. Oliver was playing with Louisa on the floor. "Ma, Nancy wants me to take this jug to Mr. Garrett, but she said I had to ask you first."

"That's fine, Andrew, but take the mare. I want you to get back here before dark."

"Yes, ma'am."

Andrew went to the barn, saddled the mare, and walked to the tree stump that he used to get up on her. He tied the sack to the saddle horn, turned the mare north, and left the cabin on a dusty ride to Sang Branch.

Mr. Garrett was a friend of his uncle and his father and was known to be a hard-living mountain man before he turned to religion and formed a church. Andrew didn't ask what was in the jug, but he assumed it was fuel. He suspected that Mr. Garrett's lantern was running low.

It was after three when Andrew reached Sang Branch, and the sun was low on the horizon. He wanted it to be a short visit so he could head home. He did not want to be out after dark and worry his mother.

Mr. Garrett lived in a rustic clapboard house in a cluster of trees within sight of Cow Creek. Andrew had been there on several occasions with his dad, delivering repaired tools or picking up broken ones. Mr. Garrett seemed like a nice man.

"Hello, Andrew! What brings you to Sang Branch?" said Mr. Garrett as Andrew rode up to the front porch of the home.

"Hello, Mr. Garrett. Nancy Hatfield asked me to bring you this." Andrew untied the sack and handed it to Garrett's extended hand.

"She did, did she? Well, that was kind of you to do that. Did she say anything about money?"

"Yessir, she said if you gave me any to bring it back to her when I could."

"Hold on just a minute. I'll be right back."

Garrett disappeared back into his house and came back moments later with a leather strap. He walked over to the mare and tied the piece of leather to the bridle, just under the mare's mane. He tucked it in so carefully that the leather looked like part of the bridle. "Just in case anybody stops you, I don't want this to cause any trouble. Just give it Nancy when you see her."

"Yessir, I'd best be on my way. I want to be home before dark."

"Thanks for coming over, Andrew. Tell your pa hello, and give my best to your uncle Anse when you see him."

"Yessir, I will. He said to tell you hello."

Andrew started back to Island Creek as shadows started forming under the tall poplar trees along the narrow trail. The mare struggled going up the steep slopes and slid occasionally going back down the far sides. Andrew had become an expert rider, learning to lean into the slope going up and back into the slope coming down. Today he would get plenty of practice; he would cross two mountain ranges between Sang Branch and his home.

As he started down the second range, just a mile from home, he saw two riders sitting in a clearing just ahead of him. One was on horseback, the other sitting on the ground holding his horse's reins. Andrew had no choice; he had to walk his horse right by them. He could not turn and go back up the slope. As he got near, the man on the ground stood up. "Where ya goin', boy?" he said.

"Home," said Andrew.

"What ya got in the sack?"

"Nothin'."

The man leaned over and grabbed the mare's reins. "You won't mind if I look then, will ya?"

Andrew said nothing. He watched as the man walked around his horse toward the gunnysack. The second rider sat on his horse and stared at Andrew. Andrew tried to look unconcerned, but he was beginning to get nervous. The rider squeezed the gunnysack, but he didn't take it off the horse. "You got any guns?"

"No, I ain't."

"You got any money?"

"No, I ain't."

"Then you won't mind if I look, will ya?"

Now Andrew was about to panic. The man holding the reins started toward him. Andrew pulled hard on the left rein, turning the mare's head in the direction of the man, keeping the horse's head between the two of them. The man became agitated and grabbed the reins on both sides of the horse's head. "Whoa," he said.

Andrew started to kick the mare to break loose from the man, when the second rider yelled, "Luke, hold on!"

The man held on to the reins, stared at Andrew, and then turned to look at the second rider.

The second rider walked his horse closer to Andrew and said, "What's your name, boy?"

"Andrew Chafin."

"Ain't you Anse Hatfield's nephew?"

"Yessir, I am. Vicy is my aunt."

The rider's demeanor changed immediately. "Let's go, Luke. Turn him loose!"

The man holding the reins did not let go. He turned and stared again at Andrew.

"Luke, goddammit, I said turn him loose. Let's go!'

The man let go of the reins, remounted his horse, glared at Andrew, and then followed the first rider back toward Cow Creek. Andrew drew a relieved breath that they did not go in his direction. He slapped the reins against the neck of the mare and started the last mile toward home. He knew for sure that he was not going to tell his mother about those two men. He wondered if he should even tell his uncle Anse. He finally decided he would not. Even Anse might become concerned about sending him out in the hills on errands if he felt that Andrew would encounter strangers like those two.

Andrew reached his home at dusk and went immediately to the corral to unsaddle the mare. He took the leather strap with him and walked in the front door to find his mother reading to Oliver. She looked up and said, "I was getting worried; it's nearly dark. Did you have any trouble?"

"No, ma'am. Mr. Garrett gave me some money to take to Nancy, and I want to take it over there before it gets dark."

"Go ahead, Andy, and then hurry home. It's almost suppertime."

"Yes, ma'am." And with that, Andrew was out the door and down the slope to Nancy's cabin, carrying the leather strap. As he reached the front step, Nancy appeared, carrying a small child. Andrew handed her the strap and said, "Mr. Garrett said to give you this."

"Thank you, Andrew, and thanks for taking the jug. It saved me a lot of trouble."

"Yes, ma'am. I didn't mind; it was a fun ride."

Andrew turned and headed across the bottoms toward home. And not a hundred yards from Nancy's door, he heard the familiar sound of a night owl. He stopped and listened. He heard it again, coming from a tree line to his right. He walked in that direction. It was nearly dark, which made Andrew a little nervous after his run-in with the two men earlier in the day, but he walked in the direction of the owl anyway. At the tree line he stopped and listened again. The sound was coming from over his right shoulder. He turned in that direction and walked into the trees. It was nearly pitch black. He waited. Directly in front of him he saw the bright light of a match. He went toward it. There, sitting on the ground, gun in hand, sat Cap.

"Andrew, anybody at my house?"

"I didn't go in, but Nancy didn't say anything about there being anybody there."

"Run back over there and be sure. If there ain't, tell Nancy I'm comin' in."

"Yessir."

Andrew backtracked and ran back to Nancy's. He was worried about getting home, afraid his mother would get nervous, but he wanted to help Cap and Nancy too. As he got near the house, dogs started barking, and Nancy walked out the front door. "What are you doin' back here, Andrew?"

"Ma'am, is there anyone else here?"

"What?"

"I just saw Cap; he wants to be sure there's nobody else here before he comes in."

"Tell him there's nobody here, Andrew."

"I'll tell him."

On the dead run again, Andrew went back into the tree line to where he had left Cap. "She said to come on in; there's nobody there."

"Andrew, I'll be up on the fence row tomorrow. Johnse is up there. Check with Nancy tomorrow after school to see if she wants you to bring us anything."

"Yessir."

It had been a long day for Andrew, from Oliver's first day of school to delivery to Mr. Garrett to the run-in with the two riders to the messages he delivered between to Nancy and Cap. All of a sudden he was tired and hungry. He left Cap and walked slowly back up the slope toward the inviting lights of home. He was glad that tomorrow was a school day. He looked forward to the slow walk to school, a normal day in class, and the slow walk home. *Normal,* he thought, *just normal.*

The School in the Bottoms was typical of most Mingo County schools in the late 1800s in that it was taught by a parent of one of the pupils. Formally educated teachers took jobs in the cities, Williamson, Logan, or Matewan. The smaller county schools took whomever they could find, formally educated or not. It had become a system of parents who went to school through the sixth grade teaching children who would also go through the sixth grade—sixth-graders teaching sixth-graders.

Andrew was normally through with his school assignments an hour into the school day. He spent the remainder of the day helping the teacher with the other students. She would take the fifth and sixth grades, and Andrew would work with the first, second, third, and fourth grades. There were exceptions. Andrew spent an inordinate amount of time with Oliver, making sure that he not only did his work, but also that he was happy. And of equal importance, he worked considerably with Rosy. It may not have been that she needed help any more than the others, but Andrew enjoyed sitting in her chair with her and teaching her the fundamentals of arithmetic using whole kernels of corn. It is doubtful that Rosy could have ever picked up the fundamentals of multiplication or division.

Andrew was indeed gifted in math. He even did math solutions for his father at the mill or on the farm. He was not blessed with size, but he was compensated by intelligence. He read easily as a first-grader, probably a result of watching Jane with her work, and did simple math by the second grade. By the third grade, he was doing multiplication and division. Because the studies came easily to him, his teacher spent very little time with him and went on to those who needed help the most. And by the fifth grade he was teaching more of the students than his teacher. Andrew felt that he was blessed to have been born in this time and place, but he probably could have done amazing things in his life if he had been born in another time and place. Sometimes life is cruel that way.

11

THE JAILBREAK

Anse Hatfield did not have to wait long for his revenge on John Rutherford. On Election Day in November 1896, Cap Hatfield was in Matewan, West Virginia, with Joe Glen, one of his wife Nancy's sons (by a previous marriage), to cast a vote for county commissioner. The reality was that Cap didn't care that much about the county commissioner's race, but he knew that Rutherford would be there. Election days were big events in the mountains of West Virginia at the turn of the century, especially in the valley, where it was as much a social gathering as an election. Cap would not normally miss an election anyway, even at the risk of running into a state or federal officer or one of the many bounty hunters still roaming the mountains. But this year he had the additional incentive of running into John Rutherford, and he came fully prepared with sidearms and a fully loaded shotgun.

Cap ran into Rutherford at the polling site, a dry-goods store, within minutes of arriving in Matewan. He approached him and started a conversation about Andrew. Cross words were exchanged, and Cap's words were few. "You're a dead man."

Reportedly, Rutherford said, "Go to hell!"

A confrontation was inevitable.

Later, as Cap and Joe Glenn were ready to leave Matewan, Cap told Joe to go on ahead, that he had unfinished business with John Rutherford. But instead of leaving, Joe retreated to a nearby tree to watch the encounter. Cap waited outside the dry-goods store, a double-barreled shotgun resting on his hip, waiting for Rutherford to come out. Rutherford did not disappoint. He came out of the door firing. Bullets flew in both directions, but Cap's aim was better, and the shotgun sent buckshot across an area that covered the entire doorway. Rutherford had no chance; he fell to the ground, dead. Rutherford's brother-in-law followed him out the door, and Cap's second shell found him as well. He fell to the ground, covered with blood. John Rutherford's brother, Elliott, was next out the door and set to fire on Cap, who now held an empty shotgun, but Joe shot and killed Elliott before he could fire on Cap.

Cap and Joe mounted their horses and rode northeast out of Matewan, without even bothering to check on the three bloody corpses that lay in front of the general store. Cap's passion for finding Rutherford and dealing with him had erased what little common sense he had. He had left himself exposed to capture, and the authorities would take advantage of it. Within hours, both Cap and Joe were found by Matewan police and arrested for murder.

After a speedy trial, both were convicted of involuntary manslaughter. There were sufficient witnesses to confirm that all parties were firing shots and that it was a matter of self-defense. Cap's manslaughter charge came, according to the jury, because he was the instigator of the gun battle, although he did not fire the first shot. He was sentenced to a year in the Mingo County jail. Joe, as a minor, was sentenced to a West Virginia reform school. Anse had other plans.

Anse and Vicy both attended the trial, which drew reporters from as far as St. Louis and New York City. Having a Hatfield in jail for murder was national news, and reporters did not want to miss the story. The reporters left town after the charges were announced, disappointed that they were not going to witness a hanging. Cap had been locked up in the Mingo County jail for days before Anse made up his mind what needed to be done. He waited for Andrew to get home from school, and as Andrew walked in the Hatfield front yard with Oliver and the Hatfield kids, Anse called him over to the front porch.

"Andrew, I have another errand for you."

"Yessir, what can I do?"

"Cap found John Rutherford in Matewan and shot him. He is in jail in Williamson, and I want you to go down there and get him out. If any of those bounty hunters get the chance, they'll take him to Kentucky, or kill him. I can't let that happen."

"When do you want me to go?"

"Go on up and talk to your pa. Tell him to come on down here; I need to talk to him. I'll explain to you both what I want you to do. I think Holbert will be all right with it after I explain it to him. Then we'll talk about when you need to go."

"Yessir, I'll go get him."

Andrew left Anse on his porch and ran home. Oliver tried to keep up, but Andrew was running too fast. Oliver wasn't in that big a hurry to get home anyway; there was nothing there but girls. Andrew found his dad chopping wood behind the cabin. "Pa, Uncle Anse needs to talk to you. Cap found John Rutherford in Matewan and killed him. They caught Cap, and he is in jail in Williamson. Uncle Anse wants me to go down there. He said he had a plan to get him out, but he didn't tell me what it was."

"What? He wants you to go get him out of jail?"

"That's what he said. He said he was sure you would be all right with it once he explained what he wants."

"When does he want to see me?"

"He said as soon as you could come."

Holbert put down his ax, picked up a saddle, and walked to his horse. He saddled the mare, got on, reached down, and pulled Andrew up behind him. They were at Anse's house in minutes.

Andrew stood by his dad, waiting for the results of the conversation. He hoped that his uncle would be able to talk his dad into letting him go. Anse began, "Holbert, I need Andrew to go to Williamson for me. Cap shot Rutherford a few days ago, and they got him in jail in Williamson, charged with manslaughter. I need Andrew to go over there and get a horse to him. I can get him out of jail without a problem."

"Anse, Andrew is too young for this. You need to send Troy or Elias or Joe."

"Holbert, when the trial was over, I talked to the jury foreman. That jury was going to acquit Cap; they agreed he was not guilty. Rutherford shot first. The problem was that Kentucky officials were outside the courtroom waiting on Cap. If the judge released him, the Kentucky folk would have arrested him on the spot. The jury convicted him of involuntary manslaughter to keep bounty hunters from getting to him."

"The sheriff won't give a damn if Cap is gone. He doesn't want him in that jail. I promise you that Andrew will be safe. I know the prosecuting attorney in Williamson very well, and all I want Andrew to do is to take a message to him and get a horse down there for Cap."

"What message?"

"Holbert, I can't tell you that. But I can tell you that Bank Hi Williamson is the prosecuting attorney in Mingo County. He is a good friend, and he will arrange to get Cap out of that jail. Andrew will not be in any danger."

"But why can't you send Joe or Troy or Elias?"

"Holbert, if either Troy or Elias goes into Williamson they may get arrested too; they're both hotheads on occasion, and they could start a ruckus at the drop of a hat. And they won't let Joe near that jail. They know he is a Hatfield, and we're not very well liked in Williamson. Andrew is just a young boy. They probably won't even notice him. And even if they do, they won't make any connection between Andrew and Cap Hatfield."

Holbert was worried about his son, but he knew that everything Anse said was true. He had but one other choice. "Anse, I'll go. I don't want to see Andrew off on a trip like that."

"Holbert, Williamson is on edge right now. If anybody notices a strange man riding into town and heading for the courthouse, they will be suspicious, and you know it. They won't even notice a ten-year-old boy."

Holbert was out of arguments. "Anse, if Lucindy finds out about this, I am in big trouble."

"We won't tell her. Just tell her that Andrew is staying here a few nights. She's used to that. We'll cover for him until he gets back. He won't be gone but a few nights."

"All right, Anse. I don't like this one bit, but I know Andrew will want to help, and I don't think we have any choice. Andy, do you want to go?"

"Yessir, I'll be careful."

"When do you want him to go, Anse?"

"He should leave before daylight tomorrow morning. That way he can get there in one night."

Holbert said good-bye to Anse and then walked over and knelt in front of Andrew. "Andy, this is a mighty big thing you are doing for the Hatfields, and I am proud of you for going, but you have to promise me to be very careful. Your ma would kill me if she knew I was letting you do this. She must never know!"

"I'll be very careful, Pa. And I won't say a word to Ma."

Holbert rubbed the top of Andrew's head, turned, and nodded good-bye to Anse as he mounted his horse. It would be a long few days, and he knew it.

Anse waited until Holbert was out of the gate. Then he started his instructions to Andrew. "Andrew, I want you to take the bay and an extra horse early in the morning. Leave one of them at Dr. Lawson's on Sycamore Creek, just this side of Williamson. Tell Dr. Lawson that I sent you. And then go on in to Williamson to Bank Hi Williamson's house off Third Avenue. Anybody can show you where he lives. I'll have a package for you to take to him. Give him the package and then do what he tells you to do. Can you do that?"

"Yessir, I understand. I can do that. I have been to Dr. Lawson's place with Pa, and I know where he lives."

"And be careful. If anything looks strange to you, come on back home."

Andrew nodded. He did not want his uncle to notice that he was getting nervous.

Andrew stayed in the Hatfield loft that night, but he couldn't sleep. He was anxious for morning and his new adventure. It didn't cross his mind to ask what was going to be in the package. He assumed that Anse did not want him to know, or he would have told him. He was going to follow orders and do what he was told. He knew that his uncle and Cap trusted him, and he was going to make sure they always did.

It was still in the early-morning hours and pitch black outside when Andrew felt a tug on his shoulder and looked up to see his uncle Anse standing over him. "Time to get up, Andrew. Vicy's got breakfast for you."

Andrew dressed and climbed down from the loft to find Vicy and Anse sitting at the table, plates of hot biscuits and country ham in front of them. Vicy got up, walked over to Andrew, and gave him a big hug. "Eat your breakfast, Andrew; you have a long day in front of you."

Before the sun cleared the horizon, Andrew was sitting on the bay, waiting on instructions from Anse. He had the bridle to the second horse in his hand and a rope around the horse's neck tied to his saddle horn. Both horses were saddled. Anse walked out with a box that was the size of a cigar box, dropped it into the saddlebag, and tied the leather straps over it. "Andrew, this is the package for Bank Hi. Give it to him as soon as you see him. You stay on Island Creek until you get to the valley. Go west on Pidgeon Creek and stay out of the trees as much as you can. You should make it to a little town called Varney by nightfall. Stay near Varney overnight. Try to find a place to keep the horses safe, and don't go into town.

"We packed enough food for you and the horses in those sacks. Stay in the valley through Varney until you get to Taylorville. On the other side of Taylorville, you'll find a clearing that will take you over to Lick Creek. That will take you into Williamson. Dr. Lawson lives just off Lick Creek on Sycamore. If you have any kind of trouble, you come on back home, you hear?"

"I'll be all right, Uncle Anse. I'll be careful."

Anse said nothing more as he picked up a rifle, walked over to the bay, and slid the rifle case under the stirrup and through the straps of the saddle. He looked up at Andrew with a look that said, "Be careful!" But he said nothing. Andrew slapped the reins against the bay's neck and started out the front gate without turning around. He did not want Anse to think he was worried—or even worse, that he was scared. He was both.

Andrew had been to Dr. Lawson's home with his dad before, delivering harnesses, but he had never been into Williamson. He was sure he would be able to find Bank Hi Williamson's home. His first worry was keeping up with the spare horse. He worried that something would spook the horse and he would lose him. And he had a long time to worry. It was going to be a long and arduous trip.

The valley south of Island Creek on the way to Varney was a major east-west passage through the mountains. The trail was wide enough for two wagons to get around each other if they were going in opposite directions. A man on horseback could easily pass a wagon without encountering water or undergrowth. Years of east-west wagon traffic had made deep ruts in the clearing that traversed the valley and kept the path free of underbrush and trees. Andrew's anxiety was that the wagon traffic would make it difficult to keep holding on to the horse that followed him.

It was noon when Andrew made it over the pass south of Island Creek and into the valley that surrounded Pidgeon Creek. He had to walk most of the way over the pass, trying to keep both horses together. The spare horse was easily spooked and jumped at every sound. Andrew was exhausted, pulling on two horses, which went in two different directions at times. The valley was a welcome sight.

He remounted the bay, slipped the rope knot back over the saddle horn, and started the long trek through the valley toward Varney. After an hour ride to the west, he encountered his first obstacle. Directly in front of him, going in the same direction, was a flat-bed wagon filled four to six feet high with cut and trimmed black pine trees. The trees were twice the length of the wagon and were hanging out over the back and scraping against the ground as the wagon slowly made its way west. The noise and the motion spooked both horses. Andrew could not get close enough to get around the wagon; neither horse would budge. The spare horse pulled against the rope and the reins Andrew held, and the bay kept turning his head to the side, trying to turn back east. Andrew was stuck.

Andrew followed the wagon from a distance for more than an hour, fighting the spare horse the entire time. His arm was numb from pulling on the reins to keep the horse in tow. The wagon finally stopped. The noise stopped. And Andrew had this one chance to pass. It was nearing two o'clock, and he would not make Varney by nightfall if he didn't get around that wagon.

He urged the bay forward. The bay was not anxious. Andrew slapped the reins against its neck and jammed his heels into its underbelly. He jumped and moved forward. The spare horse followed, reluctantly. The bay was directly alongside the wagon when the wagon started to move again, and he jumped. Andrew nearly fell, and he dropped the reins of the other horse so he could grab to the saddle horn. The other horse jumped, pulled against the rope, and trapped Andrew's hand against the horn. Andrew gasped, yanked, and pulled his hand away from the saddle horn, taking the rope with it. The second horse was free.

The wagon moved forward, not realizing that Andrew was even there. The bay turned away from the wagon and started for the trees. The other horse turned and started back east. Andrew had lost control of the bay and could not stop it from going into the trees, thick with underbrush. Andrew's right hand was beginning to swell and was useless in pulling the reins. He pulled as hard as he could, but the bay ignored him. It didn't stop until it had gone into the trees, where the underbrush stopped him. Andrew leaped off, went to the front of the bay, and started stroking across his nose with the calmest voice he could muster. The bay's eyes were bulging; his fear was obvious. Andrew continued to calm him. He looked over his shoulder for the other horse. It was nowhere in sight.

Five minutes of Andrew's soft voice settled the bay and calmed him down. Andrew took the bridle, turned the bay, and led him out into the clearing. He looked to the west; the wagon was out of sight. He looked to the east; the second horse was out of sight. Andrew found a stump, remounted the bay, and started back to the east. He rode twenty minutes before he saw the other horse, grazing near the tree line. The gunnysacks were still firmly attached to the saddle.

Andrew dismounted and calmly walked the bay toward the spare horse. The horse turned, looked at Andrew, and started slowly moving away. Andrew slowly followed saying, "Whoa," in almost a whisper. The horse continued to move away.

"Whoa."

Andrew stopped. The horse stopped. Andrew stood in front of the bay and turned his back to the other horse. He watched the bay start grazing and ignored the loose horse. Within minutes the loose horse started grazing again. Andrew glanced over his shoulder to check, and the horse seemed calm. Andrew walked slowly toward him, leading the bay as he went. The loose horse looked up but didn't move. Andrew walked to him and started rubbing his nose. He was calm now.

Andrew took the reins; slipped the rope back over his saddle horn, and walked both horses to a tree stump. He remounted the bay and turned again to the west. It was three o'clock. He had two hours of daylight left; it was too late in the day to make it to Varney.

Andrew continued west through the valley, checking the horizon as best he could for any trace of the log wagon. He did not want to run into that wagon again. He felt that he was at least two hours behind the wagon and back far enough not to catch it before he had to stop for the night. It worried Andrew that he would have to spend the night isolated on the valley trail with two horses. He was glad that his uncle had included the rifle. He would continue west as long as he could and then pull the horses into the trees and build a brush corral to surround them.

By five o'clock, the light on the horizon was gone. Andrew had another hour of daylight, and he was at least two hours from Varney. He found a small stream and decided to make camp nearby. He pulled the horses into the trees and untied the gunnysacks, using his good hand as much as possible and holding his swollen hand to his side. He left the saddles on. He led the horses to the stream and held the reins until they had their fill of fresh water. He walked them back to a small clearing that was in sight of the rutted wagon trail and tied their reins to a low tree branch. He then wrapped rope around their front legs so that they could not move.

He then proceeded to build a corral around them, starting with broken branches and shrubbery. An hour later the corral was finished, the horses were secure, and it was almost pitch black. It was dinnertime. Uncle Anse had included two feed bags and enough oats for a two-day trip. Andrew would refill them for the trip back.

After the horses were taken care of, Andrew took the rifle from the saddle, found a level spot under a tree, and settled in. He placed the rifle across his lap and opened the bag of food Vicy had packed. By then the only light he saw were the thousands of lightning bugs that flew around in circles over his head. Strangely, the darkness made him feel more secure. If he could not see anything, then nothing could see him either. He finished his meal, leaned back against the tree, and fell fast asleep. He was exhausted, and his hand was swollen and throbbing.

Andrew woke often during the night, sometimes just to look around and other times to get up and check on the horses. He was anxious for daylight; he wanted to be on his way. He had no idea of the time, but as soon as he could see the outline of the wagon trail, he set about repacking the horses and securing the gunnysacks. He was well on his way west when the first shadows of the morning sun reached across his shoulders. He ate the ham-and-biscuit breakfast on the mare's back, without the jelly.

Varney was in his sight by midmorning. It was not really a town. It was a clearing in the trail with a dozen or more rugged clapboard cabins surrounding a small creek. It was nothing more than a logging camp with slightly more permanent housing than tents. Andrew had intended to stop there and rest the horses, but he was so far behind in his schedule that he continued west without stopping. He was hoping to get to Williamson without spending another night on the trail. By midafternoon he had reached Taylorsville, another logging camp about the same size as Varney. He passed a small general store and decided to stop for directions. He wasn't sure how to get from Taylorsville to Williamson, and he didn't have time to get lost.

The general store also served as a post office, a livery stable, and church on Sundays. It was a single room large enough for a single potbelly stove, a few chairs, and rows of shelves, floor to ceiling, lining the walls. A lone man sat at the stove, smoking a pipe and watching Andrew. He said nothing as Andrew walked in the door. Andrew looked around for someone who looked like the storekeeper, but the man at the stove was the only one in the room. Andrew decided to try him. "I was wondering if you could help me with directions."

"Sure, where you goin', young man?"

"Williamson."

"Williamson? Boy, are you lost? Where's your ma and pa?"

All of a sudden Andrew felt uncomfortable. He didn't know why, but something told him that he had better tell a little white lie. The man was probably harmless, but he had a strange look on his face. "They're camped just west of here. They sent me back to make sure we were going in the right direction."

"Ain't much west of here, boy. The valley goes north out of here. Are you sure they ain't north of here?"

"I'm not so good with directions; they are just outside Taylorsville. We came through late last night."

"Yep, you'd be goin' north. Stay on that trail until you see a small sign on the side of the trail that says Lick Creek. Go south right there, and it takes you right in to Williamson. It's a couple of hours from here."

"Thank you, sir, I'll tell them."

"Can I fetch ya a bite to eat while you're here? Won't take a minute."

"Thank you, sir, but I'm already late. I told my pa I wouldn't be gone that long. They'll be lookin' for me."

"Not a bother, son. Stop in on your way back."

Andrew left the store, remounted the bay, and followed the valley to the north. He couldn't figure out why he was so nervous, but he would be glad to get back on the trail again. He looked up for the sun; it was near the horizon—nearly three o'clock. If he stepped up the pace, he would be in Williamson before it was too dark. He slapped the reins against the bay's neck and nudged his underbelly. The bay went into a quickened trot. The spare horse pulled against the reins and then joined in the quickened pace. Even the horses didn't want to spend another night on the trail.

Andrew found Lick Creek without trouble and reached the outskirts of Williamson at dusk. He knew that it was too late to get to Bank Hi Williamson's house, but if he could find Dr. Lawson's place before dark, he and his horses would be safer there than on Lick Creek. He pressed on.

Dr. Lawson saw Andrew coming before he reached the house. He walked off his porch and met Andrew at the front gate. "Good evenin', young man. You're out fairly late, aren't you? What can I do for you?"

"Good evenin', sir. Do you remember me? I was here with my pa in the spring, bringing your harnesses back."

"Holbert's boy. Sure I remember. What can I do for you?"

"Uncle Anse wants me to go into Williamson for him in the morning, and he wants to know if I can leave this horse here with you till I get back."

"Sure you can. I'll keep him in the barn. When will you be back?"

"I'm not sure. It may be sometime late in the morning or early tomorrow afternoon."

"Well, where are you gonna spend the night?"

"I was hoping I could sleep in your barn, just to make sure the horses are safe."

"Wouldn't hear of it, young man. You come on in the house, and I'll get you something to eat, and you can stay with us tonight. We'd love to have you."

"That's mighty nice of you, sir, but Vicy packed me a fine dinner, and I am too messy from the trail ride to sleep inside. I will be fine in the barn, if you don't mind."

"Suit yourself. Let me know if you need anything. It's good to see you again. Just leave your horse in the barn in the morning, and I'll see you when you get back."

"Thank you, sir. I'll see you sometime tomorrow."

Andrew left Dr. Lawson and walked his horses to the barn. He led them to the trough for water, and found two empty stalls inside the barn. He strapped on their feedbags and found a soft corner to settle into. It had been a long two days, and he was exhausted. He could not wait for the horses to finish their oats so he could unstrap the feedbags and finally sleep. His hand was still throbbing.

Andrew left Dr. Lawson's barn early the next morning and continued his trip into Williamson. The barn was a mile east of Williamson, and that mile was packed with people, buggies, and horses. Andrew had never seen so many people in one place before. The muddy, rutted roadway had been packed with gravel and small stones, which had been mashed farther into the mud by a constant stream of wagons. It made the roadway a lot more difficult for horses. Andrew kept the bay to the side of the roadway as much as he could, where the surface was firmer. The bay was struggling to keep his footing.

Andrew was not so worried about Cap at the moment; he was worried about finding Williamson's house. Andrew took the muddy street into Williamson, following the Tug River on his left until he came to a large general store in the center of town, a block from the river. Andrew pulled his horse to the front of the store, where two men stood talking. Andrew approached the two men without getting off his horse. "Sir, can you tell me where Bank Hi Williamson lives?"

The men looked at each other in disbelief that someone could ask such a stupid question, but one of them answered anyway, out of pity for the poor, stupid stranger. "Sure, young man. Go straight ahead on Third Street. Turn right and go two blocks. Bank's house is on the corner on the right. It has big white columns on the front; you can't miss it."

"Thank you, sir."

Andrew slapped the reins across his horse's neck and rode on. He did not want to engage the two in conversation.

He was amazed at what he saw in Williamson. The streets were wider than any streets he had ever seen. There were people everywhere, and they all seemed to be going in opposite directions. Stores lined the streets, one right after the other, and each had a hitching post in front. There were wooden walkways on either side of the mud-covered roadway, and they were full of people. There were even lights that could be turned on at night.

And then Andrew saw a more amazing sight: a vehicle going down the middle of the road without anything pulling it. The vehicle was making a loud noise, and smoke was coming out of the back. He could do nothing but stare. The bay jerked against the reins and backed away from the noisy contraption. *What is that?* Andrew had just seen his first automobile.

Bank Hi's house was an imposing sight compared to all the other structures around it. *No wonder those men looked at me weird*, he thought. Andrew tied his horse to the post at the street, grabbed the package, and walked up the steps. In the center of the front door was a circular medallion with a ratchet device in its center. There were two glass panels in the upper half of the door, allowing a visitor to see the parlor inside. It did not take a genius to figure out that the medallion was some sort of bell, so he turned it. A ringing sound came through the door from the inside.

Through the glass panel, Andrew could see a small woman with a rag on her head, wearing a white apron, coming toward the door. She walked to the door, turned the latch, and opened the door while backing up a step. Andrew wondered if she was frightened of him. She shouldn't have been; even at her small size, she was bigger than he was.

"Yes, can I help you?"

"Yes, ma'am, I'd like to see Bank Hi Williamson, please. I have something for him from my uncle."

"Who is your uncle?"

"Anderson Hatfield."

The woman's expression changed, and she closed the door. Andrew didn't know if she had gone to get Mr. Williamson or if she had decided she didn't want Mr. Williamson to receive anything from his uncle. But he had no choice but to wait. Minutes passed, and there was no sign of activity inside the front door. After nearly ten minutes, Andrew decided he had better ring again. As he was reaching for the ratchet device, a tall, heavyset man approached the door. Andrew watched as the man reached for the doorknob, turned it, and opened the door. "Good morning, young man. I understand you have something for me from Mr. Hatfield?"

"Yessir, this package."

"Anderson Hatfield is your uncle?"

"Yessir."

"What is your name, young man?"

"Andy Chafin."

"Are you related to Vicy?"

"Yessir, she's my aunt."

"I see. Well, you have a seat right there. I'll be back in a minute."

Andrew watched as Mr. Williamson took the package down the hall and into his office. Andrew looked around at furniture and lights that he had never seen the likes of before. He didn't know what a person would do with most of the things he saw. There were even blanket-like things on the floor and brass lanterns, like the one Nancy put fuel in, hanging on the walls. *They must use a lot of fuel,* he thought. *Bank Hi Williamson would be a real good customer for Nancy.*

Within minutes, Mr. Williamson was back.

"Andrew, come with me."

Andrew followed Mr. Williamson out the front door of his home, across the street, and into a small two-story building. "First National Bank" was etched in the glass above the door. They walked through the building and into a small room in the back. Andrew was amazed. This building was even stranger than the house. He could not take his eyes off the bars on the small windows that people were lined up in front of. He thought, *There must be a lot of important people in here that need a lot of protection.* Mr. Williamson said, "You wait right here, young man. I'll be right back. Have a seat."

Andrew waited for what seemed like fifteen or twenty minutes until Mr. Williamson came back in. "Andrew, do you have any guns on you?"

"Yessir, I got two."

"Two? Where are they?"

"In my britches."

"In your britches?"

"Yessir, inside my britches."

Mr. Williamson chuckled and said, "All right, give 'em to Cap when you get to Dr. Lawson's. Do you have a horse?"

"Yessir, I got two. I left one at Dr. Lawson's like my uncle told me to, and I tied one up out front."

"All right, take your horse back down near the courthouse. The jail is in the basement of the courthouse. Do you know where the courthouse is?"

"No, sir."

"Do you know where the general store is?"

"Yessir, I passed it on the way here."

"Take your horse back to the store, and tie it up there, and then walk over to the courthouse. It's a block away. You'll find a black bench just outside the courthouse, near the back. You go sit on that bench. Don't talk to anyone and don't move. You just sit there. Understand?"

"Yessir."

"You'll see Cap come out in a few minutes. Don't talk to him. Don't even look at him. Just follow him. Am I clear?"

"I think so. Will anybody be with him?"

"There shouldn't be. I just don't want there to be any unnecessary attention. Take him back to your horse and then go back to Dr. Lawson's. He'll have food for you when you get there."

"Yessir, I understand."

"All right, be on your way. Be careful going home, and tell your uncle hello for me."

Mr. Williamson walked to the front door, opened it for Andrew, and then closed it behind him. Andrew went to his horse, untied it, walked it to the lowest step of Mr. Williamson's porch, stood on the step, and slung his leg over the horse's back.

Andrew went straight to the general store and tied his horse to one of the numerous hitching posts that lined the street in front of the store. He looked across the street for the courthouse. There was no courthouse in sight. He walked a block to his right and looked down the street. There on his left was a large building with white columns and a heavy front door. On the glass above the door it read, "Mingo County Courthouse."

Andrew started toward the building, but he did not see a bench. He stood in front of the courthouse for a minute then turned and walked around the corner. There, almost in the back, sat two black, wooden benches. He walked immediately to one of them and sat down.

Andrew sat and scooted back on the bench to make himself more comfortable; his feet dangled in midair; they did not touch the ground. He had no idea how long he would be there. Several men walked by, but they didn't even look in his direction. Several women walked by, wearing big, wide-brimmed bonnets, and looked at him quizzically, wondering, no doubt, where his mother was. Andrew sat and waited. Twenty minutes passed. He waited.

Andrew heard a door slam. He looked up to see Cap walking slowly around the back corner of the courthouse. Cap walked right by Andrew without even looking in his direction. When Cap got to the street in front of the courthouse, he turned right and headed in the direction of the general store. When he was out of sight of the courthouse, he stopped. Andrew got up and followed. As Andrew approached, Cap turned and said, "Where are the horses?"

"I left one with Dr. Lawson and one is at the general store."

"Did you bring my guns?"

"Yessir, I got 'em in my britches."

"All right, let's go."

As they neared the horse, they heard a loud pounding noise coming from the courthouse a block away. They both turned and looked back toward the courthouse. There, just a foot above the wooden sidewalk, a hole appeared in the side of the courthouse at the jailhouse level. Andrew was stunned. Cap just laughed. Cap got on the horse, reached down, grabbed Andrew by the arm, and swung him up on the horse behind him. Cap took the horse to a full gallop, and they headed east toward Dr. Lawson's barn.

Dr. Lawson had food for Cap, Andrew, and the horses and gave both Cap and Andrew food for their trip home. As they walked out the front door with Dr. Lawson, Cap said, "Thank you, sir."

"Glad to do it," replied Dr. Lawson.

"Thank you, Dr. Lawson. And thanks for the use of your barn," said Andrew.

"You are welcome, young man. Say hi to your pa and uncle for me."

"I will, sir. Thank you."

Cap led Andrew on the bay out of Dr. Lawson's gate and turned his horse to the north. Just north of Williamson, Cap pulled his horse to a stop and waited for Andrew to catch up. "Andrew, we can't go near the house for a while—too dangerous. Let's head to Cow Creek and stay there for a few days with Uncle Melvin."

Andrew had little incentive to argue. He was following Anse's orders to get Cap out of jail and Cap's orders as to what to do next. Cow Creek seemed like a reasonable suggestion, since he would be less than a mile from his Cow Creek home. They started their long trek through Delbarton and then east through the fog-covered hills and pine-covered mountains on Rock Horse Creek toward Cow Creek.

At the top of a mountain pass, Cap stopped Andrew again. "Get down off your horse, Andrew. That pass up ahead is tricky. If someone was waitin' to ambush us, that would be the place. Walk your horse and stay behind me; if anybody starts shootin', you head back toward Williamson. Don't go through that pass until I am through it. Understand?"

"Yessir."

Cap pulled the rifle out of Andrew's saddle case, cocked it, and held the barrel straight up in the air. He walked toward the pass, carrying the rifle in one hand and holding on to the horse's reins with the other. Andrew stood and watched; he did not follow.

Cap walked beside his horse and pointed the rifle in the direction of the tree line to his right. There was not a sound except for chirping birds. Cap had gone almost a hundred yards before he turned, looked back at Andrew, and motioned for him to go on through the pass. Andrew walked his horse slowly through the pass, watching the tree line on both sides for any movement. Cap stood ahead of him, the rifle still aimed at the tree line that Andrew was passing. There was no movement. Cap helped Andrew back up on his horse, remounted, and the two started back down the eastern slope of the mountain,

They rode all night, and at daybreak the next morning they arrived on Cow Creek. They put the horses in Melvin's barn, found a quiet corner in the hayloft, and went to sleep. They slept all the next day. Early the next morning, Andrew told Cap that his parents would be getting worried and that he was going home. Cap agreed. He told Andrew that he was going to stay put for a while and that he would signal him when he needed anything. Cap saddled the bay, helped Andrew mount, and watched as Andrew rode off, headed for Anse's home on Island Creek.

It was early evening before Andrew arrived at Anse's. He found Anse in the barn, brushing Fred. From the looks of Fred, Anse had been on a long and hard ride. Fred was wet and steaming. Andrew didn't ask. "Evenin', Andrew, everything go all right?"

"Just like you said, Uncle Anse; they let Cap right outta jail."

"Where is he now?"

"He's on Cow Creek, at Melvin's place. He said he was going to stay there a few days until things cool down."

"That's probably best. Do you want to stay here tonight, or are you goin' on home?"

"I think I'll stay here tonight. I'm tired."

"Suit yourself. Joe and Rosy are inside. Andrew, thanks for goin' to Williamson for me. I'll be forever grateful, and I know your aunt and Nancy and Cap will be too."

Andrew just grinned.

He was glad for the invitation to spend the night; he did not feel up to another ride, and he did not want to answer any of his mother's questions that night. He preferred to settle in with the Hatfields and face his mother in the morning.

Andrew was up at daybreak and on his way home as the sky turned orange in the east. He didn't wait for breakfast; he wanted to see his parents and finally face his mother with her questions. And he couldn't wait to get his dad alone to tell him all that had happened in Williamson.

Lucinda was rolling out biscuits on the table, and when Andrew walked in the front door, she was covered with flour. She turned, gave Andrew a suspicious look, and said, "Well, good mornin', Andy. You're up early this mornin'."

"Yes, ma'am, I wanted to get home."

"Then why didn't you come home last night?"

"I got to Uncle Anse's house late, and I was tired. I just wanted to go to bed."

"Oh? And where had you been?"

"I took some things to Dr. Lawson for Uncle Anse, and it took a while to get back."

"You gonna tell me what you took to Dr. Lawson?"

"A bunch of stuff in a gunnysack."

Just as Lucinda started to dig for more information and as Andrew seemed to be getting more nervous, Holbert walked in. "Good mornin', Andrew. Did everything go all right?"

"Yessir, I got back to Uncle Anse's late last night."

"Well, good. Hurry up and eat a bite. I got some things I need some help with this mornin'." Lucinda realized that she had been cut out of the conversation, and she decided that maybe it involved things she didn't really want to know about anyway. She said, "I don't suppose y'all are gonna tell me what is goin' on?"

"Ain't nothin' goin' on, Lucindy. It's just man-talk."

"All right. Andy, I'll fix your breakfast and you can go help your pa. I'm glad you're home."

"Me too, Ma. Where's Oliver?"

"Still asleep. You leave him be and go wash up."

Andrew finished his breakfast as quickly as he could, hoping his mother wouldn't bring up the Dr. Lawson trip again before he could get out the door. "Thanks, Ma. I'm goin' outside." And with that, he was on his way out the door to find his dad.

Holbert was in the back with a harness across his lap, repairing a piece of leather, when Andrew came around the corner of the cabin and walked up behind him. Holbert looked behind Andrew to make sure Lucinda was nowhere in sight. "How'd it go in Williamson, Andy?"

"It went just like Uncle Anse said it would, Pa. They let Cap right out of jail. He just walked out the back door. But then they did a really weird thing. They knocked a big hole in the jail wall after Cap was already out."

"I guess they had to make it look like he escaped. Did you give the package to Mr. Williamson?"

"Yessir, I did. Then he took me over to a bank. I waited for a while, and he came back and told me to go sit on a bench at the courthouse and wait for Cap. Cap just walked out the back door, and we got on the horse and went back to Dr. Lawson's house."

"Where is Cap now?"

"He's up on Cow Creek at Uncle Melvin's place. He said he was gonna stay there a few days."

"Probably just as well. Glad to have you home, Andy. And I'm glad you didn't have any trouble. You wanna help with this harness?"

Andrew grinned. He could tell that his dad was proud of him and that he was glad to have him back home. He sat beside him and picked up one side of the harness. He was proud of himself. But more importantly, he had accomplished the mission that his uncle sent him, on and he was confident that his uncle would send him on others.

12

BOUNTY HUNTER

And when the railroad came through the valley, it brought everything from legitimate lawmen to desperate criminals with it. And every one of 'em was after the Hatfield boys. That railroad may have brought prosperity to the valley, but it brought a lot of crime with it too.

Andrew, Oliver, and the Hatfield kids walked into the one-room schoolhouse on Monday after his trip to Williamson, looking forward to another day in class. Their teacher was noticeably cooler to Andrew. She didn't give him her normal smile and a pat on the head. Oliver took his seat on the front row, and Andrew walked back to his back-row desk. The teacher followed him. "Andrew, you've been missing a lot of school lately. Do your parents know that?"

"Yes, ma'am, I've been on an errand for my uncle."

"Well, you are a bright young man, Andrew, and I don't want you to get sidetracked on other things. If you continue to miss like you have in the last few weeks, I will have to talk to your parents about it."

"Yes, ma'am."

Andrew was bothered that his teacher was fussing at him, and he felt defenseless. Rosy was watching closely. She didn't understand what was going on, but she was worried. Andrew never knew when Anse would want him to run another errand, and he sure didn't want his teacher to talk to his parents. He was afraid they would change their minds about letting him help the Hatfield family if they realized how much school he was missing. And besides, he liked school, although he was beginning to get discouraged about it as well. He was not getting any new instruction; it was as if his teacher had taught him all that she could.

Andrew's school assignments were almost always another book to read or a few pages of math problems his teacher handed him to solve. He would normally finish his first assignment within an hour and go back to her desk, asking for more work. He was getting frustrated about not learning more. And now that his teacher was unhappy with him, it might get worse.

Andrew decided to talk to his teacher and ask her to give him more work. He wanted to show her that he was really interested in school. Maybe then she would be more understanding if he had to run another overnight errand.

After school, Andrew, Oliver, and the Hatfield kids made their way along the familiar dirt road home. Andrew had talked to his teacher after school and felt that she would be more understanding of his absences and also give him more work to do when he was there. Rosy stopped Andrew on the way home and asked him what the teacher said to him, but Andrew just passed it off, saying, "Nothin', she was just talkin' about me missing school. She's all right about it now." Rosy looked at Andrew with an expression that let him know that she was not convinced by his answer. He hoped she would not say anything to his uncle.

On the way home, the kids were laughing, pushing each other, throwing rocks, and acting like all children do after a day in class, when Andrew heard a squirrel bark. He stopped and listened. He heard it again. "Oliver," he said, "go on home. And tell Ma I heard a squirrel, and I'm goin' to go find it."

Oliver was surprised. "You're going to go get a squirrel? You ain't got a gun!"

"I know that. Just tell Ma what I told you. I'll be home in a little while."

Oliver caught up with the Hatfield kids and walked on along the road. Andrew turned and ran toward the tree line. Just inside the trees, he stopped and listened. He heard the bark again over his left shoulder. He walked in that direction. There, sitting under a black pine tree, sat Cap, his rifle across his lap. Andrew was surprised to see him so soon; he thought he was going to stay longer on Cow Creek.

"You came back early," Andrew said.

"I gotta get home. Shepard is having some trouble. Go by my house and tell Nancy I'll be in after dark. And if you got time, rustle up some grub for me. I've had little to eat in a couple of days now."

"Yessir, I'll be right back with something."

"And if she's got any fuel, bring that too."

"Yessir."

Andrew turned and headed out of the woods on a dead run. He went straight home to let his mother know of his new errand, ran to saddle the mare, and left immediately for Nancy's house. Nancy saw him coming down the hill and walked out on the front porch to greet him. Her daughters followed. Andrew had spent so much time at Nancy's house over the years that her children were no longer bashful and quiet around him, and they enjoyed his company. Nancy's oldest girl, five-year-old Emma, was almost flirty, and she was even more so today. She ran off the porch and met Andrew as he was getting off the mare. She wrapped her arms around him and gave him a big hug. Andrew blushed.

Andrew told Nancy what Cap had instructed. He told her that if she didn't have any food she could give Cap, he would go back home and get something from his mother. Nancy said, "Let me see what I have. I'll be right back."

"And don't forget the fuel," Andrew reminded her.

"Oh, I wouldn't do that," Nancy said with a grin.

Andrew sat on the step to wait. Emma came over and sat beside him. "I start school next year," she said.

"I know," said Andrew. "You'll like it a lot."

"Will you help me learn to read?"

"Sure I will. When do you want to start?"

"I want to know how to read before I start to school. Can you teach me after school some days?"

"Sure I can. I'll talk to your ma and see if it's all right to come over in the afternoons."

Emma grinned and wrapped her arm around Andrew's arm and snuggled closer. Andrew blushed again.

Nancy came back out with a small sack and the lantern. Andrew put the lantern in the sack and tied the sack to the saddle horn. He walked the mare to the step and threw his leg up over the saddle. At eleven, Andrew was finally almost able to mount a horse without a step of some sort.

Andrew started back down the dusty road toward the clump of trees where Cap waited, nearly a mile away. One hundred yards from the tree line, he left the dirt road and started up the incline. Suddenly, a tall, skinny man stepped out from behind a paw-paw bush, directly in front of him, holding a rifle in his right hand. He wore a wide-brimmed hat and a leather vest. His trousers were tucked into tall boots that were scuffed and dirty. The gunman reached over as Andrew was about to pass and grabbed the horse's bridle. The mare was startled and backed away, but the man held tightly. Andrew tried to pull the horse's head away, but the man's grip was too strong. "Get off the horse," the gunman said.

Andrew did not answer. He continued pulling on the reins, trying to break the man's grip. "I said get off the goddamn horse!" the man screamed. Andrew turned the mare's head in the direction of the gunman, keeping the horse between them. The gunman dropped the rifle to the ground, reached up, grabbed Andrew by the arm, and slung him to the ground. Andrew fell on his back with a thud, still holding tightly to one of the reins.

The fall knocked the wind out of him, and he could not catch his breath. He was gasping for air. He wrapped the rein around his wrist and held on for dear life. The gunman walked over and shoved his boot heel into Andrew's chest, flattening him to the ground. He yanked at the reins, trying to rip them out of Andrew's hands, nearly lifting him off the ground. Andrew held on. "I need the goddamn horse," the gunman said. "Turn loose, or I'll put a goddamn bullet in ya!"

Andrew said nothing; he just held on. The gunman lifted his boot off Andrew's chest, raising it for a savage blow to his body. The boot never came down. Andrew heard the explosion of a rifle behind him. The gunman was lifted off the ground and slammed into the mare, blood streaming from his forehead. He fell to the ground with a thud and did not move.

Andrew looked over his shoulder to see Cap walking out of the trees. The rifle in his hand was still smoking. Cap cocked the lever-action Winchester and walked over to the gunman. He put the barrel of the rifle to the man's chest, directly over his heart, and pulled the trigger. A gush of blood shot straight up and settled on the man's shirt, turning it a deep purple.

"Are you all right, Andrew?"

"I guess so. I don't know what I would've done if you hadn't been there!"

"I was watching him. He was walking down the road toward my house when he saw you coming, and he ducked behind that bush. As soon as I saw him hide, I took off. I was just glad I could get here in time."

"Do you know who he was?"

"One of those goddamn Phelps Agency boys, I guess, or a Pinkerton. The woods are full of 'em. You go on down to Pa's house and get me a shovel while I drag this bastard into the woods. If Troy and Elias are there, bring 'em back with you. Did you bring any food?"

Andrew untied the gunnysack and handed it to Cap. Cap took the lantern out, unscrewed the fuel bowl, and took a long drink. He wiped his mouth with his sleeve and said, "Get goin', Andrew. I wanna get this bastard in the ground before dark."

Cap walked over to the mare, cupped his hands near the stirrup, and waited for Andrew's foot. Andrew lifted his foot, stepped into Cap's hands, and Cap flipped him up on the horse. Andrew was off toward Anse's house without a word. But he was trembling inside and nauseated.

Andrew walked the mare through the front gate at Anse's house and found Anse sitting on the front step, cleaning his rifle. Andrew proceeded to tell Anse the whole story of the gunman, the attempted horse theft, and Cap's rescue. Anse's reaction was one of disgust and anger, but not surprise. He got up from the step and told Andrew to follow. They walked around the house and into the barn, where Troy and Elias were cleaning stalls. "Troy, you and Elias go with Andrew, and take some shovels."

Troy and Elias dropped their pitchforks, walked over to the two shovels leaning against the side of the barn, and walked out the barn door to their horses. They said not a word. They seemed to be as unsurprised as Anse; it was just another everyday occurrence. Anse took Andrew by the shoulder and walked out of the barn toward the house. "Andrew, we're going to have to talk your ma about lettin' you carry a gun. These hills just ain't safe for nobody anymore."

"I don't think my ma would ever do that, Uncle Anse. She's scared of guns. She makes Pa keep his put away when he is at home; she doesn't even want to see it."

"I may have to talk to her then."

Anse walked Andrew to his horse, cupped his hands as Cap had done, and hoisted Andrew up on the mare. As Andrew was about to walk the horse out the gate, Anse said, "Andrew, Rosy tells me your teacher seemed to be fussing at you in school today. What was that all about?"

"Nothin' much really. She said she thought I was missing a lot of school, and she said if I missed much more she was going to have a talk to Ma and Pa."

"She did, did she? Well, we sure don't want to get your ma involved in all of this. We'll talk again in the mornin'. You just stop by here on your way to school tomorrow."

"Yessir, I will. Oliver and I usually go in with Rosy and the boys anyway. I'll see you in the morning."

Andrew walked the mare out of the gate with Troy and Elias following. They headed down the dusty road where Cap was waiting for the shovels and digging help. During the ride, Andrew thought about all the killing he had seen in the five years that he had lived on Island Creek, and he wondered how many more he would see before it was all over. He worried that he was becoming as accustomed to the killings as the Hatfields seemed to be. He thought about Anse's suggestion that he needed to carry a gun, but he knew that might never happen.

Cap was waiting just inside the trees when Troy, Elias, and Andrew arrived. There was no greeting. Troy and Elias dismounted and slung the shovels over their shoulders. Cap got up from his spot under the black pine tree, turned, and walked into the trees. Troy and Elias followed. Andrew got off the mare and started into the trees behind them, but Elias stopped him. "Andrew, you go on home now. We'll help Cap. Go tell Nancy what happened. We'll take care of things here."

Andrew didn't argue. He wasn't anxious to watch a burial. He walked the mare to a fallen tree and remounted. Then he started down the incline onto the road toward Nancy's house. He knew that he had to tell Nancy about the gunman, because Elias told him to, but he worried that word would get back to his parents, and he sure didn't want that to happen.

Nancy met him at the front door, with Louise, Emma, and Coleman crowding in the doorway beside her. "What are you back here for, Andrew? Did Cap give you another errand?"

"No, ma'am, I just wanted to let you know that a man tried to take my horse, but Cap stopped him. Cap will tell y'all about it when he gets home. Troy and Elias were with Cap when I left, and Elias said to stop by and let you know what was going on."

"Is Cap still coming home tonight?"

"Yes, ma'am. And, ma'am, it sure would be nice if my ma doesn't hear about this. She might make me stay at home more."

"I understand, Andrew. We won't say a word. You go on home now, and say hi to your ma and pa for me."

"Yes, ma'am, I will."

"And, Andrew, Emma said you would help her learn to read. You can come over and give her reading lessons any time you want to. It would be a big help to her, and we'd love to see you more often."

"Yes, ma'am. Thank you." Andrew looked down at Emma, who was grinning from ear to ear, standing by her mother and chewing on her finger. He said, "I'll see you tomorrow, Emma, and we will start your lessons." Emma grinned even wider, turned, and ran into the cabin. Louisa and Coleman ran in behind her and shut the door. Nancy looked up at Andrew and smiled.

Andrew turned and walked the mare up the incline toward home. He could see lights in the windows of his house, and they were most inviting. It had been another long and stressful day, and as much as he would have loved a comforting conversation with his mother and dad about his day, he knew that it would be better if he did not. Some things were just better left unsaid.

Lucinda met him at the door, drying her hands on her apron. Jane was at the sink, washing pots and pans from a day of canning. Oliver and Louisa were busy playing with the newest member of the Chafin family, Joshua, who was just turning three. It was a most comforting sight to see all the happy faces welcoming him home. But they had no idea of what his day had been. "Wash up, Andy, it is time for dinner. Did you get that squirrel?"

"Yes, ma'am, I found him."

Oliver asked, "What did you do with him? And you didn't have a gun."

"I just watched him for a while. I had to run an errand for Nancy, so I didn't have time to come home for a gun. Ma, do you think I am getting old enough to go squirrel hunting alone, without Pa or Uncle Anse?"

"Not yet, Andy. Maybe by the time you are twelve or thirteen your pa might let you go out alone. Don't rush it. Now go wash up." Lucinda realized that she was running out of time. Andrew would not continue taking no for an answer. He would eventually remind his mother that the other boys his age were hunting alone with permission from their parents. She was not going to be able to hold him off much longer.

Lucinda would never know all that Andrew had been through over the past few years and what he was yet to face. She knew that there was only so much a mother could do to protect her children in the hostile environment of the valley at the turn of the century.

Bright and early the next morning, Oliver and Andrew were at the Hatfield door, waiting for Rosy, Willis, and Tennis to walk on to school. His uncle met them at the door. "Andrew, I'm going in to school with you this morning. I want to make sure your teacher knows that you are running errands for me when you miss school."

"I told her that, Uncle Anse. I think she is all right with everything now. We had a long talk after school yesterday; she said she understands, so I know things are all right now."

"Maybe so, Andrew, but I just want to be sure that she understands everything so she won't get your ma and pa involved."

"You're not gonna fuss at her, are ya?"

"No, Andrew, I won't fuss at her. I just want to talk to her a few minutes."

Andrew was nervous about his uncle talking to his teacher. He felt that he had taken care of his teacher's concerns. He did not want his uncle to upset her. He had seen Anse in polite, friendly moments, and even those were somewhat hostile. He worried about how his teacher would feel about the meeting; he did not want to get her in trouble. At the same time, he could not argue with his uncle either. Anse would do what he thought right, and Andrew could do nothing about it.

Anse led the troop of youngsters along the roadway that morning, enjoying their playful walk and proud that they had a school to attend every day. He knew that they would have a much better start in life than he had, and he regretted that he had not learned to read or write himself. His mission that morning, however, was to make sure that Andrew's teacher understood the situation and would give Andrew the leeway to miss school if he needed to—without involving Lucinda.

When they reached the schoolhouse, Anse sent all the kids to the playground. He opened the door of the school and walked inside. Andrew hesitated, turned, and walked back to the schoolhouse door. It was open. He sat on the porch step as close to the open door as he could without being seen. He had to know what Anse was going to say to his teacher.

She was at her desk with a pile of papers in front of her. Anse walked up to the desk, and she stood to face him. "Good morning, Mr. Hatfield. It is nice to see you out this morning."

"Good morning, ma'am. I thought it was important that we talked after I heard about your talk with Andrew yesterday."

"My talk with Andrew?"

"Yes, ma'am, I understand that you told Andrew that if he missed any more school, you might have to talk to his parents about it."

"Mr. Hatfield, Andrew is a bright young man, and I was just encouraging him to pay more attention to his studies. He has missed several days this year, and I want him in class as much as possible. I do not want him to get behind in his studies and lose interest in school. We have too many children in the Island Creek community who have done just that. I don't want that to happen to Andrew."

"I appreciate that, ma'am, and I assure you that if Andrew had his choice, he would be in school every minute of every day. I just want you to know that on the days that he is not in school, I have sent him on an errand, and I have his pa's permission to do so. Do you have any problem with that?"

"No, sir, Mr. Hatfield, if Andrew's pa is fine with running those errands and missing school, then so am I. I will see to it that he doesn't fall behind."

"That is kind of you, ma'am. I thank you for being so understanding. Good day."

"Good day, Mr. Hatfield. It was good to see you."

"And you as well, ma'am."

Andrew jumped up, ran around the corner of the schoolhouse, and headed for the playground.

Anse turned and walked out the door, shutting it behind him.

Andrew walked into the small one-room schoolhouse with great reservation. He was unsure of how his teacher would react to her conversation with his uncle. She did not look in his direction as he passed by on his way to his seat, but he could tell she was upset. After settling the other students and getting them started on the daily assignments, she walked back to Andrew's desk and handed him a stack of math problems. He looked up at her but said nothing. She looked back at him but said nothing. As she walked away, she patted his shoulder gently. Andrew took that as a sign of peace and decided to speak with her once school was out for the day.

At the end of the school day, Andrew waited until the others had left the building. He watched Rosy walk outside, and he knew that she would be waiting on him to come out. He got up from his desk and walked by the teacher's desk, his completed assignments in his hand. He laid them on her desk and said, "Ma'am, I just wanted you to know that I didn't say anything to Uncle Anse."

"That is all right, Andrew. He explained everything to me, and I am fine with you missing school when he needs you. You are bright enough to keep up, so don't dwell on it."

"Yes, ma'am. I hope you'll let me help you teach some more. I like doing it and I promise to keep my work up."

"Sure you can help me, Andrew. I'll see you tomorrow."

Andrew walked out to find Oliver and the Hatfield kids waiting for him. They made their way down the familiar trail home without another word of the incident. Andrew knew that he would have to find a way to get close to his teacher again, and he wished that Rosy had not said anything to her pa. When Anse Hatfield fussed at a teacher, it was not the same as having other parents fussing. His presence in the community was much more powerful, and his words were much more important. Andrew knew that he would have to work extra hard to make peace. He would start tomorrow.

13

ANDREW, THE TEACHER

Those girls, they loved me too. Don't think they didn't, especially Cap's two. I was almost a replacement for a father they didn't see much of. But I would help them too; I'd do anything for them. Rosy and Emma were my favorites.

Andrew sat in class the next day daydreaming. There was something intriguing about teaching Emma to read after school. He even thought that at some time in his life he may become a schoolteacher. Andrew would be twelve in two weeks, and school would be out for the summer in three months. Teaching Emma to read would be like extending the school year, and that pleased Andrew considerably. He looked forward to the afternoon.

The school day finally ended, and Andrew, Oliver, and the Hatfields started their trek home. Andrew tried to act normal, but Rosy sensed that something was on his mind. She kept looking at him with a slight look of suspicion. Andrew laughed, threw rocks, and tried his best to be casual, but Rosy would have none of it.

"Andrew, are you all right?"

"Sure. What do you mean?"

"I don't know; you're acting funny."

"Don't mean to. I just got a lot to do today."

"Let me help you. I'll come over this afternoon and help with your chores."

Uh oh, what do I do now? Andrew decided it was best to tell the truth and get it over with. "Not much you can do, Rosy. I told Emma I would help her learn to read. I'm going over to Nancy's this afternoon to start her lessons."

Andrew waited for a reaction. He didn't get one. *Surely she won't be mad at me,* he thought. *Emma is only five.* Andrew was not old enough to know how women think. Rosy didn't speak to him for the rest of the walk home. When they reached the Hatfield front gate, Rosy took off on a dead run for the house. She ran in the door and slammed it behind her. Oliver, Tennis, and Willis looked at each other with a what-was-that-all-about look. They weren't old enough to understand women either.

Andrew was quiet for the rest of the walk home, wondering how he was going to handle tomorrow when they stopped by to meet Rosy for school. But for the moment, he was looking forward to helping Emma. When they got home, Andrew told his mother of his plans to go to Nancy's to help Emma learn to read. He took a stack of Oliver's books and started out the front door. Then he stopped, turned back to Lucinda, and said, "Ma, you don't think Rosy would be mad because I'm helping Emma, do you?"

"Why do you say that, Andy?"

"I don't know. She just acted funny when I told her what I was going to do."

"Did she say anything?"

"No, but when we got to her house, she ran in the door and slammed it."

Lucinda grinned. "She'll be fine, Andy. Don't fret over it. You go on over to Nancy's and help Emma. But be back in time for supper."

Andrew turned and ran out the door. Lucinda went back to her knitting, but she had a wide grin on her face.

Emma watched Andrew cross the bottoms and walk up to the front porch. She met him at the front door. She had on a clean dress and a ribbon in her hair. He looked at her strangely. *What is this all about,* he thought. Nancy, Coleman, and Louise were waiting inside with an anticipation that Andrew had not seen in the household before. It was as if he were some important person who came to visit.

Nancy greeted Andrew and told Coleman and Louise to go somewhere and find something else to do. The oldest son, Shepard, was in a back bedroom, apparently sleeping. Andrew rarely saw him, and almost never outside. Emma led Andrew to a braided rug in front of the fireplace and plopped down on the floor, crossing her legs and adjusting her skirt. Andrew sat in front of her and opened the first book. Louise went over to sit with her mother, but Coleman did not move. He wasn't going to miss anything.

Nancy said, "Coleman, get over here, out of the way."

Reluctantly, Coleman got up and moved across the room. He had just started the first grade and wasn't really interested in the lesson; he just wanted to be involved. Nancy was going to see to it that he wasn't.

Andrew proceeded to explain to Emma what she was seeing in the book, exactly as his teacher had instructed him some four years before. Emma was attentive. For the next forty-five minutes, Andrew instructed, Emma listened, Coleman fidgeted, and Louise ignored. When Andrew began to lose Emma's attention, both Nancy and Andrew recognized that it was time to end the lesson. Nancy got up and thanked Andrew for his time and walked him to the door. Andrew walked home proudly. He looked forward to the next session.

A few days after that lesson, Andrew heard that Shepard had died. He never knew how or why. But he remembered that Shepard was in bed that afternoon of the first lesson.

The next morning, Andrew and Oliver stopped by the Hatfield home on their way to school, as they did every day. This morning, however, Rosy was nowhere to be seen. Willis and Tennis were throwing sticks to the dogs in the front yard. Andrew asked, "Where's Rosy?"

"In the house," Willis said.

Andrew walked to the front door, and as he was about to open it, Vicy walked out. "Rosy is sick today, Andrew. She won't be going to school."

"Tell her I hope she feels better, Aunt Vicy." And with that he led his troops south to Island Creek School—for the first time without Rosy. Andrew did not know it at the time but his relationship with Rosy would never be quite the same. They would continue to be friends, but Andrew would never again get the attention from Rosy that he had enjoyed over the past few years. Had he realized it, he might have thought twice about helping Emma with her reading. He was very fond of Rosy. Maybe he should have asked her to teach Emma.

The Messenger

In early March, 1897, a major celebration took place at the Hatfield home, with the entire community invited to meet Elias's new wife, Nancy. Elias and Nancy Browning had been married on March 18, 1897 at the Logan County Courthouse in Logan Courthouse, West Virginia. Nancy Browning was an obvious choice for Elias. She was very attractive and very smart. All of the Browning girls were as cute as they could be, and the Browning family was one of the largest and most upstanding families in Logan and Mingo Counties. Logan County was full of Brownings. Lucinda was also a Browning. After the wedding, as was the Hatfield family custom, Elias received twenty acres of farmland outside of Gilbert, West Virginia, from his father.

On the last day of school, May 24, 1897, Andrew led a contingent of Hatfield and neighborhood kids along the dusty road home as he had done for the last five years. He and Oliver left Tennis and Willis at the front gate of the Hatfield home, and for the first time that he could remember, Andrew did not go in to see Anse or to say hello to Aunt Vicy. He walked on with Oliver, anxious for his afternoon session with Emma.

At home, Andrew found his mother and father sitting at the table, talking. Holbert had not been home in a week, and Andrew was glad to see him. After casual greetings, Holbert told Andrew to sit for a few minutes, because he wanted to talk to him. Andrew sat, and Holbert said, "Andy, school is out for the summer and we are all going back to Cow Creek. And this year I want to get you started helping me with the mill and the farm. You are old enough now to be a big help, and it's time you learned how things work on the farm. You'll be in the sixth grade next year and ready to go to work after that."

Andrew was thrilled. "That's great, Pa! I've wanted to help at the farm for a long time. When are we leaving?"

"We'll head out on first thing Monday. We'll spend the weekend loading the wagon and getting everybody ready for the trip."

"I told Emma that I would help her learn to read, but I am sure she will understand."

"She'll be fine, Andrew; her mother can help her some. She'll be ready for school in the fall, and you have already helped her a lot. She'll understand."

"I'm going over there right now, and I'll let her know. Thanks for letting me help, Pa. I really want to work in the mill." And with that, Andrew was out the door, books in hand, and on his way to Nancy's.

Emma greeted him at the door, smiling, and with a different ribbon in her hair. Andrew walked in behind her, and they took the same spot on the rug in front of the fireplace. Nancy took the other two Hatfield children out the front door to keep them out of the way. After the forty-five-minute lesson, Andrew walked to the door, and Emma and Nancy followed. Andrew decided that now was the time to let them know about going back to Cow Creek. "Ma and Pa told me a little while ago that we are going back to Cow Creek for the summer, so I won't be able to help Emma until we get back. Pa wants me to help in the mill."

A sad look laced Emma's face, but Nancy covered for her. "That's fine, Andrew. I know your pa needs help, and Emma can practice a lot while you're gone. I'll help her as much as I can."

"Yes, ma'am. Emma is a smart girl; she's picking up reading real fast. I think she'll be reading by the time school starts. Bye, Emma, I'll see you tomorrow."

Emma stuck one finger in her mouth and waved good-bye with the other hand. Then she turned and walked slowly into the house without a word. Andrew ran across the bottoms to his house, dropped the books on the table, and told his parents that he was off to Uncle Anse's house to give them the news.

"That's fine, Andrew," Holbert replied. "We'll have some things to get done when you get back."

Andrew saddled the mare and, using the bench outside the back door, mounted the mare, and headed south. When he reached the Hatfield home, Vicy and Rosy were on the porch cleaning vegetables. When she saw him coming, Rosy got up and went in the house. "Hi, Aunt Vicy. Where is Rosy going?"

"She'll be out in a minute, Andrew. How are you doing?"

"I'm doing fine, Aunt Vicy. Pa just told me that we are going back to Cow Creek for the summer. He wants me to help him on the farm and in the mill this summer."

"Good, Andrew. I know he can use the help. But we sure will miss you."

"I'll miss y'all a lot too. Can I go in to see Rosy? I want to tell her."

"Sure, Andrew, go ahead."

Rosy was at the sink when Andrew walked in, but she did not turn around.

"Hi, Rosy."

"Hi."

"Ma and Pa told me a few minutes ago that we are going back to Cow Creek for the summer. He wants me to help in the mill and on the farm."

Rosy turned around and looked at Andrew with a semisneer. "What about the reading lessons with Emma?"

"I won't be able to help her this summer, but she's all right with that," said Andrew.

"Well, that's nice. I'm glad *she's* happy."

"You're not mad at me for helping her, are you?"

"Of course not."

"Do you want to help her?"

"No."

"We're not leaving until Monday, so I'll see you this weekend. Do you know where Uncle Anse is? I want to tell him the news."

"No, ask Ma."

"I'll see you later." And without a good-bye from Rosy, Andrew was out the door. Vicy told him that his uncle was in the barn, so Andrew headed in that direction on a dead run.

"Uncle Anse, Ma and Pa told me today that we are going back to Cow Creek for the summer, and he wants me to help him in the mill."

"Good, Andrew. It'll be good for you and I know your pa needs the help. When are you leaving?"

"Monday morning."

"Then ask your folks if y'all can come over to eat on Sunday. Everyone will want to tell you good-bye. Andrew, this summer might be a good time to talk to your pa about carrying a gun. You ought to bring it up if you get the chance."

"Yessir, I will. I'll talk him into goin' hunting with me and show him how I can shoot. He'll let me then, I know."

"Good. Now don't forget about Sunday. I'll let Vicy know y'all are coming. I'll ask Nancy and the kids too."

"Yessir, I'll tell them."

The Chafin family spent the weekend getting ready for the trip back to Cow Creek, loading the wagon with all the essentials they would need while there and leaving behind all they wouldn't. Andrew was able to work in two more reading lessons with Emma when he wasn't helping his dad and Oliver load things in the wagon. Emma was clearly disappointed that Andrew was going to be gone for so long, and she didn't try to hide it. It was hard for her to concentrate on reading. She pouted often and cradled her chin in her hands, indicating her displeasure with Andrew's news.

On Sunday afternoon, Holbert and Lucinda loaded all five of the Chafin children into the wagon for the short trip over to Anse and Vicy's home for a Sunday afternoon dinner. They were greeted by the entire family, even Troy, Elias, and his new wife. It was a crowded house when they were all in the same room. Holbert intended to use the afternoon to talk to Anse about the cabin, and Troy intended to use the time to talk to Holbert about a job.

Holbert brought up the cabin idea at the first available time. "Anse, Lucindy and I have been giving the cabin a lot of thought lately. You have been very generous in letting us stay there, but now I want to talk to you about buying it. We're going to have kids in school for a long time, and with the politics as they are on Cow Creek, I don't see us getting a school there anytime soon. Would you have any interest in selling the cabin to us?"

"Holbert, I hadn't thought a thing about it. You know you are welcome to stay there as long as you like. You don't have to buy it."

"I know, Anse, but we really feel badly about it, and I have some things I want to do with it with more kids coming. So if you are willing to sell it, we sure would like to buy it."

"Well, Troy and Elias haven't shown any interest in it. They're both talkin' about goin' in to Matewan or Williamson to work for the railroad. So if you are serious about owning it, I am sure we can come up with a reasonable price for you."

"That would be great, Anse. We sure would like to own it. It has been a really good thing for us during the school year."

"Well then, we'll talk about it and come up with something."

It was Troy's turn. "Holbert, Elias just got on at the railroad, and I've applied for a job too, but so far I haven't heard anything. I was wondering if you needed any help at the grain mill or the sawmill to keep me busy until I hear from the railroad."

"Troy, I think we can work something out. We're going back tomorrow. So why don't you come over one day next week, and we'll sit down and talk about it."

"Yessir, I'll do that. I really appreciate it."

The rest of the afternoon was filled with running kids, slamming doors, and conversation, and lots of good food, especially Vicy's famous biscuits. By four, the conversation had moved to the porch. The pipes came out for a late after-dinner smoke. At six, most of the activity was over. The youngest Chafin, Emma, was asleep, and Holbert was carrying her to the wagon. Fifteen minutes later, the wagonload of Chafins were headed north for home. Tomorrow would be a long day.

Early on Monday morning, Holbert, Lucinda, and all their children were well on their way to Cow Creek. The wagon was loaded with kids and supplies. Holbert's horse was tied to the back of the wagon, and Andrew was riding the mare and leading the way. Andrew had not seen the farm in months, and he was anxious to see the changes. He was equally anxious to see the mill operating; it had been under construction the last time he was at home, so he had not seen it in action.

At twelve, Andrew felt like a full-fledged adult. And for the times, he was. He would finish one more year of school and then be expected to work full time and pull his own weight. The friends he had left on Cow Creek when he went to live with Anse and Vicy were five years ahead of him in work experience. Not one had attended school, even for one year. Anse had not attended school, nor had Vicy, Johnse, or Cap. Troy and Elias attended through the sixth grade. Rosy had just finished the sixth grade; Willis would finish next year; and Tennis the year after that. Andrew felt lucky that his parents had given him so much time in school, and he was determined to make the best of it.

They arrived on Cow Creek just after lunch, and Andrew was amazed to see the improvements in the farm. Holbert had been busy.

There were acres of corn growing. There was a corral behind the barn, a deep well, and ducks and chickens running loose everywhere. In the distance he could see the hog pen with dozens of hogs circling, as hogs will do. There were at least a dozen head of cattle grazing in the pastures around the house and barn. And something new had been added. Now there was a sawmill. Andrew was fascinated by the sound of a saw blade spinning and sawdust flying.

The house was immaculate, inside and out, as Andrew had expected it to be, with his father's demeanor. The beds were made, the kitchen was clean, and everything was in its place. *When I grow up, I want to be just like Pa,* Andrew thought. And he would be.

Holbert took Andrew and Oliver on an afternoon tour, beginning in the mill. The wooden, water-pushed pods were turning a stone wheel, which was grinding away at kernels of whole corn. Two workmen were busily shoveling whole corn into a moving trough while small bits of corn grits were dropping through a maze of wire screens, sifting out the small pieces and trapping the larger ones for a return trip to the grinding wheel. "Pa, I can shovel the corn kernels," Andrew offered.

"And you will, Andy. Before the summer is over I want you to know every job. That is the only way you will learn how everything works."

They watched as the workmen shoveled the grits into a funnel that poured them into burlap sacks. Then the workmen stitched the sacks with twine and set them aside. "I can do that too," Andrew said. But when a workman picked up a large bag of grits and threw it over his shoulder, Andrew said, "I'm not so sure about that part of the job."

Holbert grinned. "Maybe later, son."

Next came a tour of the sawmill. Andrew was really anxious to see it. He held his ears when they walked inside. It was much louder than the grain mill, and dirtier. Sawdust was flying everywhere and was piled up on every surface. Workmen were rolling solid, round logs into a trough that guided them to a blade that sliced them, a strip at a time, into planks. The noise was deafening, but Andrew was thrilled with all the activity.

They watched as workmen loaded the wood planks into a mule-pulled wagon, to be taken out and stored until they could be taken to a dry kiln in Barnabus. "I can do that too, Pa," Andrew said.

"Maybe for a little while, Andrew, but you would get mighty tired after an hour or so of loading those planks. We'll let you do that job next year."

The final stop on the tour was the blacksmith shop, where a single blacksmith was pounding out small pieces of red-hot metal. "What's he making?" Andrew asked.

"He's making pieces to fix a plow." The blacksmith shop was as dirty as the sawmill, and it didn't look like as much fun to Andrew. It was hot and smoky.

"I'm not sure I want to be a blacksmith," said Andrew.

"I'm sure you don't, Andrew, but you need to learn how it is done anyway."

By the time the tour was over, the sun was going down, and Andrew and his siblings were getting tired and hungry. They were all looking forward to a hot bath, a hot meal, and bed. It had been an exhausting day.

14

PINKERTON DETECTIVE AGENCY

I pointed my gun at him, but I don't know if I could have shot him or not. And I didn't have long to decide.

A week went by on Cow Creek before Andrew brought up the possibility of carrying a gun. After an afternoon in the grain mill, with Andrew shoveling grain and filling burlap sacks, Holbert approached him with words of praise. "Andrew, you are working real hard, and I am proud of you. You're doing a good job."

Andrew was quick to use the opening. "Thanks, Pa. I want to do a good job to show you I am almost grown. I hope you will think about letting me carry a rifle. Ma said that when I am thirteen or so I will be ready, and I'll be thirteen in a few months."

Holbert looked at Andrew, scratched his head, rubbed his chin, and said, "Come with me."

Holbert took Andrew behind the barn, gathered a few bottles, walked to the fence, and placed a half-dozen bottles on the top rung. He walked back to the barn and came out with a lever-action Winchester rifle. He handed it to Andrew and said, "Let's see what you can do. See how many bottles you can hit."

Andrew had been waiting for this moment for a long time. He was prepared. He raised the rifle to his shoulder, tucked it under his arm, looked through the sight, and took aim at the first bottle. He fired, the bottle exploded. He quickly cocked the rifle and fired again. The second bottle exploded. He cocked again; six shots, six exploded bottles. He turned and looked at his dad. Holbert's mouth was wide open with shock. "Where did you learn to shoot like that?"

"Uncle Anse taught me and Joe at the same time, but I can shoot better than Joe."

"You can shoot better than me! I'll talk to your mother to see what she thinks. I'll let her know that I think you are ready to carry a rifle when you need to."

Andrew was beside himself. And after a conversation between Holbert and Lucinda, from which Andrew was excused, Holbert came back with the news. "Andrew, your ma said that if I think you are ready, it is all right with her. So when we get back to Island Creek, if you have to run errands for Anse again or you want to go hunting by yourself, you can carry a rifle."

That bit of news gained Holbert a big hug. Andrew ran to the house and gave his mother a big hug as well. Andrew was officially an adult.

By the end of the summer of 1897, Andrew had experienced his first real taste of adulthood. He had worked in the grain mill, he had worked in the sawmill, he had picked corn in the fields, he had learned how to milk cows, and most importantly, he had learned how to kill hogs at harvest time. Holbert had allowed Andrew to be the one with the rifle shooting the hogs that were culled for slaughter. And best of all, he would be allowed to carry a rifle when he got back to Island Creek.

By September the family was back on Island Creek. This school year would be different for Andrew and the Hatfield children. Rosy would be gone, Andrew would be in the sixth grade, Willis in fourth grade, Oliver and Tennis in third grade, Coleman in second, and Emma and Andrew's little sister Louisa in first. Two more of Holbert and Lucinda's children, Joshua and Emma, four and two, would still be at home. Andrew was now seen as the school patriarch, and in charge, a position that delighted him. He liked being in charge.

On the first day of class, Andrew, Oliver, and Louisa walked across the bottoms to Nancy's house to gather Coleman and Emma. Nancy walked out with the two and instructed Coleman to be attentive and watch out for his little sister. Coleman took Emma's hand and walked off the steps with her. As Andrew walked closer, Emma pulled her hand away from Coleman and took hold of Andrew's hand. Louisa held on to his other hand and gave Emma a threatening look. The four walked south along the creek on the rain-soaked roadway, on the way to the Hatfield home and school. They were met at the Hatfield gate by Willis and Tennis. Rosy was nowhere in sight.

Because the one-room schoolhouse was organized by grades, with the first-graders in the front row, and followed by each successive grade all the way back to the sixth-graders in the last row, it was considered a big deal to be sitting in the back row. Andrew basked in that authority and he cajoled and instructed the younger children with zeal that the teacher could not match. They came to him with questions and brought their work to him for approval when completed. But no one was more interested in Andrew's approval than Emma. She delighted in walking to the back of the room. Andrew would blush, and Louisa would fume.

A week after Thanksgiving, as Andrew led his school procession home after a day in class, he heard the familiar bark of a squirrel. He stopped and listened. He heard it again. Andrew called on Oliver again. "Oliver, you and Coleman take Emma and Louisa home. I have to go up the hill. Tell Ma I've gone after a squirrel." By now Oliver was accustomed to the squirrel escapades and didn't argue or ask questions. He simply called on the young girls to follow. Tennis joined the walk, but Willis was not as anxious to leave. "Where you goin', Andrew?"

"I heard a squirrel. I gotta go check it out."

"I'm goin' with you!"

"I don't need you to go with me."

"I'm goin' anyway."

Andrew couldn't argue; Willis was already on his way up the mountain. Andrew joined him without another word. Just inside the tree line, they found Johnse sitting under a tree, a rifle across his lap. He had two ammo belts crisscrossing his chest. He looked at Willis with a slightly disagreeable look, but did not make an issue of his presence.

"Afternoon, Johnse," said Willis.

"Afternoon, boys. Y'all doin' all right?"

"Yessir, how are you doin'?" replied Andrew.

"I'm doin' all right. But I need you to get a message to Pa. That goddamn 'Doc' Ellis is cuttin' our trees again. I want that sonofabitch dead!"

"Pa ain't gonna be happy with Doc," said Willis.

"Damned right he ain't. Go get word to him. Andrew, I'll wait at the loggin' shack. Let me know what he says. See if you can round up some food for me. And stop by Nancy's and bring me some fuel."

"Yessir, I'll get there as soon as I can. I need to be home before dark. Ma gets worried."

"I'll be up there in a couple of hours. You just hurry on."

Willis and Andrew left on a dead run for Anse's house as Johnse got up and walked into the trees. It was just past noon, and the sun would be down in three or four hours.

Willis and Andrew found Anse in the barn behind his house. "Pa, we saw Johnse as we were coming home from school," Willis said. "He said to tell you that Doc Ellis is cuttin' our trees again."

"Where is Johnse now?"

Andrew said, "He wants me to meet him in the loggin' shack above Nancy's house in a couple of hours."

"Andrew, you tell him there'll be no guns. We'll handle this in court. Find out where Doc is cuttin' trees, and I'll go check it out myself. Tell him I said to let it be until he hears from me."

"Yessir, I'll tell 'im."

Andrew took off for home and found Lucinda inside. "Ma, I gotta get a message and some food to Johnse for Uncle Anse. You have anything I can take him to eat?"

"Where is he?"

"He's up in that loggin' shack above Nancy's house. I've been there before."

"You know you don't have much time before dark. If you're going, you'd best hurry. I'll round up some food; you go get the mare ready. Andrew, you know I don't have to tell you to be careful."

"Yes, ma'am, I will."

"I got a slab of ham you can take, and some taters left over from last night. I don't know if Nancy's got any food or not." Within fifteen minutes, Andrew was on his way to Nancy's with a gunnysack strapped to the saddle horn and a rifle under his leg.

Nancy watched Andrew approaching and met him at the front porch. He explained his errand and waited while Nancy got the fuel. The slab of ham that Andrew brought from home turned out to be all the food he could take, but Nancy did have a full bowl of fuel. Johnse would probably appreciate the fuel more anyway.

By one o'clock, Andrew was on his way up the narrow trail to the fence line and the logging shack. As he approached the spot where he had been accosted by two riders the previous year, he pulled the rifle from its case and held it straight up, the butt against his leg. He was taking no chances this time. At the fence row, he turned right and slowly walked the mare up the steep incline.

An hour and a half into his ride, he was within fifty yards of the logging shack, listening for a squirrel's bark. He heard nothing. Andrew barked. He waited. He heard nothing. He dismounted, carrying the rifle, and tied the mare to a low branch. He walked around the ridge in the trees, keeping sight of the shack fifty yards below him. He found a spot under a tree where he could see the door of the shack and sat down. He had to wait. He did not want to go near the shack until he heard from Johnse.

Andrew sat for twenty minutes with no sound. It was nearing four, and the sun was gone. It would be dark soon. He could not wait much longer. Andrew heard a twig snap in the distance. He pointed his rifle toward the shack and sat quietly. Below him, in a small clearing in front of the shack door, a lone man approached the shack with a rifle to his shoulder and aimed at the shack door. Andrew panicked. *What if Johnse is in there? Should I take a shot?* The man got even closer to the shack. Andrew aimed his rifle at the man's head.

The man stood at the door of the shack, crouched for an assault. Andrew watched, not knowing what to do next. He prayed his horse would remain quiet. The man raised his right leg and slammed it into the door, knocking the door off its hinges. A shot rang out, and the man dropped immediately to his knees. He fell forward through the open doorway, half in the shack, half out.

Johnse appeared from the tree line on the other side of the shack, his rifle still smoking. He walked up to the man lying in the doorway, put his rifle to the back of the man's head, and fired again. The body jumped and then nothing. Johnse propped his rifle against the wall of the shack and pulled the man out of the doorway by his boots. The man's rifle was still firmly grasped by two very dead hands. Johnse twisted the rifle loose and stood it against the shack wall next to his. He looked up into the trees at Andrew and motioned for him to come down. Andrew untied the mare and walked her down the incline to the shack.

"I've been watching this bastard for over an hour. That's why I couldn't signal you."

"Do you know him?"

"Nope, another one of those goddamn Pinkertons, I reckon."

"We don't have any shovels."

"You'll have to bring me one tomorrow. We can't leave him out. I'll drag him over in the trees and cover him up until I get a shovel. Did you talk to Pa?"

"Yessir. He said to tell you no guns, that he would settle it in court."

"To hell with court. They ain't gonna do nothin'."

"That's what he told me to tell you. He wanted to know where Mr. Ellis was cutting trees; he wanted to go check it out himself."

"It's in that hollow off Mate Creek near Red Jacket. But I ain't gonna leave this to the court. Pa knows they won't do nothin'. I'll take care of it myself."

"I'll tell your pa what you said, but I sure would wait till he gets back to you. He ain't gonna be happy about you not listening to him."

"You tell Pa to go check it out, and I'll wait for that, but I ain't waitin' on no goddamn courts. They don't give a damn about our trees. Did you bring the food and fuel? I need a drink!"

Andrew got the gunnysack off the mare and handed it to Johnse. Then he said, "I gotta get home now; it'll be dark soon. I'll come back up tomorrow with a shovel. And I'll tell your pa what you said."

"I'll be here. You tell 'im what I said. That sonofabitch has gotta pay! If Elias or Troy is at home, send 'em up here with the shovel. I'll need some help."

Andrew remounted the mare and started down the long incline toward home. He had about another hour of daylight. He did not want his mother to be worried.

The lights were on in the cabin when Andrew got home, but it was not dark enough yet for his mother to be worried. He left the mare at the front porch and went in to report on his errand. "Ma, Johnse sent me with a message for Uncle Anse, and I gotta go tell him tonight. I'll be right back."

"Don't you want to eat first?"

"No, ma'am, I'll eat when I get back."

Andrew walked out the front door, mounted the mare, and turned south for Anse's house. He dismounted at the front gate and led the horse through the gate as the dogs started barking. The bear had been moved to a pin behind the barn, so Andrew saw no pacing.

Anse walked out of the front door carrying a rifle. Tennis and Willis followed. "I talked to Johnse, Uncle Anse. He said the timber was being cut over in the hollow off Mate Creek near Red Jacket."

"Did you tell him what I said about no guns?"

"Yessir, I did, but he wasn't too happy about it. He said he did not trust the courts and he would handle it himself. But he said he would wait until you checked it out before he did anything."

"Is he still at the loggin' shack?"

"Yessir, a man tried to break in the shack and Johnse shot him. The man kicked the door in. I gotta take a shovel up to him tomorrow."

"Did he know the man?"

"No, sir, he thought he was a Pinkerton."

The Pinkerton Detective Agency, hired by Anse's enemies in Kentucky, was rumored to have sent a half-dozen men to the mountains in the past six years in search of Cap and Johnse Hatfield. Not one ever came back.

"Willis, you go with Andrew tomorrow after school and take a couple of shovels. If Troy or Elias shows up in the morning, I'll send them. Come by here after school, Andrew. Go on home now; we'll talk again in the morning. I'll be heading out to Red Jacket early tomorrow."

"Yessir, I'll be here."

"Andrew, thanks for goin' up there. I appreciate it. I see your pa is lettin' you carry a gun now. I'm glad about that too."

"Yessir, me too. Willis, I'll see you in the morning. I'll come by after school, Uncle Anse."

Andrew mounted the mare, walked her through the gate, and headed north for home. Lucinda had food on the table when Andrew got there. His dinner with the family was almost strange; there he sat with all of his siblings, laughing and talking about school, after having just witnessed a killing. And he had to help with a burial tomorrow. Life could be brutal in the Tug Fork Valley.

After school the next day, Andrew and his crew stopped by the Anse house to see if he needed to take shovels back to Johnse. Rosy met him at the front steps. "Andrew, Pa said to tell you that Elias has gone up to help Johnse. You don't need to go. Pa's gone off to Red Jacket for some reason, said he would be back later tonight."

"Damn, I wanted to go with him," said Willis.

"I'm going home then," said Andrew. "Tell Uncle Anse I'll come by after dinner to see what he found out. I'll see you later, Willis."

Andrew gathered his group and started north for home—Emma on one arm, Louisa on the other. Oliver and Coleman ran on ahead, delighted that they didn't have girls hanging all over them.

15

HUMPHREY "DOC" ELLIS

Johnse wasn't so bright anyway, but going into Gilbert after Doc Ellis was one of the dumbest things he ever did.

Anse was not home from Red Jacket the next morning when Andrew led his group to school. Andrew told Vicy to let Anse know that he would stop by after school in case Anse needed him for anything.

It was a long day in school for Andrew, as he was anxious for news from his uncle. Finally, at the end of a long day, he found himself in the barn with his uncle, finding out all he could about Doc Ellis, the cut timber, and what was to happen next. Andrew had sent Oliver, Louisa, and Nancy's two kids on home so he would have time to talk.

"Doc did cut some of our timber, Andrew," Anse said. "He leases the ridge next to mine outside of Red Jacket. He cut the whole ridge and then came across the bottoms and cut about eighteen acres of mine. The problem is that the property lines in that bottom are hazy. I stopped by the assessor's office yesterday afternoon; he checked his records and they ain't all that clear. But I know what land I am paying rent on, and the trees are gone on some of that land."

"So what are you gonna do now?"

"You go find Johnse for me in the morning. Tell him I ain't gonna tell him not to go after Doc, but if he does, I want him to take Ock with him. I don't want him goin' into Gilbert alone. It's too dangerous. He should know that Doc will be expecting something from the Hatfields, and he'd better be prepared. And I need to know if Johnse is still going after Doc or not. Tell him to let me know."

Ock Damron was one of the hired hands that Anse kept around his home or in the timberlines. Andrew knew little about him except that he seemed loyal to the Hatfield family and kept to himself most of the time.

When Andrew got home, he told his mother that he had to run another errand for his uncle the next morning and that he would be missing school. Lucinda was not happy about his missing school or about his roaming through the mountains, but she understood the loyalty that he had to Anse and the trust that Anse had in him. She did not argue.

Andrew stopped by Nancy's the next morning to let her know his plan to meet with Johnse and that he would not be walking the girls to school. Emma was disappointed that she would have to hold Coleman's hand on the way to school, but she said nothing. Nancy gave Andrew a jug of fuel and several strips of dried beef, and he headed west up the mountain to the logging shack.

Andrew was worried that Johnse would be gone from the shack and that he wouldn't know where to look for him. He worried needlessly. At the fence line, just as Andrew started up the mountain to the shack, he heard the familiar bark of a squirrel. He stopped, listened, and heard it again. He walked the mare toward the sound and found Johnse sitting under a tree, watching Andrew's progress.

"Did you bring any food, Andrew?"

"Yessir, I got some dried beef."

"I'll take it. What's the news from home?"

"Your pa checked out the timber day before yesterday and said to tell you that you were right. Doc has been cutting trees on that land."

"I told 'im!"

"But he said that he checked and that the lines in that bottom are not all that clear."

"They're clear to me. That bastard cut our trees, and he knows it."

"Uncle Anse said he won't tell you not to deal with Doc, but if you do, he wants you to take Ock with you. He doesn't want you going into Gilbert alone. He said that Doc would know that the Hatfields would do something about the trees and be ready for you."

"All right, I'll take Ock. You tell Pa I ain't going into Gilbert until after Christmas. But I am goin' after that sonofabitch, and I'm gonna kill his ass."

"I'll tell him what you said."

"What's he gonna do about the courts?"

"I don't know that; he didn't tell me."

"I'll find out from Pa. You tell Ma that I'm coming in sometime around Christmas, and I'll talk to Pa then."

"I'll tell them."

Johnse walked over to the mare and cupped his hands near the saddle for Andrew's boot. Andrew mounted and then turned the mare down the slope for home. Johnse shouted, "Andrew, thanks for the food—and the fuel."

"Yessir. You want me to take the lantern back to Nancy?"

"Ya, do that."

Andrew turned the mare, went back to Johnse, and watched as Johnse dropped the lantern back into the sack. "Tell Nancy thanks for me!"

"Yessir, I will."

It was snowing when Johnse and Ock left the Hatfield home and started southeast to Gilbert. Johnse had convinced Anse that the courts were no good in this dispute and that Doc Ellis would continue stealing trees if he were not stopped. Anse did not agree with Johnse's plan, but he did not try to stop him either. Anse was as unsure of court action as Johnse, but he assured Johnse that he would pursue it legally in the courts anyway. Johnse chose not to wait.

Johnse and Ock headed south along Island Creek and turned east toward Gilbert. They stayed in the trees during the day and spent the nights around campfires deep in the forest. They reached Gilbert after a night in the frigid forest and made camp a mile outside of town. They started a surveillance of Doc's home and watched for two days. There was no unusual activity, with people coming and going throughout the days. But there was no sign of Doc Ellis.

On the third day, Doc appeared. He stepped out of a buggy and walked into his house with two burly men—bodyguards. Johnse and Ock made their plans. They waited until well after dark and went, on foot, to an overgrown pasture adjacent to Doc's house. Both men stretched out on the ground, surrounded by tall weeds. Johnse held a rifle aimed at a window in the Ellis home. Shadows would pass constantly across the shaded window, but there was no good sign of Doc. They waited.

An hour went by and then two. Johnse's new plan was to rush the house after all were asleep. He had not counted on the bodyguards. He told Ock that if the bodyguards didn't leave, they would have to come up with a new plan. Two men walked out of the front door at eleven, loaded into the buggy, and rode out of sight. Johnse whispered to Ock that they would wait fifteen minutes and then go to the house. Johnse was to blast the back door with his shotgun and then storm the house with his sidearms.

As Johnse was about to give the order to advance to the house, he heard a click behind his right ear. He froze. Standing above him, with a pistol just an inch from his head, stood one of the two burly men who had loaded into the buggy. "Don't move," the man said.

Johnse dropped his head in disgust. Ock jumped up and ran, not the smartest of moves—but then, Ock was not the smartest of men. The man with the gun told the second man, who turned out to be Doc Ellis, to watch Johnse while he went after Ock. Doc sat down on Johnse's back and placed the gun directly against the back of Johnse's head. He said, "Please move!" Johnse did not.

The other man, who was a federal agent, was working an unrelated case in West Virginia when he got word that Johnse or Cap may be gunning for Doc and decided to stay close to Doc to see if they showed up. He returned shortly with Ock in tow. Johnse and Ock were arrested on the spot and taken to the Gilbert City Jail for the night.

At daybreak, the federal agent and two police officers of the Gilbert City Police Department were on their way west with two highly visible prisoners: one a son of Anderson "Devil Anse" Hatfield and the other an employee of his, each charged with attempted murder by a Logan County judge. The federal officer, the two Gilbert city policemen, and their two well-known prisoners reached Matewan at noon and crossed the Tug River shortly after on their way to Pikeville, Kentucky. They would face a local judge and jury, who had no love for Hatfields and who wanted to see all of them in jail. Johnse's idea for revenge against Doc Ellis was not well thought out, and he would pay the price.

For reasons that were never made clear, but suspicious, Ock was released by the Kentucky judge and never charged. He returned to the West Virginia side of the Tug River and remained on Anse's payroll.

News travels fast in the mountains of West Virginia, even faster for the Hatfields. Anse knew of Johnse's capture before the prisoner and his guards had reached Matewan. Anse decided to do nothing about it. The day after Johnse's arrest, Andrew walked into Anse's house to a heated conversation between Anse and his sons, Troy and Elias, concerning his reaction to the arrest. Anse was clearly against doing anything, while Troy and Elias were hell-bent to rescue Johnse.

"We are not going to take on the federal government. It was a federal agent that arrested Johnse, not Doc Ellis," Anse argued.

"But if they get him to Kentucky, we may never see him again," replied Troy.

Andrew just sat and listened.

Elias was even more threatening. "If I ever find that bastard Ellis, I'll take him out, federal agents or no."

"We'll deal through the courts," Anse insisted. "We'll get him a good lawyer and let it play out in court. I still have the court battle with Doc on my trees too. It's the court's job to handle this now, whether it is in Kentucky or here."

Troy and Elias knew that there would be no arguing with their dad; once he had a position on any matter that was the way it was going to be. Anse got up and walked out of the room, meaning that the conversation was over. Troy and Elias walked out the front door, unhappy with the decision, but resolved that Anse would have his way. Joe motioned for Andrew to follow and walked out behind Troy and Elias. As the two rode away, Joe said to Andrew, "Pa may have stopped them from going after Johnse, but I sure wouldn't want to be Doc Ellis after today."

Andrew agreed.

Andrew turned thirteen on March 30, 1899, and as he got older, his after-school hours began to become a bore. His best friend, Joe Hatfield, now sixteen, worked in Anse's lumber business and had little time for him; Troy, now eighteen, worked in Holbert's sawmill and spent most of his time on Cow Creek; and Elias, twenty-one, worked as an officer for the N&W Railroad. Rosy, still smarting from Andrew's attachment to Emma, would have little to do with him.

So his options in the afternoon included chores around the house, exploring the neighborhood with Oliver, playing in Anse's barn with Tennis and Willis, or helping Emma and Louisa with their homework. None of the choices were as appealing as helping his dad in the grain mill or sawmill on Cow Creek.

With these few options, Andrew convinced his mother to let him travel to Cow Creek on weekends to work with his dad. So on Friday afternoons, Andrew would saddle the mare, head west over the mountain range behind their home, connect with Left Fork or Sang Branch south of Cow Creek, and be home in just under three hours; it was a four-mile ride through the mountains. Andrew made the trip every Friday afternoon and returned over the same route every Sunday.

On Cow Creek, Andrew was introduced to every aspect of the mill business and the farm. He loved the work, the responsibility, and being at home. A bonus was getting to spend more time with Troy, who had accepted a job from Holbert to work in the sawmill. Troy ate and slept in the Chafin home and worked as a box setter during the day. Andrew enjoyed his time with Troy, and they became as close as brothers.

Troy was an excellent worker, and Holbert was glad to have him, but Troy still longed for the excitement of a railroad job. Elias told stories of the train trips he made and the people he met, all of which intrigued Troy and increased his desire to one day work for the N&W Railroad.

It was near quitting time in the sawmill on a late Saturday afternoon. Andrew was sweeping up sawdust, and Troy was finishing a project on the box line. Movement at the door caught Andrew's eye, and he looked up to see a man walk in with a drawn pistol. Troy's back was turned, and the man was walking right up to him with the pistol aimed at Troy's head. Andrew screamed, "Troy!"

Troy's reaction was pure instinct; he turned and dropped to one knee in one quick motion. He pulled a pistol from his belt and fired so fast that Andrew did not even see it. The bullet hit the assailant in the center of his chest, directly over his heart. He fell to his knees and then rolled over on his side, the gun still in his hand, unfired.

Troy walked up to the fallen man, put the pistol on his forehead, and fired again—a West Virginia mountain ritual, much like taking a scalp. The body jerked; the gun rolled out of the man's hand; and he lay motionless. Troy put his gun back in his belt and went back to his project as if nothing had happened. He left the dead man right where he had dropped, not bothering to move him. Blood was spilling out on the floor and dropping through the cracks to the ground below.

Andrew stood for a minute, shaking. Troy looked at him and asked, "You all right, Andrew?"

"Y-yes-s, I'm all right."

Holbert heard the shots and came running into the mill. He looked down at the body, then at Andrew, and then at Troy. Troy was busy at his project; he didn't even turn around when Holbert came in the shop. "What happened?" Holbert finally said.

Andrew answered, "That man was going to shoot Troy, but Troy beat him to it. Pa, Troy fired so fast I didn't even see him pull his gun."

"Troy, are you all right?"

"Yessir, I'm fine."

"Do you know him?"

"No, sir, ain't never seen him before."

Holbert went over to the fallen body and started going through his pockets, looking for identification. He found nothing. "Andrew, go get the wagon and a couple of men. We're taking this fellow to the sheriff in Barnabus."

Andrew ran to the grain mill, sent two workmen over to the sawmill, and went to the corral for the mules. Holbert and the workmen hitched the mules to the wagon and then loaded the assailant in the back, covering him with a torn piece of tarp. Holbert said, "Andrew, I'm taking this fellow to Barnabus. Do you want to go?"

"Yessir, I do."

"Troy, will you be all right until we get back?"

"Yessir, I'll be fine. Don't know why we don't just bury the bastard up in the trees though."

"He was shot in a business establishment, Troy. I want to report it to the sheriff, tell him how it happened, and turn this man over to the morgue to deal with. We have enough witnesses to prove self-defense, but we gotta handle it the right way."

"Whatever you say, Mr. Chafin; you want me to go with you?"

"Either way you want to do it, Troy. I assume the sheriff will want to talk to you one way or the other. He can either come out here or you can come in with us."

"I'll come with you; might as well get this thing over with."

Andrew climbed up on the wagon bench beside his dad. Troy mounted his horse and fell in behind the wagon. They started northeast toward Barnabus without conversation. An hour later, they were in front of the sheriff's office. Holbert went in, while Andrew and Troy waited with the wagon.

Holbert found the sheriff sitting at a large desk in the back of the office. "Sheriff, I got a dead body outside. Some fellow just walked in my shop and tried to shoot one of my employees. The employee shot him first. We got plenty of witnesses."

The sheriff got up and said, "Let's go have a look." They walked out to the wagon. As soon as the sheriff saw Troy, he said, "Troy, I take it you were the employee."

"Yessir, I was," Troy said.

"And he shot at you first?"

"No, sir, he never shot. He was aiming at me, but I hit him first."

The sheriff walked over to the dead body in the wagon, pulled the tarp away, and rolled him over to see his face. "This fella was in my jail night before last. He got drunk and picked a fight. Almost beat a fella to death before they pulled him off. I threw him in jail to sober him up. I thought I was through with him when I let him out this mornin'. I suspect he came in lookin' for Hatfields and heard Troy was workin' for you, Holbert."

"Probably. What do you want us to do with the body, Sheriff?" Holbert said.

"Take him down the street to the morgue. They'll take care of him."

"Are you through with us, Sheriff?"

"I am for the time being. Troy, I might have questions later, but it seems like justifiable to me. I know where to find you if I need you."

Holbert tipped his hat. "Thank you, Sheriff. Let me know if you need anything more. We'll drop this bastard off and head on home."

"Have a safe trip, Holbert. Troy, it's good to see you again."

"Same here, Sheriff," said Troy in his most congenial voice.

Holbert took the wagon and its deceased passenger a hundred yards east to the morgue, turned the body over to two morgue employees, and turned back to the southwest for the hour ride home. There was no conversation for the rest of the trip.

16

TROY HATFIELD

The last day of formal education for Andrew Lee Chafin was May 23, 1899. Andrew walked out of the School in the Bottoms for the last time, leading his entourage of younger kids along the same dirt road he had traveled for the past six years. By West Virginia standards, before the turn of the century, thirteen was the age of adulthood. Andrew would now be expected to be employed somewhere and to support himself from then on.

West Virginia females had two choices: live forever with their parents or attract the attention of a young (or old) male who would be willing to support them, married or otherwise. It was not unusual for a West Virginia household to house multiple families under one roof. Parents lived with their offspring, along with spouses and their offspring. Andrew was fortunate that Holbert had provided him with a better start.

Andrew's future was set, or so it would seem. He would go back to Cow Creek full time and work with his dad in the mill, sawmill, or farm. He was excited about the prospect. Lucinda would remain in the Island Creek home until the last of her children had finished school. Oliver would start in the fourth grade in the fall, and Louisa would start the second grade. Next year, they would be joined by Joshua, and in three years, Emma.

Andrew would have two more siblings after Emma: Tennis would be one year old in the spring, and Cecil would be born in five years, 1904. The best that Lucinda could hope for was a school closer to Barnabus or Cow Creek. But the prospects did not look good. Holbert was insistent that they keep the farm, so the living arrangements they had with places on Cow Creek and Island Creek would have to do for some time to come.

On Andrew's first day back on Cow Creek, he was met with disappointment: Troy was gone. The railroad job that Troy so dearly wanted finally came through, and he joined Elias as an officer of the railroad, a position that required carrying a gun and keeping the peace on and around the trains, much like a private security guard. Troy was thrilled, and Elias could not have been happier. Andrew was not so happy.

On hearing the news, he became hesitant about his new job. All of a sudden it did not hold the fascination it had before. He decided to discuss the situation with his father. "Pa, I have been thinking about my job here. We both know that once I start, I will be here forever and never know what else is out there. I love working here, but I would like to see what is beyond Cow Creek."

"What do you have in mind, Andy? Have you given any thought to what you would like to do or where you would like to go?"

"Yessir, I think I would like to get a job with the railroad."

"You might be a little young to be an officer, Andy."

"I know, but there has to be something I can do. And maybe Elias and Troy can help me find something."

"Why don't you go talk to Anse? He can let Elias and Troy know that you are interested, and maybe they put in a good word for you with the railroad."

"Do you mind if I try? If it doesn't work out, I'll come back to the farm and work here."

"No, son, I don't mind. A man has to seek his own fortune. You do what you have to do. I'll be fine here if it works out for you and you like the railroad. And if you don't, just come on back."

Andrew was too old for giving his dad a hug, but he felt like doing it. He settled for a handshake.

Early the next morning, Andrew was on his way back to Island Creek to visit with Anse. He told his dad that he would stay on Island Creek until he heard something from Elias or Troy, and if it didn't work out, he would be back to Cow Creek.

It was noon when Andrew walked into his Island Creek home. Lucinda was surprised to see him; she had expected him to be on Cow Creek until at least the weekend. "What's going on, Andrew? Is there something wrong?"

"No, ma'am, nothing is wrong. I talked to Pa about maybe getting a job with the railroad before I started working for him."

"Why?"

"Ma, I told Pa that if I start working in the mill or on the farm right now, I am there for life, and I will never know what goes on outside of Cow Creek. I would like to find out if there is anything outside Cow Creek for me before I settle in for life. Troy left the mill to go work for the railroad, so now both Elias and Troy work there. I just want to see what it is like, and if I can't get a job there or don't like it, then I can go back to the farm. I just need to find out."

"Was your Pa upset?"

"No, ma'am. He understood. He told me that everybody has to seek his own fortune. That's what you and Pa did when you moved to Cow Creek."

"Yes, we did, Andy, and I didn't have the same confidence that it would work out that your Pa did. But he knew what he was doing, didn't he?"

"Yes, ma'am, he did. And I hope it works out for me too. But even if it don't, I have to try it. I'm going to ask Troy and Elias to help me look for something at the railroad."

"Andrew, I would feel better knowing you were on the farm. I don't know anything about the railroad. But I can't ask you not to do it. You have to do what you think is best for you."

"I'm gonna try, Ma, and if it doesn't work out, I will come back to Cow Creek. I'm going over to talk to Uncle Anse right now, so he can let Elias and Troy know what I'm doing."

"Tell them hello for me, Andy."

After a short hug good-bye, Andrew was off to Anse's house a mile away. He was getting more determined by the minute.

Rosy and Vicy were shucking corn on the front porch when Andrew rode up to the gate, dismounted, and walked the mare to the steps. "Afternoon," he said.

"What are you doing back here, Andrew? We thought you were going to work at the farm," Vicy asked. Rosy said nothing; she continued to shuck corn without looking up. Andrew could not understand how Rosy could still be upset that he had helped Emma learn to read. He was getting disgusted with her attitude.

"Aunt Vicy, when Troy left the mill to go to work at the railroad, I told Pa I wanted to try to get on there too. I'm hoping Elias or Troy can help me. Do you know when they're coming home?"

"Elias said they were coming for the weekend, so I expect them tomorrow."

"Is Uncle Anse home? I want to talk to him about this too."

"No, but he'll be back shortly. Just have a seat. He'll be along."

Andrew sat beside Rosy, picked up an ear of corn, and started shucking. "How you doin', Rosy?"

"Fine."

"Are you having a good summer?"

"Fine."

"So, would you like to go for a walk?"

"No thanks."

Andrew decided to give up.

"Vicy, where are Willis and Tennis?"

"They're in the barn, Andrew. They'll be glad to see you."

"Thanks, I'll go see them." Andrew was not going to let Rosy get off so easily; he got in one more word. "Bye, Rosy, it was good seeing you."

"Bye."

Andrew left the porch and headed for the barn. *"Women!"*

He was still in the barn when Anse appeared. "Afternoon, Andrew. Vicy tells me you want to work at the railroad."

"Yessir, I was hoping that Troy and Elias could help me get on."

"Well, they'll be in tomorrow. Come over for dinner and talk to 'em. I'm sure they'll be glad to help if they can."

"Yessir, I'll do that. Thank you."

Andrew was on his way home at dusk and could see lights on in the house as he was taking the saddle off the mare. He could smell the food too. It would be good to have some of his mother's cooking again. She was preparing his favorite meal: chicken and dumplings, and baked apple pie with a cinnamon crumb topping.

The next day was a long one for Andrew, waiting for dinnertime and his chance to talk to Elias and Troy, but finally the time arrived.

Andrew walked the mare through the Hatfield gate and greeted the entire Hatfield family, who were all sitting on the porch. Troy got up to greet him. "Evenin', Andrew, how you doin'?"

"Fine, Troy. Good to see you."

That greeting started an hour-long conversation about the prospects of Andrew getting on with the N&W Railroad. When the conversation was over, it was decided that Andrew would go back to Williamson with Elias and Troy and interview with the railroad company early the next week. He would stay with Elias and Troy for the interview—and permanently if he got the job. It was an exciting conversation for Andrew, and he could not wait until Sunday to start his journey to Williamson. He hoped that it would not be a journey just to Williamson, but it would be a journey into a brand-new life.

Andrew's days on Island Creek held wonderful memories for him. The farm on Cow Creek would be hard to replace, but Andrew was seeing the prospects of a new world out there, and he could hardly wait be a part of it.

To Andrew, Williamson, West Virginia, had to be the biggest city in the state. He had no idea what the world was all about outside of the communities he knew. His entire world was confined to the mountain ranges that encircled Cow Creek and Island Creek. He couldn't dream that the sun didn't go down at three in the afternoon in all parts of the world or that there were actually lights on the streets after dark in some cities, so that you didn't have to carry a lantern everywhere you went. And most of all, he had no idea that school actually lasted longer than the sixth grade. He could not even dream that in his lifetime he would get around without the thought of a horse. Andrew had a lot to experience.

17

THE N&W RAILROAD

No, it wasn't much money, but I was tickled to death. Troy hadn't said anything about paying him rent, and I figured I could eat and pay the stable to keep my horse out of what I was making. That's all I cared about.

Andrew thought the interview went well. The man interviewing him seemed interested in everything Andrew said, and he was asking interesting questions:

Did he own a gun?
Could he travel out of state?
Could he read and write?
What did his parents think of this venture?
Did he own a horse?
Did he have a place to live?
What relatives worked at the railroad?

Andrew felt that was the question that would get him the job.

He was instructed to return to the N&W office the next morning, when they would have an answer for him. It would be a long evening and night. And Andrew used the time to walk the streets of Williamson.

He decided to go by the general store, the Mingo County Courthouse, and Bank Hi Williamson's house to see what they looked like now. He remembered virtually every step of his venture there just over three years before, when he had gotten Cap out of jail. The city had grown considerably since then, including a brand-new train depot within sight of the Tug River. The depot would become the center of Williamson activities.

There were new homes being built everywhere and a new shop on practically every corner. There were more horses, more automobiles, and many more people. And there was more to come, with suburb communities like Victoria Court, Fairview, and Chattaroy. It was an exciting time to be in Williamson, West Virginia.

Andrew arrived earlier than expected at the N&W offices, a lesson he learned early from his father. Andrew would tell his own kids often that when you are late to a meeting, that tells the one waiting on you that you think your time is more valuable than theirs. That was true at the turn of the twentieth century, and it is true today.

Andrew sat in the lobby, right where he was instructed to sit, and waited to be called. The wait was not as long as it seemed to be to him.

"Andrew Chafin?"

"Yes, ma'am, right here."

"Come with me, please."

The woman ushered Andrew into the office where he had spent the better part of an hour being interviewed. The same interviewer sat behind the big oak desk, writing. The desk was extraordinarily neat. There was not a piece of paper on it, save for the pieces the interviewer was writing on. There was an ink well, a picture of something or someone that Andrew couldn't see, and an ink blotter in the center of the desk that was perfectly clean.

Andrew waited to be invited to sit. The interviewer finally finished writing, stood up, and invited Andrew to have a seat in front of him. Andrew sat. "Young man, we have decided to give you a chance to build a career with the railroad. It won't be a lot of money at first, and it will depend on how well you do your job as to where you go from here. But it will be a start, and you will be able to grow with the railroad as we grow. Are you interested?"

"Yessir, I am."

"Good, we're going to put you on as a call boy. That means you will be given the names and addresses of every crew member for every shift. It will be up to you to make sure that each one is here on time for their shift. And if, for some reason, they can't make their shift, it will be up to you to find a substitute. You think you can do that?"

"Yessir, I can."

"Fine, we're going to give you a chance at it. Troy and Elias spoke highly of you, and they think you will do a fine job. We'll pay you twenty-five dollars a week, and you can ride free on the train anytime you want or go wherever you want to go. You'll start on Wednesday. There are a bunch of papers for you to sign, so if you will see the young lady out front, she will get you started."

"Yessir, where do I report? Here?"

"Oh, no, you'll be working out of Gray Station. It's just west of here about fifteen minutes. Ask either Elias or Troy. They'll tell you where it is."

"Yessir, and thank you very much."

"You're welcome, son. Welcome on board, and good luck to you."

Andrew was an employee of the N&W Railroad Company, and he was as proud as he could be. He just wished he had enough time to go home and tell his folks, but that would have to wait.

He went back to the boardinghouse to tell Troy and Elias the news. They playfully picked him up and threw him around their shoulders while they all laughed in celebration. Andrew had become a favorite of Troy and Elias, and they had become his favorites as well.

Andrew quickly learned his job as a call boy, and he did it well. He clearly had Holbert's work ethic, one of the many valuable traits that Holbert passed on to his sons. In two months Andrew knew the names and addresses of every crew member who worked for the N&W. He could find every house. He knew their wives' names and their children's names. He knew where they liked to hang out when they were off duty, including their favorite bars. He knew who would be on time and who wouldn't. He knew who he would have to go drag out of bed and who would be sitting on the check-in bench, ready to go to work. He was earning his twenty-five dollars a week.

After two months on the job, he had established a routine. Troy and Elias were out most of the week, and he would have the boardinghouse room to himself. On the weekends when he was off duty, he would travel back to Cow Creek or Island Creek to visit his family. And when he had enough time off during the week, he would board a train bound for Catlettsburg, Kentucky, or Ironton, Ohio, to see what the rest of the world looked like. He loved working for the N&W.

In late September, Andrew was sitting on the arrival dock at Gray Station, waiting for Elias to come in from a week-long assignment to Columbus, Ohio. Troy had arrived earlier from Catlettsburg, Kentucky, and the three were off to Island Creek for a long weekend. As the train pulled in, Andrew saw Elias standing on the rear platform of the train, leaning over the side to make sure that all was clear. The train stopped, and Elias hopped off and reached for Andrew's hand. Andrew was facing the rear car as he greeted Elias and saw a man stick his head out the rear door and then duck back in. Andrew shouted, "Elias, there's Doc Ellis!"

Elias whipped his head around to see Doc disappear back into the last train car. Elias took the pistol out of his holster, pointed it at the back door of the car, and started walking in that direction.

Doc came to the door with his gun drawn, pointing straight at Elias. Elias had seen this action before, and he was in no hurry. He walked steadily toward Doc, his gun aimed at his head, and then he fired. Ellis dropped to his knees, fell down the three steps of the railcar, and lay motionless on the rail dock, one foot still lodged on the first step of the car. In that instant, two shots had been fired, one from Doc's gun that missed Elias and one from Elias's gun that found its mark, dead center in Doc's forehead.

Elias said, "Andrew, git home and tell Pa that I killed Doc. Tell him I gotta stick around here and take care of this. I won't be comin' home this weekend. And let Troy know too."

Andrew hesitated. "Hold on a minute, Elias. I gotta see what happens first."

Elias walked over to one very dead Humphrey "Doc" Ellis and twisted the gun out of his very dead hand. He put his own gun back in its holster and stuck Ellis's gun in his gun belt in front of the holster. He was tempted to put another bullet in the back of Doc's head but with lots of people watching, he decided it probably would not be a very good idea.

By then a crowd had gathered, and the Williamson police had arrived, guns drawn. They aimed their guns at Elias and demanded that he drop his weapon. Elias raised his hands and leaned over to place his pistol gently on the ground. Andrew watched. He wanted to give his uncle Anse a full report of what happened.

Elias stood in front of the Williamson police officers, holding both hands in the air. Andrew was close enough to hear the conversation. Elias said, "I am an officer of the N&W Railroad. This gentleman shot at me, and I returned fire."

The policeman said, "That gentleman was Humphrey Ellis. Why would he be shooting at you?"

Elias answered, "I don't know, Officer. He came out of that last car, firing. I returned fire."

A second officer went toward the crowd that had gathered. "Any of you see the shooting?" Several hands went up. The officer went over to one man, took out his pad, and started asking questions and writing. He then went to a second man and then a woman. He was obviously collecting the names of the witnesses to be used later in front of a judge. Andrew could not hear what was going on, but the hand gestures that the witnesses were making seemed to indicate that they thought Elias was at fault. It probably didn't help that Elias was a Hatfield.

The police officers were clearly confused. They didn't know whether to arrest Elias or let him go. They finally chose the safest option. An officer picked up Elias's gun and said, "You come with us. We'll straighten it out at the station. We'll let a judge decide."

Elias walked away with the Williamson officers, and as he walked by Andrew, he said, "Go!"

The officers stopped at Andrew. "Young man, did you see the shooting?"

"Yessir, I did. I was standing right by Elias when Mr. Ellis came out."

"What is your name, young man?"

"Andrew Chafin."

"Do you know this gentleman?"

"Yessir, he's my cousin. I live with him and I work for the railroad too."

The officer said, "Well, I don't know how much your testimony will mean to the judge, but you'd better make yourself available in case he wants to talk to you."

"Yessir, I will. I'll be there for the hearing."

The officers took Elias toward the Mingo County Courthouse, and Andrew left immediately for the boardinghouse where Troy was preparing for the trip to Island Creek.

"Troy, Elias just shot Doc Ellis!"

"What?"

"He did. Doc came at him shooting, and Elias returned fire and killed him. The police have taken Elias to the station for questioning."

"Dammit! I'm going down to the station. You get on to Island Creek and let Pa know. I may come in, or I may not. Depends on what they do with Elias."

"Yessir, I'm on my way."

Andrew had a long ride in front of him. He rode east out of Williamson, past Dr. Lawson's house, on to Lick Creek, and then north through Taylorsville and Varney. An hour east of Varney, he stopped at a small clearing to water the mare. The sun had gone down behind him, and it was beginning to get dark. Andrew decided to push on as he and Cap had done three years before. He wanted to get word to Anse as quickly as he could.

Another hour into the ride, total darkness had settled in. The forest was a thick, black mass with not even a moon to help him see. The mare just plugged along, stepping over and around objects as she came to them, objects that Andrew could not even see. Another hour into the ride Andrew had reached his limit. He stopped the mare, dismounted, and looked around. He needed someplace to tie his horse, and she needed water.

Andrew had no lantern and no matches. His only light was a reflection of stars off a shallow creek south of the trail. Andrew took the mare to the creek. As the mare started to drink, Andrew dropped to his knees, lay on his stomach, and drank from the creek right beside the mare. He then got up and looked around for a place to settle in. He had decided to wait for daylight; it was too dark to go on.

A twig snapped in the trees directly in front of him. He heard the rustle of leaves and underbrush on the other side of the creek. Andrew backed up and took his rifle out of its case, which was attached to the saddle. The mare stopped drinking and started backing up. She was getting nervous. Another twig snapped. Andrew cocked the rifle and pointed it toward the noise. He waited.

The mare was pulling against the reins. Andrew tightened his grip on the reins and put his hand across the mare's nose, petting her. He strained his eyes, looking in the direction of the noise, but he could see nothing. He backed up another three or four feet, staring at the creek, looking for anything that would disturb the water flow and give him a hint that something had crossed the creek.

He saw movement. Something had crossed the creek, but he could not see it, and he could not tell what it was. The mare kept backing up. He heard a hissing sound. He pointed the rifle toward the sound. The mare bolted, pulling the reins out of his hand. He reached for the bridle before the mare could get free, and held on.

Andrew was holding the horse with one hand and the rifle with the other, looking for the source of the hissing sound. Finally, two bright-green eyes appeared directly in front of him, almost at his feet—a bobcat. He leveled the rifle with one hand and fired in the direction of the green eyes. The bullet dug into the ground just inches from the green eyes, but it was close enough. He heard water splashing as the cat ran back across the creek and into the trees. This was clearly not the place to stop.

Andrew walked the mare to a tree stump and remounted. They had to go on, whether he wanted to or not. He was afraid the cat would return and spook the mare. He could not afford to lose his horse.

Andrew could not see the trail in front of him, but the mare could. He would just have to trust her. They headed east.

At daybreak, Andrew was atop the mountain ridge just west of Island Creek. He started the mare down the slope toward Right Fork Creek. The sky was a bright red-orange above the trees in the distance. *What a beautiful sight*, Andrew thought. He was thirty minutes from his uncle's house.

Anse would be expecting three riders that morning, although not that early. Andrew sensed that it was nearing five and that he should be at Anse's house just after sunup. Anse would be waiting in his rocking chair on the front porch. Vicy would be in the kitchen, preparing those wonderful biscuits and frying slabs of country ham in the large, black, cast-iron skillet she kept near the fire. There would be honey, red-eye gravy, and fresh eggs. Andrew was salivating.

The Messenger

Andrew could see the house in the distance. He could smell the cooking. He was exhausted. He dismounted at the gate, opened it, and walked the mare through it on the way to the porch. Anse was watching. The rifle that normally occupied Anse's lap was resting against the wall behind him. In his hand instead was a steaming cup of black coffee.

Andrew stopped right in front of the porch step and looked up at his uncle. Anse looked back at the gate, looking for his sons. He said nothing, but the expression in his eyes said that he knew something was wrong. Vicy came out the front door, wiping her hands on the apron she always wore; she looked toward the gate. Anse looked at Andrew and said, "This don't look good."

Andrew explained. "Elias shot Doc Ellis yesterday, Uncle Anse. The police took him off to jail, and Troy stayed behind to check on him. They don't know if they are going to make it home or not."

"How'd it happen?"

"Elias was just getting off the train when Doc came out the back door on the last car. He saw Elias and went back into the car, I guess to get his gun. Elias walked toward the car, and when Doc came out again, Elias shot him."

"Did Doc shoot?"

"Yessir, he did. But he didn't hit anything. Elias killed him with one shot."

"Then why the hell did they take him to jail?"

"I don't know if they kept him or not. One of the police officers said they would let the judge figure it out."

"You musta rode all night," said Anse.

"Yessir, I did. I wanted to tell you about it as soon as I could. My mare is pretty tired. Can I stable her here for a while?"

"I'll take care of the mare, Andrew. You go on in with Vicy and get you something to eat. We'll just have to wait to see if Troy comes in, and then we'll figure out what to do."

"Yessir."

Andrew gladly followed Vicy to the kitchen. He could smell the food, and he was starving. Rosy and Willis were at the table when Vicy and Andrew walked in, and Rosy surprisingly got up, came over to Andrew, and gave him a hug. Andrew grinned; it was good to see her smile again. Willis greeted him without getting up. He was busy on a plate of ham and biscuits.

Late Saturday afternoon, Troy rode up alone to the Hatfield home. Andrew and Joe were sitting together under a tree in the front yard when Troy arrived, and they jumped up to follow him to the house. Anse walked out of the house as the three came up the front steps. Troy walked over to his father and hugged him, and then both went inside the house. Joe and Andrew followed, curious as to Elias's fate in Williamson.

"Pa, the sheriff decided to keep Elias until they can see the judge on Monday morning," Troy said. "He is not convinced that killing Doc wasn't premeditated."

Anse asked, "Have they talked to any witnesses? Andrew said that Doc came after Elias and that he fired a shot too."

"There are witnesses, but they swear that Elias was the only one who shot. I know Andrew says it different, but that is the word of a thirteen-year-old boy compared to a half dozen who don't like the Hatfields anyway. I'm not sure what chance we have in court."

Anse looked at Andrew. "Andrew, are you sure that both fired?"

"Yessir, Uncle Anse, I saw smoke come out of both guns. Doc fired before he was all the way out of the back car door. Elias fired at the same time, but I know that both guns fired."

"Troy, I'm going back to Williamson with you. I want to be there when the judge hears this thing. Andrew, I want you there too."

"Yessir, I'll be there."

Before sunrise on Sunday morning, Anse, Troy, and Andrew were on their way out of Island Creek, following Rock Horse Fork through Delbarton and into Williamson. They arrived after dark and settled into Troy's boardinghouse. Anse left Troy and Andrew at the boardinghouse and went into town to call on Bank Hi Williamson, who was the prosecuting attorney in the Elias Hatfield-Humphrey Ellis matter. He returned two hours later.

"Bank Hi said the judge is a fair man," Anse said. "And he felt like Elias would be all right. I told him Andrew's story about both of them firing. He had not heard that. He said the mistake that Elias made was picking up Doc's gun and sticking it in his belt. If he had left the gun alone, they would have had evidence that Doc had fired it. However, the arrest record showed one shell missing from the gun, and the barrel was still warm when the arresting officers checked it. He said Elias's biggest problem is that Doc is pretty well liked in Williamson."

"When will he see the judge?" asked Troy.

"Ten in the morning," answered Anse. "It will be a closed hearing, which means we won't get to tell our side of things, unless the judge asks for us. Bank Hi is going to tell him about Andrew's side of things, but that don't mean he'll pay attention. We'll just have to wait and see."

At nine thirty the next morning, Anse, Troy, and Andrew joined Elias's wife, Nancy, on the first row of benches in the Mingo County Courthouse, Division III, in downtown Williamson. At ten sharp, Elias was escorted into the judge's chambers by two armed officers, followed by prosecuting attorney, Bank Hi Williamson. There was no lawyer for the defendant.

The courtroom was filled with spectators. Some were there to see the murderous Hatfield. Some were friends of Humphrey Ellis. And there were reporters from the local newspaper as well as the *Huntington Herald* and the *Charleston Gazette*. At 10:20, one of the escorting officers came out of the judge's chambers and called for Andrew Chafin.

Andrew looked at Troy and Anse, and trembled slightly. Anse patted him on the shoulder and said, "It will be fine. Just tell your story." Andrew got up and went to the officer, who escorted him into the judge's chambers.

Thirty minutes went by before Andrew came out of the chambers and took his seat next to Troy. An hour later, Elias reappeared, escorted by the two officers and Bank Hi Williamson. Bank Hi told the officers to hold on for a minute and motioned for Anse's group to join them. Cameras flashed in all directions. Nancy walked over to Elias and Bank Hi, followed by Anse, Troy, and Andrew. Bank Hi said, "Anse, they are taking Elias back to the jail. You can see him there as soon as they get him checked in. I'll explain the judge's decision in my office; we don't want to talk about it in the courtroom. I was just allowing you to speak to your son."

Nancy hugged Elias, and then Anse hugged his son, backed away, and headed out the front door of the courtroom. Troy hugged Elias and followed Anse and Nancy. Andrew followed the group down the hall to Bank Hi's office, who met them at the door and said, "Come in and have a seat." All four found chairs and sat down, waiting on the decision. Nancy was in tears and did not say a word. She sat quietly, a handkerchief dabbing her eyes.

Bank Hi said, "First, let me explain that this is the result of a plea bargain, which I have agreed to for the state. If Elias does not agree, he is entitled to stand before a jury. The judge took into account Andrew's story and accepted it. But it is common knowledge throughout the county that Elias was gunning for Doc after he got Johnse locked up. Elias didn't help himself any by picking up Doc's gun; the judge charged him with tampering with evidence.

"The judge also considered that Elias was not acting in his service to the railroad—that this was a personal matter, not official business. But on the other hand, the judge also took into account that Elias was newly married, had gainful employment, and got high marks from his employer.

"So, in the end, Elias was given a thirty-day sentence in the county jail, shortened by the three days he has already served. So he will be out in twenty-seven days. The state has accepted that, and if you and Elias go along, he will be free in twenty-seven days. I suggest you go downstairs and visit with him now, and let me know your decision."

Anse said, "Bank, I'll go talk to Elias. I know he ain't gonna be happy spending any time in jail, but I'll try to talk some sense into him. Give me an hour or so, and I'll be back."

Anse led the group down two flights of stairs into the courthouse basement and the county jail. Nancy continued crying. Anse, Nancy, Troy, and Andrew were checked in and were escorted into a small meeting room. Ten minutes later, Elias was escorted into the room by the same two officers. Nancy jumped from her seat and ran to him. They stood in an embrace before joining the others at a long table. The officers stood outside the closed door, glancing in on occasion to see that all was in order.

Anse said, "Elias, we ain't gonna get any better terms from a jury."

"May be Pa, but I shouldn't have to serve no time. He was shootin' at me too."

The Messenger

"It's your decision, Elias, but I say serve the twenty-seven days and get outta here."

Elias looked at Nancy. "What do you think?"

"Elias, I agree with your pa. It could get a lot worse in front of a jury. Hatfields are not all that well liked in Williamson. I'll be fine on the farm till you get out."

Elias then looked at Troy. "Troy?"

"Elias, I agree with Pa too. You ain't gonna get a better deal from a jury. Not in this town, where they think Doc is a good man. I say take the twenty-seven days."

There was silence in the room for the next few minutes, broken up by an officer sticking his head in the door to say, "Ten more minutes, folks."

"Okay, I'll take the twenty-seven days. Tell Bank Hi I'll take the time offered."

The group said their good-byes and walked back up the two flights of stairs to Bank Hi's office. Anse went in while the others waited in the hall. When he returned, Anse said, "It's done. Bank Hi will notify the judge, and we can pick Elias up in twenty-seven days."

18

BOOMER, WEST VIRGINIA

There were lots of reports about Anse owning a saloon and I guess in a way he did. But Anse was against taxing whiskey. He thought it was the same as the government legally stealing from its citizens, so he wouldn't have anything to do with buying or selling whiskey. He wasn't going to pay Charleston any taxes.

The official release time from the Mingo County jail was noon. And so, on August 20, 1899, at noon, Andrew joined Nancy, Troy, and Joe on the same black bench outside of the Mingo County Courthouse, where Andrew had waited for Cap three years before. Andrew could still see the outline of a large hole in the wall of the courthouse that had been patched just above the sidewalk. On the inside of that patched wall was the jail cell that Cap had occupied three years earlier.

Elias walked out of the same back door of the courthouse that Cap used, walked around the corner, and waited for Nancy, who was on the dead run toward him with her arms extended. They hugged for a period while Troy, Joe, and Andrew walked slowly toward them. Elias then hugged Troy, then Joe, and then Andrew. They didn't linger, as there was a crowd in front of the courthouse curious to see Elias and voice their displeasure over the short length of time he served for Humphrey Ellis's death. They started the seven-block walk to the boardinghouse, ignoring the crowd.

Twenty-seven days is not long, unless you happen to be a prisoner in jail. Then, to be sure, it can seem forever. Elias had a lot of catching up to do. The conversation at the boardinghouse was casual, on purpose, with Nancy having the most to say about things at home. Troy filled Elias in on what was going on at the railroad, and Joe filled in the details of Island Creek. Andrew just listened. The conversation turned more serious when it was Elias's turn. "Troy, while I was a guest of the county, I met a guy from Boomer."

Andrew asked, "Where is Boomer?"

"It's a small town in Kanawha County, right outside of Logan County on the Kanawha River," Elias said. "This fellow was in jail for public drunkenness and disorderly conduct. It seems he had a little too much to drink in that old saloon down by the Tug River."

"I don't think I would put much stock in what that fellow had to say, Elias," said Troy.

"Well, that's what started the conversation, Troy," Elias said. "The fellow said he didn't like Williamson because he would never be thrown in jail for public drunkenness in Boomer. He told me there is this saloon in Boomer that is the hottest place to be. There are lots of fights and all sorts of action because of the river traffic from Charleston."

"So, what's the catch? What was so interesting about this fellow?" asked Troy.

"He said the saloon is owned by a friend of his, Alvin Simms, and Alvin's brother, and they are looking for a buyer. The bar has such a bad reputation in Boomer that he can't find anybody there that will put up with all that goes on there. Apparently, Alvin is in poor health and he wants to get out of Boomer and move up to Charleston. His brother doesn't want to run the bar."

"So?"

"It's perfect for us!"

"How's that?"

"Well, first of all, we don't care about all that goes on there. Can't be any worse than what goes on here. And second, I need to get the hell out of Mingo County. You know damned well the railroad ain't goin' to keep me on after killin' Doc. I'm gonna need a place to go."

"What about the money? What are we gonna use for money to buy it with?"

"Pa."

"What?"

"We'll ask Pa to front us the money."

"I ain't movin' to Boomer," Nancy said.

"No need to, Nancy. We'll keep the farm, and you can stay there if you want, and I'll come in on weekends, or you can come in to Boomer with me."

Joe added his support. "And I can come work for ya in the saloon."

"Look, Troy, just think about it," Elias said. "I'm goin' by the rail office tomorrow morning to see what my work status is and whether or not I have a job. If I ain't, I'm goin' to Boomer to check it out. If it looks promising, we'll go talk to Pa."

"I'll think about it, Elias, but I'm not so sure about being in the bar business. And besides, I think the railroad will keep you on. They've been mighty good to me."

"We'll know tomorrow. But you just think about it. I gotta leave this county if I ain't got a job, and I need you to go with me."

The conversation ended without Troy committing to going into the bar business with Elias. He would withhold that decision until he could see the bar and how it operated.

Troy and Andrew accompanied Elias to the N&W Railroad office the next morning and sat in the outside lobby while Elias went into the field supervisor's office to check on his employment status. His employment status was all too obvious when he walked out. The expression on his face revealed the decision. "I'm out," he said.

"What did he say?" asked Troy.

"He said that there was no way they could keep me on after the Humphrey Ellis killing, that there was too much public sentiment and hostility over it."

"He knows it was self-defense?"

"He said what he thinks don't matter. The public don't think so."

"So, what about my job? Am I in trouble too?"

"I didn't ask about your job. You best go check it out yourself."

"And my job," added Andrew.

Troy walked immediately through the supervisor's door. Elias and Andrew sat. The outer lobby got very quiet.

Ten minutes later, Troy walked out. "He said I am still in. And I asked about your job too, Andrew, and he said you were fine. So, Elias, I guess the saloon ain't such a bad idea."

"Troy, if it works out, will you come up to Boomer with me?" Elias asked. "I'm not sure I want this thing if you ain't there with me. This is a two-person deal."

"We'll check it out first, Elias, and we'll see. We ain't gonna mention nothin' to Pa until then. In the meantime, I'm stayin' with the railroad."

"Me too," added Andrew.

Elias and Nancy returned to their farm after he promised Troy that he would journey to Boomer later in the year to see about the possibility of purchasing the saloon. Troy continued his employment as officer for the N&W Railroad, and Andrew continued his duties as call boy, residing with Troy in the boardinghouse off Third Avenue in Williamson, West Virginia.

Williamson grew rapidly at the turn of the century, a result of the ever-expanding railroad. Coal and lumber businesses were booming, now that the railroads were there and coal and timber could be easily moved into Kentucky and Ohio. There were new hotels and restaurants springing up all along the Tug Fork Valley, and more new homes being built on every available lot. The train depot became the focal point of the town, which bustled with people for every train arrival and departure. A second general store opened and then a third.

Soon the streets became wider, and there were more of them. Horse traffic became less and less as automobiles became more and more popular. There was even a new hospital under construction. Andrew might have been raised on a farm, but he loved all the activity in Williamson and could picture himself becoming a resident of the city someday, should he get the chance.

Elias returned to Williamson after the first of the year and boarded a train bound for Charleston, West Virginia, where he would transfer for the short train trip to Boomer. He looked up the Simms brother's saloon and made the short walk there from the train depot, a matter of blocks. On the afternoon he arrived, the saloon was full of customers, and it was loud—very loud. Elias asked to see Alvin Simms and was taken to see a frail little man with white curly hair. Elias introduced himself. Not surprisingly, Alvin had heard of the Hatfields.

Alvin took Elias to a backroom office, where they discussed the possibility of Elias purchasing the saloon. The cell mate in the Mingo County jail had been correct; Alvin did indeed want to sell the saloon and move to Charleston. The activity in the saloon and the noise were appealing to Elias. So there was an owner wanting to sell and a buyer wanting to buy. All they lacked was an agreement on price.

The two agreed that Alvin would gather all his financial records, bank receipts, and expenses and forward them to Elias. He would also include a proposed purchase price. They shook hands, and Elias caught the last train out to Charleston before the sun went down.

It was be February before Alvin's documents made their way to Elias. When Elias studied them, he was disappointed. Before he even analyzed all the receipts and expenses, it was clear that purchase price itself was more than Elias thought it would be. The decision to buy or not to buy would require careful consideration and consultation with Troy and his father.

The first opportunity for that consultation occurred in early March when Troy and Andrew were back on Island Creek for a long weekend. Elias made the trip to Island Creek with all of Alvin's documents. He would talk to Troy first. If Troy had no interest, there would be no reason to pursue the idea with Anse.

Andrew was using the long weekend to visit his parents and siblings on Island Creek. There had been a new addition to the family since he finished the sixth grade and started employment with the N&W; his brother Tennis was born in 1898, bringing the number of siblings to six. One more was to come. Holbert was in for the weekend, and the family was to go to the Hatfields for dinner on Sunday. There would be a very full house at Uncle Anse's on Sunday, as Cap and Nancy would be there with their three children.

Cap's problems with law enforcement and bounty hunters had eased considerably since both the State of West Virginia and the Commonwealth of Kentucky had withdrawn all bounties for his capture as well as the capture of Johnse, who was still serving time in the Kentucky State Penitentiary. It had been over seven years since the feud ended and over ten years since Cap and Johnse had gone on their killing spree against the McCoy family. The statute of limitations had expired, and the Commonwealth had changed political parties twice. There was no longer any interest in the cases.

Cap had moved back home and was learning to read and write at Nancy's insistence. Andrew's favorite student, Emma, was finishing the second grade at Island Creek School, and Coleman was finishing the third grade.

On Sunday, at the first opportunity, Elias summoned Troy for a quiet session to look over Alvin's financials. They quietly retreated to an upstairs bedroom and lay the paperwork out on a bed. Troy was very uncomfortable with the string of documents. He had little or no training on financials and had no idea what he was trying to analyze. Elias had studied the documents over the past month, but he was almost as uncomfortable as Troy. Some of the figures meant nothing to him. Discussing the financials with Anse would be difficult, since he could not read anything.

Troy suggested they have Andrew look at them, reminding Elias that Andrew was great with figures. And while they realized that Andrew knew nothing about the saloon business, he might at least understand what some of the figures meant. They asked Andrew to join them upstairs.

Troy initiated the conversation. "Andrew, do you know anything about financial records?"

"Just what Pa has shown me about the mill and the farm."

"Would you look at these figures and see if you can make out what they mean?"

Andrew took the stack of documents and quickly shuffled through them. "Troy, I am the wrong one to ask. Why don't we get my pa up here? He knows a lot more about these numbers than I do. He would be glad to look at them."

Elias said, "I hadn't even thought about Holbert. Let me go get him."

Elias left and was back in a matter of minutes with Holbert. "Holbert, would you take a look at these and tell us what some of this means?"

Holbert took the stack, sat on the bed, and started sifting through the paperwork. Troy, Elias, and Andrew stood watching. After a few minutes, Holbert said, "I see all the figures, but what is this all about?"

"Troy and I are looking at the possibility of buying this saloon in Boomer," Elias said. "I asked for the financials, but I'm not sure what I am looking at."

"Well," Holbert said, "the saloon is making money. I guess it would depend on what they want for it."

Elias told him.

"Well, if you do the simple math," which Holbert did, "it would take ten years to pay for itself if the revenue and expenses stay the same."

"Ten years?"

"That's what it looks like to me. Of course the owners are taking money out of the business too, so that adds some back into the pot. But if the two of you take money out, it will be the same."

Troy asked, "Holbert, would you buy a business that was going to take ten years to pay for itself?"

"I don't think I would be interested, but then I don't know anything about the saloon business either. Just seems like a lot of time and money to me."

"Me too," added Troy.

"Well, I'll make him an offer. What would you consider a reasonable payout time, Holbert?"

"I'd say no more than five to seven years would be reasonable."

Elias said, "Then we'll have to talk to Pa. If I put an offer in writing and he accepts it, we are in trouble if Pa says no. We'll talk to him after dinner."

It was well after dark before Holbert and Lucinda had their brood safely tucked into the wagon and on their way home from the Hatfields. Jane and Andrew were the only siblings awake. The younger ones had been worn to a frazzle and were sound asleep in the back of the wagon, except Tennis, who was asleep in Lucinda's arms.

After the mules were unhitched, the wagon put away, and the kids safely in bed, Holbert, Lucinda, Jane, and Andrew sat on the front porch, reliving the evening at the Hatfields. Andrew brought up the saloon. "Pa, do you think the saloon would be a good deal?"

"Not at the price he told me, I don't. But if he can get the price down a little, possibly so. Nonetheless, it will be a hard sell to your uncle Anse."

"Why?"

"Several reasons: first, Anse doesn't like the saloon business; second, he won't want to see his boys that far away; and third, the saloon business is a dangerous business. The customers are an unknown. They mostly have a chip on their shoulder when they are drinking, and they go out of control easily. I don't think Anse wants his boys around that crowd."

"You think Elias and Troy can talk him into it?"

"If anyone can, they can. But I suspect that if they do, they all may regret it one day."

Bright and early Monday morning, Troy and Andrew were on their way back to Williamson. Their long weekend was over, and they would report to the supervisor's office the next morning to begin the new week.

Andrew asked, "Troy, did you and Elias get to talk to Uncle Anse about the saloon?"

"We talked to him, Andrew, but we didn't get an answer. He wants to think about it, he said. I don't think he wants us that far away. And he thinks the saloon business is dangerous. He said we would talk some more."

Andrew smiled to himself. Where had he heard that before?

19

SARAH RICHARDS

You know, things just have a way of working out. If I had stayed with the railroad and not gone back to Cow Creek, you and I wouldn't be having this conversation right now, Claude. I wouldn't have met your grandmother, and you wouldn't be here.

The years went by swiftly in Williamson, West Virginia, for young Andrew. He continued to work for the railroad and live with Troy in the boardinghouse just off the Tug River. Young Andrew traveled extensively—often to Catlettsburg, Kentucky; to Charleston and Huntington, West Virginia; and on occasion as far away as Cincinnati, Ohio, all compliments of the N&W Railroad's free fare policy. He spent his free weekends watching those cities grow larger and seeing Williamson become the commercial hub of southern West Virginia. He loved his job with the railroad and the life he was living. But it was about to come to an end.

Andrew had just turned sixteen when he got the news. Elias had completed negotiations with Alvin Simms, and the Boomer Saloon now belonged to Elias and Troy. The negotiations with Alvin were easy compared to the negotiations with their father. Anse was strongly against the saloon endeavor and tried his best to talk Elias out of it. Elias brought Holbert and Andrew with him for his discussion with his dad for support and to show Anse the financial information that Alvin had sent him. Holbert did not voice an opinion as to whether or not Elias should buy the saloon. He only voiced an opinion on the financials, proving that Elias could make money in the business if he could buy it at the right price.

Anse was not convinced. "Elias, selling whiskey is a dangerous business. You are dealing with the lowest of the low, and when they are drinking, they are out of control. And in Boomer, there isn't much the family can do to help you. You know that outside of Mingo County you are at risk."

Elias countered, "Pa, Troy will be with me, and we both know that he is the best shot in the state. Nobody is goin' to mess with him. The Simms brothers have owned this saloon for years without any trouble; I don't know why we would be any different."

"If Troy is with you, that makes it even worse. I could lose you both! And it ain't the same as it is for the Simms brothers. They ain't Hatfields."

Eventually, because Elias and Troy were such favorites of Anse, he found it hard to say no. He conceded after an afternoon of debate and agreed to front Elias the money. But in what would prove to be prophetic, he said, "Elias, I know in my heart I should not do this. I could lose you both."

Elias and Troy would take over the establishment in June, which meant that Troy would be moving to Boomer. Andrew was out of a place to live. The N&W Railroad supervisor could not find a job for someone Andrew's age that would pay him enough money to live alone, so Andrew's options were few. Until he could figure it out, he would be on his way back to Cow Creek to work with his dad. It was May 1902.

The Cow Creek farm was not Williamson, West Virginia, but it was better than most places Andrew could think of to live. The mountains were beautiful, and he was at home. He loved working in the grain mill, and he got to see his family often. He sometimes wondered why he missed the activity of N&W Railroad and the bustle of Williamson. The weekends were special as well, when Andrew and his dad would travel into Island Creek to see his mother, brothers, and sisters.

Oliver would be starting the sixth grade in the fall. Louisa would be in fourth, Joshua in second, and Emma in first. Of Uncle Anse's kids, only Tennis was still in school. Rosy still lived at home and was seeing a young man that worked for Anse on the timberline. Three of

Cap's children were in school, and Emma, Andrew's favorite pupil, would be in the fourth grade with Louisa. Andrew wondered if Louisa was still jealous of Emma for holding his hand.

Andrew still loved his visits with his uncle Anse and looked forward to their bear, rabbit, and coon hunts. It seemed that Anse and Andrew were on a hunt every weekend that Andrew got back to Island Creek. When they weren't on a hunt, they were sitting with Vicy on the porch, talking and laughing about days that had been. Even Vicy would grin on rare occasions.

Anse moved around slower, but he still had a keen eye and a steady hand on a rifle. He could still hit a coon or a rabbit from fifty yards away. The only difference in their hunts now was that Andrew always carried the coons or rabbits home, even if Uncle Anse killed them. Though Anse had always insisted that if you killed it, you carried it, he'd had a change of heart. Now Anse would say, "Can't be proud forever!"

The feud with the McCoys seemed so long ago that most of the community had forgotten about it. There hadn't been a bounty hunter in the mountains in a couple of years. The only remnant of the McCoy conflict and the bounty hunters was the old fort behind Anse's house that Andrew had never seen used. Anse built the fort in anticipation that the feud would follow him from Grapevine Creek and the fort would be a final defense. But the feud did not follow him, and the fort was eventually swallowed up by the massive undergrowth. Anse never went up there anymore unless he was looking for coons or rabbits.

Andrew still loved the stories of the feud, and if he could catch Uncle Anse in the right mood after a good hunt, Anse would fill in a few details for him. Otherwise it was never mentioned. Anse and Andrew would sit on the porch and talk solemnly about those things that happened after the feud, and it seemed to ease Anse's mind to get them off his chest. Andrew told his uncle that he just knew that Anse and his sons had worn out a dozen shovels after he went to live with them.

The Hatfield home was much quieter now. Aunt Vicy still cooked all day, always in that feed-sack apron. Joe had moved on and worked in the lumber business in Logan, traveling with Willis to Boomer on weekends to work for Elias and Troy. Rosy had moved to Logan and was getting married in the spring. And Tennis, the most studious of the bunch, kept his nose in a book full time.

Andrew had become accustomed to the faster pace of Williamson. And Island Creek certainly did not hold the same fascination for him. He could not get over the dull sensation in his stomach that there had to be more to life than that. He could not see himself spending the rest of his life on Island Creek or, for that matter, on Cow Creek. He had a sick feeling that he would be there forever and that there was nothing he could do about it. *What does life have in store for me?* he thought. *Whatever it is, I wish it would hurry up.*

Andrew and his uncle Anse had spent a hot August weekend on a two-day hunt, and Andrew was on his way back to Cow Creek—a trip he would long remember. He crossed the ridge behind their home on Island Creek and was following Sang Branch just south of Cow Creek. He saw someone ahead of him, watering a horse at the creek. He saw more horse than rider; the horse was blocking his view. He walked toward the rider without taking his eyes off the stranger. *Who is that?* he asked himself. As he got nearer, he realized it was a girl. Her back was to him, so he could not make out who it was. He thought he knew every girl on Cow Creek. *Who is that?* Whoever it was had the most beautiful hair he had ever seen. It came down almost to her waist.

Andrew rode up behind her, but she still had not turned around. He stopped. He knew that if he spoke he would scare the life out of her. He also knew that if he didn't speak, he would scare the life out of her when she did turn around. So he had two choices: he could ride on and say nothing, or he would scare the life out of her. He was not about to ride on. He would take his chances on scaring the life out of her.

"Hello."

She screamed an ear-splitting scream and turned around.

Whoa! Who is this? She is beautiful! Andrew was enchanted, but he had no idea with whom. She was as thin as a pencil, with bright blue eyes, high cheek bones, and eye lashes that curled almost into her thick bangs. Her ankle-length dress was too tight, which he loved, and she had on boots.

"I'm sorry. I didn't mean to scare you. My name is Andrew."

She said nothing. She turned her back to Andrew, put her boot in the stirrup, and remounted the horse. She turned the horse away from the creek and walked it away.

Andrew yelled, "I said I was sorry!"

She did not turn around.

"Can I at least have your name?"

Nothing. She did not even acknowledge his presence. She rode toward Cow Creek and turned west. She never looked back.

Andrew just sat. How depressing. The love of his life had just ridden away, and he would probably never see her again. His sorry life had just gotten a lot worse. When she was completely out of sight, Andrew turned the mare toward home, slapped the reins against her neck, and headed for Cow Creek. *Damn!*

Andrew found his dad in the kitchen, frying chicken for dinner. He loved his dad's cooking and hoped that someday he would learn to cook like him, or find someone who could—like the girl he just lost. "Pa, do you know every family on Cow Creek?"

"Pretty much, Andy. Why?"

"Do you know a family that has a girl about my age with beautiful, long hair? She's tall, maybe taller than I am, and really thin."

"No one comes to mind, Andy. Why?"

"I just saw her on the way here, but I scared the life out of her, and she rode away."

"How did you scare the life out of her?"

"She was watering her horse on Sang Branch, and I just rode up behind her. She must have been deep in thought, because she didn't hear me coming up. So when I spoke to her, she jumped."

"She was probably just embarrassed, Andy. If she lives on Cow Creek, I am sure you will see her again."

"I sure hope so. She was beautiful!"

Holbert just grinned.

Two weeks went by, and Andrew could not get the girl off his mind. At least once a day he would ride back to Sang Branch and sit. He threw pebbles in the creek, he daydreamed, he paced, and he waited. And then he went home.

Another two weeks went by, and Andrew gave up. He rarely thought about the girl anymore. Well, almost. At least he could get her out of his mind if he was busy. So he tried to stay busy. It was almost lunchtime, and Andrew was working in the grain mill. A man walked in the door, carrying a bridle. "Excuse me, can you tell me where I can find Holbert?"

Andrew answered, "Yessir, he's over in the blacksmith's shop. Do you know where that is?"

"No, I don't."

Andrew walked to the door, with the man following. "Go toward the house over there. The shop is behind it."

"Thank you." The man started in the direction of the house.

Andrew turned and started back into the mill when something caught his eye. He looked back over his shoulder. There, in front of the house, on the front bench of a buggy, sat the girl. Her back was to him, but the hair was unmistakable. Andrew's knees got weak. He wiped his forehead with the rag he had in his hand, leaving a thick, greasy strip across his forehead. He walked toward the buggy, this time making a wide circle so that the girl had plenty of time to see him coming.

If she saw him before he reached the buggy, she didn't show it. She stared straight ahead. Andrew walked up beside the buggy, wiping his hands on the greasy rag, making his hands greasier than they were before he wiped them. He stopped right beside her. Finally, in what seemed like forever to Andrew, she turned her head and looked at him. She looked up at the greasy streak on his forehead, put her hand over her mouth, and chuckled.

She is beautiful, thought Andrew.

She said nothing. Andrew said, "Hi, my name is Andrew."

She spoke. "I know that."

"How do you know that?"

"You told me at the creek."

"Then why didn't you tell me your name?"

"I don't know. Didn't feel like it."

"Did I scare you?"

"A little. I didn't know you were there. And besides, I don't know you; I don't just speak to everybody."

"You knew my name!"

"It's not the same."

"Okay, now you know me. I live here. This is our home. Where do you live?"

"On Cow Creek, a mile or so west of here."

"How long have you lived there?"

"I got there a while ago. I live with the Lees."

"Are you going to stay here?"

"I don't know."

Andrew was getting nowhere in this conversation. He was about to give up again when the man came back with his dad. Holbert said, "Andy, did you meet Mr. Lee?"

"No, sir, I did not."

"This is the gentleman I named you after. This is Andrew Lee."

Andrew walked around the buggy, wiping his hands on the greasy rag, and stuck out his hand to shake Mr. Lee's hand. Then he looked down at his hand and realized what he had been doing, so he simply said, "Nice to meet you, sir."

"You too, Andrew. Holbert, thanks for your help. I'll come by next week and pick it up."

Mr. Lee got back in the buggy and pulled on the reins to turn the horse toward the gate. Andrew stood by his father, watching the maneuver. As the buggy started to pull away from them, Andrew panicked. He screamed, "Wait!"

Mr. Lee pulled on the reins and brought the horse and buggy to a stop. Andrew ran up to the girl sitting on the bench. She was smiling.

Andrew said, "I still don't know your name. What is your name?"

The girl smiled. "Sarah. Sarah Richards."

Andrew smiled and backed away from the buggy. Mr. Lee cracked the reins against the horse's back, and the buggy started moving again. They drove away. Sarah did not turn around; Andrew did not take his eyes off her.

Holbert put his arm across Andrew's shoulder. "You're right, Andy. She *is* beautiful."

A few days after Sarah's visit, Andrew went to his father. "Pa, I want to take the bridle back to Mr. Lee when you finish with it."

"I thought you might, Andy. I finished it, and it's hanging in the barn. Take it anytime you want."

"Where do they live?"

"West of here about a mile or so—it's a small, white house that sits in a clump of trees, and it has a split-rail fence around it."

"I'm going over right now," said the very impatient Andrew.

He found the house without trouble and rode up to the front steps. He was getting off his horse when the front door opened and a frail-looking woman walked out on the step. "Whatcha want?" she asked sharply.

Andrew went back to his saddlebag and pulled out the bridle. "I'm Holbert Chafin's son. My name is Andrew, and I brought Mr. Lee's bridle back."

The very frail, but very feisty, little woman said, "I'll give it to him."

Andrew was getting nervous. *Would he not get to see Sarah?* "Thank you, ma'am. I appreciate it. Is Sarah at home?"

"She's busy," said the woman as she turned, walked back in the house, and shut the door.

Andrew was sick. *This just isn't right*. He walked up on the porch and knocked on the door. The woman reappeared. Before she could say anything, Andrew said, "Ma'am, I really want to see Sarah if you don't mind. She's the reason I came over here."

She was starting to respond when Sarah walked up beside her. "Hi, Andrew!"

"Hi, Sarah. I brought Mr. Lee's bridle back and wanted to say hello," said a much-relieved Andrew.

Sarah started to open the door, but the woman put her hand out and said, "You got chores, young lady!"

Sarah looked at her with a look that Andrew felt was a look of desperation. "I'm going out!" Sarah said. The woman backed away.

Sarah walked out the door, off the porch, and toward the creek. Andrew took the reins of his horse and followed.

"Did I get you in trouble?" Andrew asked.

"Probably, but I don't care anymore."

With those words Sarah had declared her independence. She had been an unwilling housemaid and farmhand for long enough. She was not going to be a prisoner any longer. "They took me in when my dad went away, Andrew, but I'm not going to live like this anymore. If they throw me out, I'll find somewhere else to live."

That conversation began a very short courtship. Sarah was determined to live her own life, and Andrew might be her best chance. She was not going to let that chance get away.

On April 5, 1905, Sarah Richards became Mrs. Andrew Lee Chafin, married just outside of Logan, West Virginia. She and Andrew were both nineteen. Sarah had lived a very difficult life before she met Andrew. Her mother died when she was very young, and her father was left, reluctantly, to raise her and her siblings alone. He was an alcoholic and abusive. He was rarely at home, and when he was, the children were terrified.

Sarah and her younger siblings went hungry most of the time, with little or no food available. Years later she would admit to trapping and killing birds to eat, just to stay alive. There was no medicine and no doctors. When Sarah or one of her younger siblings became sick with the normal childhood diseases, they had to nurse themselves back to health.

After years of not even pretending to care for his children, her father, George Richards, decided that even having them around was too much. He simply gave them away. No family would take all three, so he gave them to three different families. Sarah went to Andrew Lee and his wife. In her new home, Sarah had food, but she was required to work for it. She was not allowed to go to school, even Sunday school, and she was not allowed to have friends. She stayed in the house or garden and worked from the moment she was out of bed until she collapsed into bed after dark. The next day she started work all over again. Andrew Chafin must have seemed like true salvation.

Andrew and Sarah began their lives together on the farm on Cow Creek, and it didn't take Sarah long to show her spunk. Her previous life had hardened her, and she knew she had paid her dues. As Andrew and Sarah were hoeing in the garden one hot afternoon, Sarah stopped, looked at Andrew, and said, "Is this what we will be doing all our lives? Is this all there is to life?"

Andrew got the message. She was right; there had to be more to life than a garden on Cow Creek. And Andrew knew he had to find it. He once again visited with Holbert and once again made the decision to see what else was out there in the world. Holbert understood and wished his son well.

Andrew and Sarah moved to Williamson, where Andrew began his adult life working in the business community, ultimately the automobile business. He later owned one of the first Packard dealerships in the state, which he lost during the Depression. After the Depression, he worked as an accountant for Price Motors, one of the city's best-known businesses. Andrew and Sarah bought a home in downtown Williamson, on Prichard Street, right behind the Methodist church, where they raised seven children: Arvil, Raymond [the author's father], Thelma, Opal, Edith, Andrew Lee, and Ruth Ann.

Andrew and Sarah continued their visits to Uncle Anse on Island Creek, including a weekly Sunday afternoon lunch with their three oldest children in tow. Only those visits were to the large, two-story home that Anse built a quarter of a mile south of the cabin they occupied when Andrew lived with them.

Andrew was a Mason (O'Brien Lodge 101) and deeply involved in the Williamson business community. To this day a picture of Andrew, with other city leaders, hangs in the Mountaineer Hotel in downtown Williamson. He was devoted to the Methodist church and never missed a Sunday, always sitting with Sarah on the same front row pew. Andrew played violin for most services while Sarah played the piano.

In his later years, Andrew was an avid collector. His coin collection was worth thousands, his pipe collection was a coveted keepsake for family members, and his tool collection was pampered and polished with great regularity. He kept a detailed diary in his later years, noting everything from what he spent and where, to visitor's names, and special events. His bookkeeping background served him well until his death.

Andrew and Sarah remained married and devoted to each other from their marriage in 1905 until Andrew's death in 1977. He was devoted to his family and as the stories in this book show, he was equally devoted to the Hatfield family.

Sarah Chafin
circa 1911

Andrew Chafin
circa 1911

EPILOGUE

It was the hardest thing I have ever done in my life, and I would have given anything if I weren't the one having to do it. But I didn't have any choice. Anse and Vicy did not deserve to hear it from strangers.

On Tuesday afternoon, October 17, 1911, Andrew received a wire from Joe Hatfield, sent from Harewood, West Virginia:

> Elias and Troy shot to death today, stop
> cannot get home to tell folks, stop
> please go let them know, stop

This would be the last and most difficult message he would ever deliver for the Hatfields.

Andrew left Logan on that Tuesday afternoon in one of those "newfangled horseless carriages" for an eighteen-mile ride to Island Creek. He arrived at the Anse Hatfield home in the middle of the afternoon. He walked to the front gate and stopped. Anse was not in his familiar spot, in a rocker on the front porch, but the memories of him sitting there swept over Andrew like a cold chill. He recalled the number of times he had passed through that gate, sometimes with bad news and sometimes with good news. But today would be the most painful news. And he did not want to deliver it.

Andrew crossed the small yard and walked up the three steps to the long front porch. He knocked on the screened door and waited. Vicy opened the door, wearing that ever-present apron, and looked at Andrew. He had never been there midweek, and the look in Vicy's eyes told him that she knew something was wrong. She opened the screen door without a word and stood to the side as Andrew removed his hat, passed by Aunt Vicy, and walked into the large room. Anse was sitting in front of an open fire, holding a cane. When Andrew walked in, Anse started to get up. Andrew said, "Don't get up, Uncle Anse. I want to sit down."

Anse sat back and watched as Andrew walked across the room and sat beside him. Vicy followed. She sat in a small chair, watching Andrew, and waited. Anse had the same look in his eyes that Andrew had seen in Vicy's just a minute before. There was no greeting. There was a resolve in the air that both Anse and Vicy shared. They were simply waiting on the bad news that they both felt was coming.

Andrew started to speak, but his lip was quivering and he could not get the words out. Vicy put her hand to her mouth; a tear appeared in her eye. Andrew started again. "Uncle Anse, I got a wire from Joe this morning. He asked me to let you know that—" Andrew stopped again. Anse turned his head away; he knew he did not want to hear what was coming.

Andrew started again, but Anse stopped him. "It's Elias or Troy, isn't it?"

"Uncle Anse, this is the most painful thing I have ever tried to do. I'm not even sure how to say it." There was a long and painful pause. And then, finally, Andrew got it out. "Elias and Troy were both killed this morning."

Vicy buried her head in the apron and sobbed. Anse put his head down on the top of the cane standing in front of him and closed his eyes. He sat there without a word for countless minutes. A single teardrop fell from his closed eyes to the floor. Andrew said nothing else. He did not know what else to say. He just sat.

Finally, Anse forced enough courage to speak. "Do you know how it happened?"

"No, sir, I don't know. I am sure that Joe is on his way here to fill us in. He wanted to get word to you before you heard it from somebody else."

Anse got up and walked to the front door. He stood there staring outside, resting on his cane. He was shaking badly. After several minutes he walked back to Andrew and said, "Andrew, thank you for letting us know. I understand it wasn't an easy thing to do, and we appreciate it. If you don't mind, I want to go lie down for a bit. I'm not feeling so good."

Andrew got up from his chair, walked to Anse, cradled his sagging shoulders into his chest, and held him. He then went to Vicy and hugged her for as long as he could. She was crying uncontrollably. Anse walked through his bedroom door and closed it quietly behind him.

Andrew had just seen a beaten man. In his life, Anse Hatfield had faced the meanest men on earth, and hadn't blinked. He had shot and killed without a moment of regret or sadness. He had faced hostilities that most humans would never understand, and stood up to them with an almost supernatural strength. But the death of Elias and Troy had reduced him to a whimper.

Anse would never get over the deaths of Elias and Troy, not only because he had lost two sons but because he blamed himself for their deaths. He felt that if he had been stronger, he would never have given them the money to go into the saloon business. Anse was one of the strongest men that God ever put on this earth, but his weak link was the love of his family, and Elias had taken full advantage of it. Anse would take the pain of losing Elias and Troy to his grave, never forgiving himself for causing it.

Elias and Troy were involved in a gunfight over the territorial rights for liquor sales in Boomer. They went to the home of the man they knew was infringing on their territory; and a gunfight ensued. All three men were killed in a hail of bullets.

Over the past twenty years, Andrew had watched his uncle Anse's children grow up and his uncle grow old. He had sheltered the sons from harm and protected the Hatfield family as if they were his own. And as he left the front gate of the Hatfield home, he had but one final thought: *Could I have done more?*

Elias and Troy Hatfield at the time of their death

The Andrew Lee Chafin Family, circa 1948
Andrew Lee (A. L.) front row
Arvil, Thelma, Edith, Ruth, Opal, Raymond, second row
Sarah and Andrew, back row

Sources

Author's personal interviews with Andrew Lee Chafin, 1965–1970
Taped interview, Andrew Lee Chafin, Thanksgiving, 1972
"Feud-Hatfields, McCoys, and Social Change in Appalachia, 1860–1900," Altina L. Waller
"The Hatfields and the McCoys," Otis K. Rice
"Ordinary Hero," Andrew Chafin
The Feud: The Hatfields and McCoys: The True Story, Dean King
Descendants of Holbert Chafin, Laura Loding
Logan County Genealogical Society, 1870, Logan County, West Virginia Census
West Virginia State Archives
United States Census, 1890, 1900, 1910
West Virginia Census, 1890, 1900, 1910
Hatfields and McCoys: A Comparison with the Oral Family History, Appalachian Lady in History
West Virginia Marriages Index, Ancestry.com
National Geographic, Artifacts Research
Kentucky Archaeological Survey
West Virginia Burial Index, Ancestry.com
US Department of the Interior, US Geological Survey, Island Creek School (historical)
An Early History of Mingo County, West Virginia, Nancy Sue Smith
"The Hatfield and McCoy Feud," West Virginia Genealogy Trails
West Virginia Archives and History
Arabel Hatfield, granddaughter of Cap Hatfield
US Genealogy Bank
"The Devil Turned to Stone," Robert Spence, Goldenseal

Made in the USA
Lexington, KY
15 February 2014